FREIGHT TRAIN

INTERNATIONAL BESTSELLING AUTHOR
SAPPHIRE KNIGHT

Sapphire Knight

Freight Train

Copyright © 2017 by Sapphire Knight

Cover Design by CT Cover Creations
Editing by Mitzi Carroll

This book is a work of fiction. The names, characters, places, and incidents are products of the writer's imagination or have been used fictitiously and are not to be construed as real. Any resemblance to persons, living or dead, actual events, locales or organizations is entirely coincidental.

All rights reserved. With the exception of quotes used in reviews, this book may not be reproduced or used in whole or in part by any means existing without written permission from the author.

The author acknowledges the trademarked status and trademark owners of various products referenced in this work of fiction, which have been used without permission. The publication/use of these trademarks is not authorized, associated with, or sponsored by the trademark owners.

ACKNOWLEDGEMENTS

My husband - I love you more than words can express. Thank you for the support you've shown me.

My boys - You are my whole world. I love you both. This never changes, and you better not be reading these books until you're thirty and tell yourself your momma did not write them!

My Beta Babes - Thank you for all the love you've shown me. You've all helped me grow tremendously in my writing, and I'm forever grateful. I was seriously freaking out over this book and y'all gave me the reassurance and confidence that I needed to keep trucking on. This wouldn't be possible without your input and suggestions.

Photographer and friend Wander Aguiar - Thank you for your friendship and sharing your talent with the world. You're truly a class act.

Model Conor Cushing - Thank you for being my Tyler Owens in Freight Train!

Editor Mitzi Carroll - Your hard work makes mine stand out, and I'm so grateful! Thank you for pouring tons of hours into my passion and being so wonderful to me. One day I'll meet you and one day I'll squishy hug you!

Sapphire's Naughty Princesses - You ladies are brilliant; thank you for everything that you do to help promote my work and for all your support and encouragement. Some days it's one of you that keeps me writing my next book, excited to bring you a small escape in this world. Thank you for giving me a piece of your heart—I adore you!

Sapphire Knight

My Blogger Friends -YOU ARE AMAZING! I LOVE YOU! No really, I do!!! You take a new chance on me with each book and in return share my passion with the world. You never truly get enough credit, and I'm forever grateful!

My Readers - I love you. You make my life possible, thank you.

Freight Train

Some people have to wait their entire lives to meet their favorite player.

I raised mine.

-Football moms everywhere

Sapphire Knight

DEDICATED to –

My kid.

Jr, this one's for you.

My first born, my momma's boy. I love you more than you'll ever know.

Thank you for making me proud, for making my life wonderful.

My existence wouldn't be complete if you weren't a part of it.

Sapphire Knight

ALSO BY SAPPHIRE

Oath Keepers MC Series
Exposed
Relinquish
Forsaken Control
Friction
Princess
Daydream
Baby
Chevelle
Cherry
Oath Keepers MC Collection
Oath Keepers MC Hybrid Collection

Russkaya Mafiya Series
Secrets
Corrupted
Unwanted Sacrifices
Undercover Intentions
Russian Roulette

Vendetti Family
The Vendetti Empire
The Vendetti Queen
Vendetti duet

Dirty Down South
Freight Train
3 Times the Heat

Standalones
Unexpected Forfeit
Tease
Gangster

WARNING

This novel includes graphic language and adult situations. It may be offensive to some readers and includes situations that may be hotspots for certain individuals. This book is intended for ages 16 and older due to some steamy spots. This work is fictional. The story is meant to entertain the reader and may not always be completely accurate. Being a New England Patriots' fan isn't required to read this, but Sapphire highly recommends you become one as soon as possible. Any reproduction of these works without Author Sapphire Knight's written consent is pirating and will be punished to the fullest extent of the law.

Football is like life;

it requires perseverance, self-denial, hard work, sacrifice,

dedication and respect for authority.

- Vince Lombardi

KADENCE

Another day in the life of a college student equals me doing loads of homework and reading the next preorder that hits my Kindle tonight. The homework bit sucks, but not the reading; I've been waiting three months for this new release from one of my favorite authors. I'll happily be staying up until my eyes feel like needles are scraping against them with each blink while I busily flip page after page of what's sure to be an amazing read.

Tomorrow's Saturday so at least I'll get to sleep later than I usually do during the week. That has to be one of the hardest parts about going to college—making myself go to bed so I can peel my lids apart the next morning. Being in my second year, I still haven't learned my lesson, and I don't see it changing anytime in the near future either.

I'm a bit of an overachiever when it comes to classes and reading. I've always been that way though and still love getting good grades at the end of each semester, so I continue to study my butt off when others are out living it up. Most people come to college for the 'experience,' also known as hooking up with lots of men, partying, and overall acting a little crazy.

Not me. I enjoy my quiet life and being a bookworm. I'm not a saint by any means; I've had dick before, but not much. Around the dorms here, it seems like everyone and their best friend loves to brag about who they're dating or sleeping with. I think it's a bit trashy, to be honest. I'm not stuck up, really; I just have standards.

So far the college guys around campus haven't been up to par to meeting my criteria, unfortunately. Granted, I haven't actually *looked* for a guy since I've been here. The past few, brief boyfriends were plenty for me.

Life seems so much smoother when you just go with the flow. My best friend is different on the other hand, always gushing over someone new. I'll only be here for another year so what's the point of putting myself out there, you know?

Not to mention, my father would probably shit a brick if he got wind of me doing the same stuff everyone else does. We didn't qualify for any financial help besides my partial scholarship, so he forks out my college fund. The only thing he asks in return is for me to do my best. I think that's pretty reasonable and he doesn't bug me too much. A call here or there and the rest of the time is just me on my own in Alabama. He's a few states away if I ever need him, and I love visiting him when I have breaks, but we aren't that close anymore.

It's the weekends that are the hardest, I reckon. Once my schoolwork's all caught up, and my latest book is read, it can get lonely. I have my bestie, Brianne, with whom I share my dorm, but she stays busy with plans. Don't get me wrong, I'm always invited, but that's not my thing.

I wish I were the more outgoing type, but a few friends have always been plenty to me. It's the whole quality over quantity logic, and then throw in the fact that I can be a bit of a smartass most of the time; well, only some people seem to get me.

"Hey lady, you hanging out here tonight?" Brianne nods towards my twin-sized bed. It's shoved over in the opposite corner of hers and piled with throw pillows. I freaking love throw pillows; you can stack them any which way to get comfy. Those things are important when you're an avid reader.

She grabs her purse and slides on her sandals, floating around the room.

"Yep, a new book to read." Smiling, I wave my Kindle at her like it's an actual paperback or something.

"Well, have fun and tell me about it later, okay? I'm off with Justin!"

"Who's Justin?"

She shrugs, shooting me a goofy smile.

Laughing, I call, "Be safe," as she heads out the door.

Another night to myself. Thank God for my next book boyfriend to keep me company.

Saturday, Game Three

Tyler

I'm down after the snap.

Fuck.

This lineman is crushing my chest and feels like a goddamn fridge on top of me. "Get off me, man." Grumbling, I push against the mammoth, attempting to get the huge guy to roll off without squishing me further.

Marlyns—number eighty-eight—struts past us to line back up and gets me with a swift kick to the ribs on his way. Praise God for pads or these assholes would hit me with cheap shots every flipping game.

Jumping to my feet, I head towards the line. "Briggs, switch," I call out to my teammate.

"What?"

Freight Train

"Take RB."

"I'm not a running back, dude!" His eyes grow wide, the black paint on his cheeks smeared down part of his cheeks from him wiping away sweat.

"I'm team cap, right? Switch."

"Fine, but you tell Coach this bullshit's on you."

He shakes his head, but listens and takes my position. I hit the line, pointing at Marlyns, ready to get some payback.

It's on; I'm getting your ass for that shot.

The snap's called, and in no time, I'm on Marlyns. Grabbing him right around the ribs—in my ever-perfect tackle—he hits the ground. Hard.

Rising, I start to climb off him right away. Enough of those powerful drives from me and he'll feel it later. His ass will be stuck in an ice bath all day tomorrow trying to erase the battering his body will take in this game. Fair is fair in football. He wants to hurt me. I'll give it back tenfold.

"That all you got Owens? You hit like a bitch, yo! Did your mom teach you that shit? Bet her dumb ass can outdo you. You a fuckup like your momma, boy?"

My mind jumps to my mom's smiling face in the backyard with me. We'd toss the football every evening so I could practice my catching. Different flashes hit me from my entire childhood. One after another—her grinning at my antics; laughing when I'd act foolishly; cheering me on at every single game and telling me that I was her star. I couldn't imagine a more caring person than her.

Shaking the thoughts off, I come back to the here and now, realizing that my hands are wrapped around his chin guard—yanking and pulling until the snaps rip free. I jerk his helmet completely off and toss it to the side, landing blow after blow to his face. Right to the nose, left to the cheek, right to the front teeth, and another right to the mouth.

I get some good punches in before I'm pulled off him, and he's on his feet, yelling with blood covering his face.

"Fuck you, bitch! Watch your back, son; I got you, just wait!" he hollers, spitting a tooth out that has me chuckling.

"Better thank my momma, Marlyns; she's the one who taught me how to throw a hook."

Shooting him the bird, three angry refs are suddenly in my face shouting to get off their field. Coach Stratton runs over, arguing and screaming back at them about uncalled flags against me all night. Regardless of the cheap shots, the refs have to kick me out. I get it, rules are rules, and this is college football.

My buddy, JJ wraps his arm over my shoulders and walks me over toward our bench, "I have your back, Ty. You good, bro?"

Meeting his concerned brown eyes, I nod and sit on the hard metal seat.

I'm not really all right, though. I'm never okay without my family watching me from the stands. But I have to suck it up out here because I'm Tyler 'The Freight Train' motherfuckin' Owens and I run college football. Welcome to *my* life.

Freight Train

Four days later...

Climbing the stairs to my parents' weathered house, my brother Nate meets me on the porch.

There's nothing quite like being home, no matter how used to the college life I get. The feeling of driving onto the property alone feeds my soul. There's the sweet scent of the grassy fields lingering in the air, along with old, towering trees and plenty of land surrounding. It all makes my chest warm, my stomach finally settling from knowing that my family's here.

I'm a strong man on my own but aligned with my two older brothers, we're a force to be reckoned with.

"Back for the weekend?" Nate grumbles, gesturing to my duffle bag.

I figured he'd be giving me grief as soon as I arrived. I find it hard to believe he didn't hear about me wigging out at the game and going crazy on eighty-eight from Duke. I was suspended for this weekend's game, and I'm lucky that's the extent of it. The school attempted to push for me to have to sit out of four games but Coach fought with the board over it and got the punishment reduced. Still, one game could do some damage come draft time.

"Nope, I have practice on Sunday. Coach is gearing up; he thinks Dame One is tough this year."

He chuckles shaking his head, "When will that old man learn that no one's as dedicated as Bama boys to football?"

"Fuck if I know. He's making the whole team geek out about it." Complaining, a shudder shakes me inside, thinking back over the hectic training he's been inflicting upon us daily; my calves still hurt from running the stairs and my biceps have had to be iced everyday this past week.

"Chill Ty, we all know you'll lead them to a win." He waves me off, used to watching me play throughout the years. He knows how dedicated I am to the team and the sport.

My room's littered with trophies not only for winning football games but also for being the most valuable player and for defense as well. I have some from when I was younger from track also before I bulked up. Once I hit my junior year in high school, the track coach cut me. I was faster than everyone, but our football coach wanted me completely dedicated to his sport only, and in Alabama, football takes priority.

Nodding, I toss my duffle bag at him and chuckle. It hits him in the stomach and falls to the floor as his eyes grow wide, his eyebrows shooting up.

Freight Train

"Oh, I thought by that, you'd at least carry my bag for me, since I'm getting the win and all," I cheekily retort, like I've done many times before to pester him when we were growing up.

He shakes his head, lunging at me over the bag and I jump across the few stairs on the old rickety porch, taking off in a full sprint. Football player and grown man or not, my brother will frog me like no other if he gets the chance, and Nate is not a small guy. He's like me, used to working the ranch and playing some type of sport growing up. He loved them all and floated between different sports each season.

When it all boils down to it, this is how Nate and I are, the constant teasing and one-upping each other. I've always been the pesky younger brother, bothering my two brothers, Nate and Clyde. We've stayed pretty close growing up together. We all have our own lives but guard each other with a fierceness no one wants to cross. You don't get one brother after you, but all three. We've always been that way; well, at least since my parents passed away.

"Slow down, you chickenshit!" Nate hollers behind me, and I let loose a loud laugh.

Both of my brothers played high school ball; we're all athletically talented. However, I've been the only one to get scouted and offered a full scholarship—they only got partials. My oldest brother takes care of my parents' house and ranch while Nate does...Well, whatever it is that Nate does. He helps Clyde out, but otherwise, he likes to skirt off and do his own thing, probably chase chicks around town without telling us about it.

Huffing out a breath from running, I get about a good mile or so from the house. There's nothing out here but my family's land. My dad had two hundred acres, and it's been passed down to us in his will.

Glancing back, Nate's no longer chasing me, but lying on his back on the ground, panting away, so I slow my quick stride, relaxing my overused muscles. Turning toward the house, I do a light jog back, full-on laughing at Nate as I pass him by. He's huffing and puffing like an old geezer.

"Geez, man, you need some cardio in your life. This explains why you're still single. You better not be giving us Owens a bad reputation 'cause you can't keep up."

"Screw you," he chuckles, flipping me off as I eventually make it to the porch.

I'm the fastest out of all three of us, no matter how much they like to argue with me about it. I'm glad too because it's gotten me out of some tight spots back in the day when I would try to prank them. Let's just say they weren't amused, even if my mom thought it was funny and I learned to make good use of my speed.

She's the one who taught me how to get back at my brothers too; it was never anything destructive or malicious. However, buying fake bugs and putting them in my brothers' beds, filling their shoes with sugar, and letting air out of their truck tires, that was all her. She kept things fun around here and helped me retaliate being the youngest in the house.

My mom was everything to me. I was just like her, favoring her most with my light hair and eyes and we both loved the same foods and colors too. Clyde was always closer to my dad. He's the oldest so he would help my dad work the ranch most days, while Nate, just sort of bounced between the two of them. He didn't really favor just one parent, but more of a mixture of them both.

Freight Train

Stomping up the rickety stairs, my feet make the loud thudding noises that my mother would say sounded like horses running into the house. She'd yell at us to slow down as boys, and then lecture that we didn't always need to rush everywhere. She liked to preach that life wasn't always a race and that sometimes you needed to slow it down to appreciate what you have.

Yes, I was a momma's boy, and I couldn't be more proud of that fact. I miss her. I wish I could've slowed time down for her.

A newspaper that's resting on the kitchen table's exactly what I've been dreading. Front and center is a picture of me on top of Marlyns, straddling him, about to land a punch. As much as I hate what happened, it's a pretty badass photo of me, but it's also not how I would want my parents to see me. I knew my brothers had to know about it happening. I can't believe Nate didn't rib me over it, though.

Stopping in front of the article, the title catches my attention.

Alabama's golden boy, Tyler 'The Freight Train' finally shows us he's an Owens after all, taking after his big brother during last Saturday's game against Duke.

Tyler Owens, number twelve for Alabama, was spotted during Saturday's game, assaulting number eighty-eight, Wade Marlyns from Duke. Bama once bragged about Tyler being their homegrown country boy with unmeasurable talent on and off the football field. Judging by Saturday's game, it appears he may be just like his older brother, Clyde Owens, who was once quite the football star himself.

You may remember, six years ago Clyde Owens coming up on criminal charges for assaulting a rival player on the field during a game which led to Drew Bledsoe being rushed to the emergency room with life-threatening injuries. Clyde was stripped of all scholarships previously awarded and expelled as well from the campus. We later found out that his rage was brought on by a tragic accident where both of his parents perished.

Justin Owens, forty-four, ranch owner, and his wife Katie Owens, forty-two, were pronounced dead at...

Turning away, I stop reading as they go on in detail, explaining what happened to my parents on that horrible day.

God, I wish I could go back. If I had the chance to, I'd appreciate my mother and father more. We never realized just how blessed we were until we no longer had them in our lives. Then the state showed up, nosing around. They'd tried to take over everything, but Clyde wasn't having it, thank God. I don't know where I'd be if it weren't for my brother being stubborn about it all.

I was a freshman in high school when it all happened. Nate was in his third year as a junior and Clyde was in college, busy playing football himself. My brother withdrew from classes immediately. The school had begged him to play that last game, and in the end, he'd agreed. If only he'd have listened to us and not gone through with it.

The articles they'd published were all wrong, and he wasn't expelled. Drew was my brother's best friend back then. He never pressed any charges, and he stood up for Clyde the moment he was able too. Drew had been pushing my brother all night for playing that game, saying he should be home after his parents died. Clyde just snapped. It's not a valid excuse for the damage he inflicted on Drew, but a man can only take so much before he reaches his limit.

That goes for all men.

Clyde stood up for us and went to court on our behalf. He fought for Nate and me, using some of my family's money that they'd left for us in the will. He was determined to keep us in our own home, going to the same school and around family. He claimed that our parents would want us to keep on track and he was able to make that happen. Clyde didn't just lose our parents, though. With the fights and the state after us, he gave up everything to start a life taking care of his family.

The judge wasn't too thrilled, but he was an old friend of my father's, so he gave in. It turned out to be the best decision for all of us.

Clyde struggled in the beginning with my brother and me, but he was so young himself. Nate wanted to get in trouble, while I went the opposite direction. I was determined to be perfect, to make my mother proud of me if there was any chance she could be watching me from Heaven. I don't know if there is a Heaven, but if so, my mother was the best type of woman, and I know she would have been taken there right away.

Smiling to myself as I think about my mom, I grab the jug of red Kool-Aid out of the fridge, chugging half of the liquid down in big gulps. I'm sure whoever made it will be heated, but they can always make more. It's not like I'm home all the time anyhow, just when I have a day or two off and can help out around here.

A throat clears while I'm mid-chug and I know it's my eldest brother, Clyde. Lowering the pitcher, I'm met with amused eyes and my brother lightly holding a shotgun.

"You got him out there like an old heifer, lying in the grass." He nods toward the door, and I grin widely. I'm sure it's stained red from the Kool-Aid, but it's all good. Clyde doesn't mind; he's happy when I'm back home, and the family is together.

Shrugging, I set the plastic container on the counter next to me, and Clyde tosses me the shotgun. I easily catch the barrels with one hand; the gun pointed toward the ceiling just in case something was to happen, and it went off by mistake.

"Load up in the back of the pickup and have him drive so y'all can do a sweep around the property. Obviously, he needs to rest and catch his breath." He chuckles and walks toward the back door before I reply. He's not a man of many words, and we've always gotten along.

Nate and I will occasionally get into it over something, but not often. If there's anyone who we all argue with, it's my cousin Dallas. Not that I can complain, he's been one of my closest friends growing up at a year older than me and a year younger than Nate. We haven't seen each other much since he decided not to go to college. I was hoping he'd go to AU when time came for me to go, but he never enrolled.

The screen door slams again, and I'm met with Nate's stare.

"Clyde talk to you?" I ask and pick up the pitcher for another swig.

"Nope, and use a glass, fucker."

Ever since my mom passed, he's taken over trying to correct us on stuff. Funny since he was the one who went sort of opposite when they died. We all roll with it since it seems important to him that we abide by Mom's house rules even if we are grown men now.

Pulling the drink away, I wipe my face on my arm. "Nah, I'm done. He wants us to do rounds."

"Does your pretty boy self remember how to use that shotgun you got there or has football and college completely taken over everything?"

"I remember smoking you just fine last weekend when I was here, but I'm down to shoot if you want to get shown up again." Laughing, I put the drink back in the fridge and head toward the front door.

"I was out all night when you were here last weekend. If I'd actually gotten some sleep, then you wouldn't have won; we both know this," he argues and follows me to my father's old beat-up Chevy he used as a ranch truck.

Hopping into the back, I egg him on some more through the small open back window, "And what were you doing exactly last weekend, or should I say who?"

"Shut it, Ty," he grumbles, climbing into the truck and firing the engine up.

"Do I know her?"

"Drop it, Ty. Let's go."

He still hasn't admitted to me who the new chick is that he's been seeing. That's the only explanation I can come up with for the past few weekends when he's come home at like four a.m. smelling like perfume, and one night he even had glitter on him. He doesn't drink much unless we have a bonfire and he wasn't hung over, so I know he wasn't partying. I'll get him to fess up to who the cutie is he's seeing—eventually.

We ride along the outskirts of the property, making sure that the fence is holding up and that there isn't anything amiss. Clyde's tried to keep the majority of my dad's animals, but there aren't many left. We have three horses now; two others went to my uncle when my parents died. Sucks, but I think it was for the best. The ranch is a lot of work without the added animals.

To make some extra money for the ranch, my dad used to break horses amongst other business ventures. My uncle would often bring his horses over to have my dad work his magic. Clyde tried it out for a while but wasn't able to get into it much. He just doesn't have the way with the horses that my dad did.

Clyde's headstrong and never realizes when he has too much on his plate. He can never just do one thing at a time. I don't know if he wanted to try and take over absolutely everything my father did, but he just can't do it all.

Nate and I make it back to the house as the sun's setting. I can smell the meat on the grill that Clyde must have started cooking already. Being so active, we eat a lot of protein, especially when I'm home. Thankfully my brothers respect my diet requirements. Through the shit they give me about being a football player, they encourage me to be at my best. We usually eat whatever I need to, and I love Clyde's barbecue. I could practically live off the stuff. We pretty much did, too, when he first took over things; that and pizza.

"What's going on tonight, man?" I turn to Nate as we climb the stairs on the front porch.

"Not much, probably just watching a movie in my room," he mumbles as we head to the kitchen.

Nodding, I wash my hands in the kitchen sink and make my way out the back door to see if Clyde needs any help.

I was right, he's cooking, and it's perfect timing. "Thank God; I'm starving. You need me to do anything?"

"No, I got everything we need already. You can plate up your salad and take a seat. This chicken's almost finished."

Freight Train

Sitting in my normal spot, I load a heaping spoonful of greens just as a large white truck comes barreling down the dirt road leading to our house. We both watch it for a few seconds as it gets closer, and Clyde gripes something under his breath about it.

"Are we having company?" I gesture to the vehicle with my thumb.

"No, damn it," he glowers, watching the truck pull to a stop. A tiny woman hops down from the driver's side. "It's the woman for the taxes again. She's relentless."

"What's wrong with the taxes? Do we owe money?"

"Don't worry about it, Ty. Watch the grill," he orders and quickly strides over to the smoking hot lady.

Whatever they're talking about seems to get pretty heated, making Clyde gesture and huff at her. Whenever Clyde is upset, he doesn't show many emotions like my father used to do, so this chick must be pissing him off pretty badly. I wonder what she has to say about taxes that would bring her all the way out here and have him so wound up.

Flipping the meat, I sprinkle some seasoning on it all as the back screen door slams closed and Nate comes outside. He flops down in a seat at the old table, already dishing salad onto his plate.

"Her again?" he complains rolling his eyes.

"Who is she? It's the first time I've seen her."

Shrugging, he takes a drink of his glass of Kool-Aid and then finishes. "Some woman that keeps showing up and pissing Clyde off. I thought maybe he was seeing someone. I don't know when he's had the chance, but I asked anyway. He said she wants him to pay a bunch of taxes or else sell her the house. Too bad cause she's hot."

"She is gorgeous. But is she crazy? Why would we sell her the house? It's paid for."

"I don't know. I could be wrong, but it's something like that. You know how he is, though; he always tries to keep us out of anything he's got going on. She's persistent, though, showing up here at least once a week for about a month now. Gets him like that every time too." He nods to our brother, who appears to currently be towering over the small woman, growling something to the poor lady.

"I can't believe this has been going on for an entire month and no one's mentioned anything to me about it. This should be discussed between all of us."

"Don't worry about it; he'll take care of it."

That's always been my brother's attitude, skirting away from anything that could give him a bit of responsibility. Me, on the other hand? It drives me crazy not knowing what's going on. We've lost so much already; I don't ever want to be blindsided like that again.

Keeping the rest of my thoughts to myself, I concentrate on dishing up our barbecue even though it irritates me that Nate can so easily let Clyde take on all the stress of this place. He should be handling everything right alongside Clyde; he's here twenty-four seven with him.

Setting the platter down, I load up my own plate and watch Clyde until he joins us to eat. "So who's that?" I nod to the blonde chick, now driving away.

"No one important," he rumbles, attempting to put an end to my questions, while he busily loads his food onto a plate.

"I can help if you need it."

"No, Tyler. You can concentrate on school and football; you're the real deal. I can handle Shyla all by myself. I don't want you worrying about anything other than school and playing ball."

"So you know her then?"

"Yep. We went to high school together." He stops talking, stuffing a large bite of greens in his mouth just as Nate meets my gaze wearing a mischievous smirk.

I shake my head, but it doesn't stop him from asking, "You have a history with her, huh?"

Clyde answers with a grunt, meaning he's not going to talk about it, but my money's on yes. Something probably went down between them, and now she most likely loves it that she can make his life hell at the moment. If that's the case, hopefully, their drama wasn't so bad that she has it out for him. He needs to make amends, so she'll move on or whatever.

First chance I get when I'm on my next break, I'm finding out exactly who this chick is. Maybe she's just the type of distraction my brother needs in his life. It's time he does something for himself and stops worrying so much about and Nate and me. In fact, we could all use a distraction. I wonder if Shyla has any cute friends for the rest of us?

Sapphire Knight

There are four seasons in the South:
Winter, Spring, Summer and Football.

University of Alabama

Monday...

Hiking my camo print backpack over my shoulder, I rush through the hall after class. I'm always cutting it close to practice on Mondays and Wednesdays with the lectures running overtime. Mr. Matthews likes to talk, even after his time is supposed to be over. It drives me crazy; I hate being late.

I've attempted to speak to Coach about it, hoping to get the time issue worked out. That did no good, though; he told me to buck up. He said I need to get with the college program and that it wasn't for whine asses. So, I shut my mouth quickly and adapted the best I could.

This isn't high school; the instructors don't make exceptions for you or help you out with your grades, so that they can see you play on Friday nights. Here, college ball is on Saturdays and most of the professors couldn't give a rat's ass about whether you show up to class or not. They get paid either way, and it's completely up to you if you want to succeed.

It was difficult for me to adjust to everything my freshman year. This year I'm not only a sophomore, but I'm also a starting player and a team captain. The coaches have seen my skills over the past year and have begun to come around a little more. Now if only the professors would do the same.

I paid my dues last year riding the bench a few times. I was pretty angry at first, not understanding what it was that I was doing wrong. Then one day my buddy broke it down that no matter how good you are, you ride the bench. Everyone has to—at least once—to sort of break you in and dig it in deep that each position is earned.

Nothing is given freely here. If you're good and you bust your ass, then you get playing time. However, if you screw up or screw off, then you dwindle away until one day you're no longer at practice or sitting on the bench at all. I've worked too hard, for too long to give my spot away.

My parents were so proud of my athletic ability when I was growing up; I refuse to let them be disappointed in me now that I'm getting somewhere with it. The fight last weekend wasn't like me at all. I've had haters my entire life, but they usually aren't able to get through to me like that. I can only imagine the disappointment my parents must've been feeling if they were watching from above.

One thing that hasn't changed from when I was in high school is the amount of women giving it up freely whenever I want it. Chicks seem to flock to me whether I'm on the bench or playing the entire game. It's not the small high school or away girls anymore; it's anyone and everyone sending me the 'I'd fuck you' looks. I've even had a few dudes hit on me. Freaked me the hell out at first, but I learned to roll with it.

College is a new life in itself. Being in my second year, I'm still adapting. My brothers have no clue what I deal with. Well, Clyde has some, since he went for a while; however, I prefer the normalcy of when I'm at home and can decompress. Here at school, I'm always *on*.

"Ty! My man!" DaShwan yells, throwing me a peace sign as he passes by, full of a bright smile.

"Get it, Gator!" I holler back, using his nickname and chuckling. I don't know him well, but he's been someone who's cheered me on since I first got here. For those people, I'm grateful. They helped me power through the tougher times of being at a new school and not knowing anyone.

JJ catches up at my side, and we bump each other's forearms in greeting. "Bro, we fucking missed you Saturday."

"Yeah, tell me about it. That game was some bullshit." I tried not to watch it, but gave in and turned it on in time to see Bama get creamed. I'm sure Coach flipped out on the entire team.

"Stratton was so hot that you weren't playing. He was going apeshit on everyone, riding the guys like nothing else."

That's what I figured, but what else is new, Coach flips out if I miss a warm up, let alone an entire game. "So everyone's going to be pissed at me today then." Not being able to play was punishment enough; I don't need to catch any flak from the guys as well. Bad enough a few of them texted me Saturday evening telling me to eat shit the next time I want to get kicked out of a game.

"Or they're going to be thanking God that you're back in the locker room and on the field so that Coach will chill the fuck out. I'm telling you bro, when you get picked up in the draft, I think Stratton's going to have to retire early from a stroke. He thinks you hung the moon, pretty boy," he teases, and I roll my eyes. Laughing, I shake my head as my other buddy, Chandler approaches us.

"What-the-fuck-ever, dude. He likes me now. Wait till we get someone better, then I'll be scrubbing toilets and running the field every time I look at him wrong."

"Sup, Ty, JJ," Chandler interrupts, and we bump forearms with him next. "Christ, Ty, I don't think I've ever been happier that you're coming to practice before." He huffs.

JJ turns to me. "See bro, told you. Bama's golden boy and all that jazz."

"Stop! You know I hate hearing that shit," I grumble, too busy paying attention to the guys while my body harshly slams into something.

"Oof!" A female voice squeaks as she lands on her butt, sprawling out to catch herself with her hands. Standing in front of her, students veer around us without offering her any help like a bunch of dicks.

"Shit! I'm so sorry," I stammer out—concerned—and reach down to get her back up on her feet. Her heated chocolate gaze glares up at me full of fire, irritated like I'm the one who bumped into her and not the other way around.

Freight Train

After a moment, she finally places her soft palm in my hand. Her fingers are so small enclosed in my own, and as her skin makes contact with mine, I get a jolt. The shock relaying all the way to my toes is powerful enough to force me to do a double take.

Running my eyes over her again, I note her slightly flushed cheeks. Her skin's creamy, and with the blush peppering her skin it's almost as if she's turned on. Her heaving chest is much more noticeable when paying attention too; she's not overly big in the bust area, but more like the perfect handful. Top it all off with a pair of plain reading glasses, the type you'd see a chick dressed up as a naughty school teacher wear. I'd skimmed over it all on the first glance I had of her, but she's stunning, truly, in an understated way.

"Are you okay, sweetheart?" I ask again, my voice coming out a bit rougher after taking a better look at her and help her to her feet. The shock still has me a bit shaken.

I quickly lift her bag as well, showing the manners my parents instilled in me as a kid. She still hasn't spoken, and I'm dying inside to finally hear her, to see if she has a sultry voice to match the slight pout her peach lips make while she quickly takes stock of my body. Time seems to slow as her gaze runs up my body and then flutters back down it. My chest puffs in her perusal. I definitely like what I see, and I'm suspecting that she realizes just who she ran into.

The guys both stand next to me, quiet and grinning at our exchange. I'm surprised they haven't butted in and tried to introduce themselves or made some smartass joke to embarrass me.

"Umm, yeah. I'm fine, I guess," she grumbles, clearly still irritated as she stares at my hand as if she felt the zap also. I wonder if she did. It was probably just static or something, right? I don't normally shock people when we touch, but maybe I didn't use enough fabric softener this time. I wonder what she's thinking.

"Your bag." I hold the blue straps out toward her, noticing a lime green quote on the front pocket. 'Fuck off, I'm reading. Seriously, off you fuck!' I read aloud, chuckling. She clearly has a thing for books.

"What?" Her gaze finally meets mine, and she instantly consumes every thought I have at the moment, the quote and her bust size fading to the back of my mind as I take in the most gorgeous set of irises I've ever seen.

As quickly as possible, I catalog the little beauty mark on her cheek. Then onto the soft pale peach 'kiss me' lips that are again in a slight pout as she stares at me and fuck if I don't wish that I could press mine to them. Her perfectly shaped brows that I'm sure other women spend way too much time worrying about, all framed by long chestnut locks with a few stripes of peek-a-boo red showing through. "What?" She repeats, and I blink, coming back down to earth. She has the type of features a man could get lost in.

"Um, here's your bag."

"Oh, right. Thanks." She snatches it up, careful to avoid touching my palm again. Once it's shouldered, she hurries around me in the opposite direction.

"Wait!" escapes in a yell before I can catch myself and hear JJ quietly chuckle behind me.

"Yeah?" she calls as she walks backward, and I'm amazed she doesn't bump into anyone else.

"Are you all right?" It's the only thing I can come up with to ask, never mind that I keep repeating myself. It's like I'm in second grade again and I'm attempting to talk to the first pretty girl I've seen before.

"I'm fine," she yells back, ending with my nickname, "Freight Train." Her short form gets swallowed up amongst the students, effectively making me lose her. *I can't believe she knows my name... Wait, of course, she knows who I am. Shit, who is she?*

Turning back to the JJ and Chandler, I mutter, "Who was that? And how have I only just noticed her? Do we know her?"

The guys both laugh louder at me and Chandler tugs on my bag. "Come on; we're going to have to run to the field unless you want to do burpees after practice. And no, we don't know her."

JJ groans, "Fuck that nonsense, come on!"

"Owens!" Someone shouts from down the hallway, but I ignore it, glancing at my watch.

Shit. I'm definitely going to get my ass in more trouble at this rate.

Placing my other arm through my backpack strap, I take off in a sprint to the athletic center. JJ and Chandler follow, catching up and running beside me. Time isn't on our side right now, and I refuse to run suicides or do flipping burpees for being late. Who knows what Coach has in store already for me missing the game.

KADENCE

Tyler Owens of all the people for me to choose to run into today! Why couldn't it be the science geek again from last week? Of course, it's my luck to run into Alabama's freaking star athlete when

I'm rushing to class. I bet he was appalled being the spoiled football jock and all.

And what was that exactly when we touched? Did he feel it, too, or was it just me? It had to be me; he didn't let on that it affected him. I need to stop dragging my feet, or I'll go around static shocking anyone I come in contact with. So freaking embarrassing, I swear.

Everyone talks about how good looking Tyler is, but I've never had the pleasure of seeing him in person. Sure I watch football, but not college games. I wouldn't have even known it was him had I not seen the posters and banners with his face plastered on them as 'Bama's Golden Boy.'

Blegh.

Don't get me wrong; he has a nice face—prominent nose, high cheekbones, eyes full of mischief with lips promising to uphold his naughty thoughts. All topped off with a ball cap pulled down low, giving him just an ounce of mystery. It's enough so that you want to lift it and see the rest of him. When he spoke to me, it took everything in me not to reach up and push his hat off. I felt like I was in a trance and his teeth were so damn white; how is that possible?

He was probably disgusted to have someone normal slam into him and not a football player. I've heard the 'too perfect's' talk before. You know the fake-boobed-bimbo types blabbing around campus, about how they like to fawn all over him whenever he 'allows' it. At least I get it now why they worship him, well looks-wise anyhow.

I was struck dumb for a moment myself. And he's massive in size, like a tower over you and makes you feel tiny, type of big. Not in a rough, scary way, but more of a holy shit he's buff and strong and super hot.

And Jesus, I was completely shocked when it first happened, and I glanced up to find that the solid chest belonged to him of all people. I wasn't expecting his help either, that threw me for a loop even more. Kindly offering me his hand to stand back up was polite, considering it was my fault and most students would've been cursing me had it been them instead. His grip was tight but not enough to hurt me, just enough to offer the support I needed. I'll admit it; I may have slightly swooned when my palm met his.

He had this goofy smile when he asked if I was okay and it was sorta cute. I'm not used to guys looking at me like that too much, maybe if I'm at the pool in my swimsuit with my glasses off. Then they may, but not when I'm in my comfy school clothes. I just blend in with all the other faceless students I guess. I kinda like it that way, though.

God, who am I kidding, it wasn't just *'sorta cute,'* but more like he was completely adorable with that grin when he called me sweetheart. I swear my heart skipped a beat when he said it. No one's ever called me sweetheart before—not even my dad.

No wonder why women throw themselves at him. I've heard the stories around campus; he's like a dog in heat. There are rumors that he's even shuffled multiple conquests through his door on the same night. All the females claim that he's a stallion in the sack with a body to die for. The chicks love to brag that they got him off or whatever.

Personally, I think it's gross no matter how gorgeous he may be. I know one thing is for sure, I will never be one of them. Not that he'd want me to be or anything, I'm just reassuring myself after coming in contact with his killer smile and Superman-like body.

Superman…Geez, that perfectly explains how hard his body felt. I bet if you peeled that shirt off he'd be shredded like most of the guys on my book covers.

Shit, maybe I should use some sanitizer after touching those hands. Thinking about him and all of his conquests has me shuddering. Speaking of his hands, they were surprisingly rougher than I would expect, even if he does handle a football regularly.

And those muscles in his arms, flexing when he pulled me up. Sweet baby Jesus, I could've fanned myself right then. Thank goodness I didn't; that would've been even more embarrassing.

Now, I understand how women can get sucked in so easily with him. Oh God, I hope he doesn't think I ran into him on purpose. I bet he totally does and that's why he was smiling like that. He most likely thinks I'm freaking pathetic.

Shit.

Huffing out a tired breath from my short jog to class, I plop down in my usual seat, happy I at least made it here on time today. I don't get it why they had to make the campus so freaking big. I feel like I have to walk a mile just to get to any of my classes. I love it here, though, minus the size. The professors are great, and I've made a few friends in passing. Well, maybe not actual friends, but I do say hi to a few familiar faces.

Geesh, I need to push the 'Freight Train' out of my mind. He's just a stupid jock, even if he was polite. My best friend is going to freak when I tell her about this.

Taking my cell out, I quickly punch out a text to Brianne so that I can fill her in on what just happened.

Me: I just face-planted straight into Tyler Owens!

She shouldn't be surprised about the face plant part; that happens like once a week to me. Only it's not usually this entertaining.

My phone lights up with her calling me instantly, but I hit 'deny' since the class is fixing to start. The last thing I want is more attention.

Brianne: Ty? No way! What did he say?

Me: Umm...Ty? Since when is he Ty to you?

Brianne: That's what he tells everyone here to call him.

Me: Wait, you've spoken to him before?

Brianne: Yes, he's in my creative writing course.

Me: Tyler Owens takes creative writing? And how come you haven't told me about this before now?

Brianne: IDK, I didn't think you'd care or I would have. He's a smart guy. What did he say when you ran him over?

Professor Reynolds walks in, clearing his throat, so I type out one last text, quieting my phone.

Me: I didn't run him over!!!!! It's class time now, but you're filling me in later!

Mr. Reynolds starts talking right away, so I don't check her response. I shove my phone into my bag and grab my pen and notebook, scribbling notes down quickly as the instructor rambles on. I learned my first year that if I don't take a lot of notes, then I forget everything. Half of the curriculum is so boring; I could be watching paint dry with more excitement. I tried the recording device thing, and it wasn't for me, I need the process of actually writing it down.

The connection of pen to paper—physically writing the notes—seem to implement everything more accurately for me.

 Mr. Reynolds drones on with his lesson plan, and I zone out, missing the majority of his lecture. I can't help it; I keep replaying the way Tyler felt, the timbre of his voice, and how I wish I could see him again. Pretty weird considering he's not my usual type—at all. God, he was handsome and sweet.

 Why do I want to see him again anyway? The first time wasn't embarrassing enough? I think I figured out what's bothering me the most, though. I never apologized to him, and it's those damn southern manners kicking in, making me feel guilty about it. I shouldn't feel bad because he seemed to be in just as much of a hurry with his friends as I was. If anything, we're both at fault, and I should just drop it. That's a good plan, partial ownership and all, so he's guilty too.

 Ty's just so different than I'd expected and it has my head spinning. It's making it harder to stop thinking about him, why couldn't he have just been rude? Then I would've moved right along like nothing.

 It's been awhile since I thought of my type. Do I even have one? I suppose it's rather varied.

 The last guy I dated was a cute writer. He would think up these sweet poems and give them to me. I loved that part of him, just not the idea of him liking men more than he did women. It kind of defeated the purpose of us being together. No hard feelings in the end and we remain friends, and he's happily dating a scruffy painter.

 Before the writer was Jake.

 Agh Jake.

Freight Train

He was a summer boy. The type that comes to visit his grandparents, and when it's time to return to school, he goes back home and then you never see him again. Gosh, he was good-looking and tanned from the hours he spent as a lifeguard at the local pool. After the pool would close, he'd sneak me in, and we'd swim for hours. I had so much fun with him.

Before Jake was the guy I lost my virginity to. He was your typical high school bad boy. He rode a dirt bike and had an old, beat-up leather jacket. His ear and tongue were pierced, and I thought he was amazing at the time. Well, at least until we slept together and then I caught him making out with a cheerleader a few days later. He's lucky my father didn't find out about him. That would've been ugly.

I cried like it was the end of the world at the time. However, I got over it after a short period of time and became dedicated to my schoolwork. It all worked out for me too; I got a partial scholarship, and if the rumors that went around the school are true, he got syphilis.

Payback's a bitch—even more of a reason to be a decent human being!

Not only that, but it taught me to be more careful. I was entirely too naïve and trusting back then. I learned the hard way, unfortunately.

I've never had a thing for athletes before, more like the opposite. They're egotistical, smug, and too much work. On the plus side, they do have nice butts and cute smiles, eyes, voice…Well, everything it would seem when I think of Tyler. And, surprisingly, he also had manners. I wonder if all the talk about his 'package' is true too. Hung like a horse, makes me blush just thinking about it.

Packing up my book bag, I head out to meet up with Brianne at our spot. We've been best friends our entire lives. While everyone else was busy growing up and splitting apart, we stuck together like glue, becoming closer over the years.

Even after I moved away from Boston with my dad, we kept in touch, and she decided to follow me here to college. She thought it'd be an adventure being that far from her home. She's become more of a sister to me now. We were both skinny little book nerds when we started out in second grade, and the teacher had us sit next to each other in class for the very first time. Within two days Mrs. Muncy was threatening to move us because we talked to each other too much. I've pretty much stayed the same shy person as back then, but she's grown even more outgoing and assertive.

Dropping my bag under *our tree,* I plop down and watch as Brianne walks towards me, beaming brightly about something.

"Hey!" she says and throws her stuff down beside me.

"Hey, how was your morning?"

"It was good, the same as always. How was Reynolds' class?" She took him last year. I wish we had waited and taken him together. He's one of those professors that changes material and assignments nearly every semester so you can't share notes or work. We thought we'd have a one-up by taking different classes then sharing notes, but not so much.

"So freaking boring, I drifted the whole time."

"Yeah? That's not like you. Was it because of the run-in with Ty?"

I roll my eyes at her run-in comment. "I told you I didn't run him over, I swear—he wasn't paying attention either. He was just as surprised as I was. If he weren't so dang massive, then he would've hit the floor right alongside me."

She starts laughing, and I roll my eyes again. It happens a lot when I'm with her. "I couldn't stop thinking about him either. How do you make it through an entire class with him?"

Of course, she's going to find this amusing; she doesn't have any issues talking to guys. I'm just a normal person—quiet and keep to myself for the most part. She's the one with all the nerve to openly flirt and say what's on her mind; not me.

"Getting through class is easy." She waves her hand like it's not a big deal. "He's really nice and like I mentioned before—smart. So as long as the skanks are quiet, then it's fine. A few of them try to actually sit on his lap for the class period. He plays it off, but I could tell earlier that he was embarrassed about it. Don't get me wrong; he likes the attention. He's definitely used to it, but there's also another side to him too. I think he's amused with the women falling over themselves for him, but he also gets annoyed when they try to be all over-the-top and fake."

"I'm just surprised to find out that you know him and have never said anything about it."

"Were you wearing that when you two collided?"

Glancing down, I take in my black flip-flops, skinny jeans and favorite Game of Thrones t-shirt that declares I'm a Khaleesi supporter.

What's wrong with my outfit?

Taking off my glasses, I use a tissue from my bag to clean the plain Jane black framed specs and reply, "Yes, I love this shirt, why?" Putting my glasses back on, I meet her amused gaze.

She shrugs and drinks the last few sips of her latte. "Are you going back to the dorm?"

"Right now?"

"Yeah, I have to get ready for work."

"I'll go with you. I have plenty of homework to catch up on."

We both grab our stuff and start heading across campus to our building.

"I get off late tonight, but we could stop by the cafeteria tomorrow for lunch if you want?"

"That sounds good."

"It's a date then."

"So what's wrong with what I'm wearing?" I can't stop myself from asking; now she has me curious.

"Kadence, you probably gave the guy a nerdgasm." She giggles. "He's used to these 'Barbie Dolls' all over him, and I guess he didn't have any idea what to do with you when he saw you."

"Oh God." My hand flies to my forehead, thinking about being a huge dork compared to what he's used to. Am I really that nerdy, though?

"No, babe. Trust me; it's a good thing."

"But I don't want him to like me and how is that a good quality?" It's a total lie. I'd be over the moon if he felt that way about me. I don't know why I don't just say it out loud, though.

"Why not, what's wrong with him liking you?"

"Because have you seen him? I could never handle everything that comes along with him. This whole conversation is ridiculous anyhow. There's no way Tyler Owens would ever be into someone like me."

"Ugh, no kidding. Look in the mirror," Stacia one of our neighbors comments as she walks by.

"Screw you, whore!" Brianne calls after her. Stacia keeps walking but throws up her middle finger. "Ignore her. She's hateful because Ty's best friend slept with her and then her sister."

"Oh, wonderful." This is a perfect example of why I don't do jocks and why I don't want to like Tyler Owens.

We get to our room, and as soon as I find my headphones, I put some Cold War Kids on and get to work. Pushing the guy troubles to the back of my mind, I try to focus, 'cause nobody has time for that mess.

Sapphire Knight

**Winners are not people who never fail,
but people who never quit.**

Tyler

"But why do we have to eat here? You guys are done with practice; can't we go somewhere fun?" Jada whines as we all sit in the middle of the cafeteria, trays loaded down with a ton of food.

Swear to Christ her voice annoys me to no end. "You can go. Nobody's stopping you," I reply loud enough so that her friends can hear me also. Maybe they'll finally get the hint; I've been pushing her off me for forever it seems. She's even this way in class, and it's old already.

Jada's been a big-time hang around of mine since I rode the bench for our first game last year and it's grown worse over time. We've hooked up a total of two times now, and she wants to be more. I swear she already thinks that she's my girlfriend or something.

However, I'm not about to date a chick who gives the team blow jobs when she's drunk. They're all grateful for her team spirit, but I find it disgusting. No matter how many times I've told her that I'm not interested, she doesn't give up. She probably thinks that she'll wear me down, but it's never going to happen.

"That's not true Ty!" She giggles in her fake high-pitched voice. "You know food tastes better with me around." Smiling coyly, she plays it off by taking my fork and feeding me a bite of my cheese fries. I usually eat pretty decently but I was craving cheese fries topped with gravy something fierce. She thinks that she's cute and attentive by feeding me, but it just gets on my nerves. It'd be nice if she'd actually get out of my way so I can really eat before it gets cold. I've said this out loud before, yet she ignores it.

Sitting at the head of the table, Jada perches on my lap, feeding me a bite and then carrying on about makeup to her friends. JJ and Chandler are in their seats on each side of me, a few of Jada's girls trying to do the same thing as her in monkey-see, monkey-do fashion. A couple of other teammates sit in the remaining chairs with random girls as well. This is usually dinner and makes me miss my brothers damn near every night.

Don't get me wrong, the guys and I loved it at first, and then we got sick of it. Now we've just gotten used to it. This is how mealtime normally turns out if we're not at our house and we're usually so exhausted from practice that we don't want to cook, so we end up here a lot since it's quick and easy.

Freight Train

JJ and Chandler aren't just my teammates; they're my best friends on campus. I'm close with my cousin Dallas too, but he doesn't go to school here. I met both guys while playing ball in high school. They went to other schools, but when my team would travel, we'd play against their teams. In the off-season, we'd take turns visiting each other and screw around together. They practically lived at my house during summer vacations.

When it came time to choosing schools, they both knew I had one selection. I would go where my parents and Clyde went no matter how hard I had to work to get there. When I showed up to my first football practice for AU, my two best friends were there waiting for me. I almost broke down into tears. I know it was my mom that made it all happen for me. She'd be the only person who'd know that I'd need them with me and be able to actually make something like that happen.

"Hey Freight Train, no more kicking guys' asses on the field. Next time, tell one of us and we'll do it for you. Coach killed us while you were out," Niner grumbles, then chugs his chocolate flavored protein mix he just finished shaking up.

He's a defensive lineman we've become cool with. The man's massive at six foot-five and three hundred forty pounds. He came all the way from Nebraska. He played one season for them and decided he'd rather play for a southern team. Can't say I blame him; we are the best when it comes to college football.

"I heard. Did he make you call him Daddy too, Niner, and it hurt your feelings?" I razz and the guys all laugh, Niner included.

"Shut the fuck up man," he grumbles, and we keep chuckling.

Glancing around, I catch sight of familiar chestnut locks and a curious face watching our table. Her eyes meet mine briefly then she quickly averts them, turning away and talking to a friend who's with her. I can't believe I'm getting to see her twice in one week. Has she been right in front of me this entire time? Have I really been that self-absorbed and blind? How many other gorgeous chicks have I missed around campus?

"Jada, how about you sit over there so I can finish eating?" I don't want her all over me with the pretty girl from yesterday around to see it.

"No worries, I'll make sure you eat. You need to rest after such a tough practice," she argues, and I glance at JJ, frustrated. The girl on his lap feeds him, and he happily goes along with it, smirking and egging her on. Turning to Chandler, he rolls his eyes and moves his face away when the girl on his lap attempts to give him a drink of soda.

At least he feels my annoyance.

Ignoring everything else going on around me, my gaze stays trained on the gorgeous female that ran into me yesterday. I open my mouth and chew each time Jada feeds me a bite, on autopilot but otherwise completely ignore her, staring at mystery girl. She eats a banana and yogurt while her friend across from her chomps down a few pieces of pizza.

Shit, I know her friend. She's in my class. I think her name is Brianne.

Standing suddenly, Jada falls off my lap in a comical manner with her feet and arms flailing. She catches herself with the table, and the guys chuckle at her bright red face. "I'm done," I declare and push my half-eaten tray of food toward Jada. "Thanks for the help, ladies. Jada, be a babe and toss this for me."

Freight Train

I'm a dick. I don't glance her way as I practically order her to get rid of my trash for me. Maybe it'll piss her off, and she'll leave with her little group of hoochies. The last thing I want is her to follow me around some more.

JJ and Chandler stare at me confused until they see that my sight's trained on the other table with the two beautiful young women. Once they notice the other chicks, they both stand, doing the same as me.

They've had to listen to me go on about her all day. I've been wondering who she was and how I'd be able to see her again. I'm not about to let this chance pass me by. I need to figure out who the hell she is and why I haven't noticed her around before yesterday. I never meet any women that get under my skin enough to have me thinking of them so much.

"Niner, Briggs, Grey, and ladies—we'll catch you guys later." We each say our goodbyes, and I make a beeline straight for Brianne and her mousy friend.

Stopping behind my little assailant, I place my hands on the back of the standard-issue cafeteria chair. My fingertips and knuckles rest against the warmness of her back, and I can feel her muscles tense up. Brianne beams her usual friendly smile, even as JJ and Chandler take seats on either side of her.

"Hey, Brianne. Thought we'd come say what's up to you and your friend." Grinning, I peer down at the top of the statue-still head of miss chestnut locks. The peek-a-boo red barely shows through, but it's enough to know she's probably a wild one inside. I love the chicks with all the pent-up frustration in them; they're the good girls that always go oh-so-bad with a little motivation. I'm just the type to do the motivating.

Brianne's smile widens, amusement shining brightly in her gaze, as I'm sure she's heard all about what happened between her friend and me. "Hey, Ty. Who are these big stud muffins you've been hiding?" Her head tilts to each side of her.

"Chandler," I nod to my friend on the left who's sitting up properly. Good posture and all that. He grins a friendly smile at her with his perfectly straight teeth and dimple on full display. "JJ," I nod to the right. And he flashes a cocky smirk, completely full of himself. Officially introducing them, I signal toward the top of the gorgeous head below me. "And who's this pretty lady?"

"Nice to meet you, handsome number one." Brianne trails her fingers over JJ's muscular arm. "And you too, handsome number two." She winks at Chan, not the least bit shy to flirt with the both of them. "This is my best friend, Kadence Winters. Kay, meet Ty Owens." She motions for Kadence to turn and look behind her.

Instead of moving around, she leans her head back until our eyes meet. She's sexy as all hell with that tiny beauty mark on her face. I'd love just to bend over and plant my lips against her sinful little mouth. I fantasized about that pucker and her sultry peach gloss all damn night last night while in bed; she had me jerking my dick so hard, that I thought I'd eventually rip it off. It's still there, and I'll happily show it to her too.

"Hey, Pretty." My lips turn up into my signature smile that makes the girls' panties drop. They can never resist it when I turn up the charm. It's an Owens family trait.

She makes a disgusted look, clearly not amused. "Sorry for running into you yesterday."

Not the response I was expecting. It has me choking up a little; it's something I'm not used to happening—like ever.

Freight Train

Just shake it off and play it cool.

"It was more of a pleasure if anything." The wink I give her comes natural, the flirting leaving my tongue like the skillful flirt I am.

She squints her eyes like she's trying to figure me out or something. As she does, I'm able to make out tiny golden specks mixed in with her rich coffee colored irises. They're an absolutely stunning feature, but she keeps them hidden away from the world behind a pair of plain, black-framed glasses. I'm sure the color would be much more noticeable if she'd take them off and wear contacts. I don't mind, though; if anything, those specs make me think of her in a naughty schoolgirl uniform being bent over and spanked.

I doubt people realize how beautiful she truly is and it's their loss. At first glance, she's kind of plain, but when you stop and really look at her, she's magnificent. Is she the cheerleaders or sorority girls running around with a face full of makeup and barely-there clothes, kind of hot? No. She's so much better. She has very little, or no makeup on, besides that edible peach gloss. And she's dressed like herself, not trying to impress anyone. It's so fucking sexy—her confidence, not caring what anyone but herself thinks.

I wish more chicks were that way. Then there'd be a variety, instead of a group all trying to be the same thing. Dress the same, wear the same makeup, drive the same cars, act the same. *So fucking boring.*

"I'm full," she announces suddenly, looking over at Brianne and shutting me back out. "Are you ready to go?"

She's pulling the same move I did back at the other table with Jada, and I can't believe it. Is she still pissed from us colliding earlier? I thought it wasn't a big deal since neither of us were hurt. Did I remember to apologize? Shit, should I? Even if it wasn't my fault?

"I'm ugh...sorry about earlier, sweetheart." The words leave my mouth a bit gruff, just as a pair of hands scale up and over my back.

Jada appears beside me, wrapping her arms around my body like a snake claiming its next meal. "Let's go have dessert. Also, about our convo we were having earlier about being called 'daddy,' I can call you whatever you'd like me too. You know I'm easy." She ends with an annoying giggle, and I damn near gag.

"I don't know what the fuck you're talking about, but 'daddy' is the last thing I'd want you to call me."

Kadence's chair pushes backward, right into my groin as she stands. It feels fucking brilliantly painful and stars dance in my vision as I choke through the feeling of being punched in the stomach.

"Yep, I'm done. I couldn't eat after that if I tried," she declares, disgusted, and quickly strides toward the trash can.

Momentarily dazed from being hit in the dick, I try to collect myself when Brianne jumps up and hurries after Kadence, calling back, "I'm sorry, guys! It was nice meeting you."

I can't compose a coherent goodbye through the throbbing sensation radiating in my nuts, but the guys both wave their goodbyes.

Just like earlier, she's gone again.

At least now I have a name. It's a start, and I know who her best friend is too. I'll find her...Right after I can breathe correctly again.

"Aww, poor baby! Do you need me to rub it and make it all better for you? We don't even have to leave; we can use the bathroom here if you want." Jada's palm runs down over each ridge of my abs—on a mission—and I jump back away from her touch.

Freight Train

"I'm busy tonight and every night." She reaches for me again, rubbing over my stomach. I stop her hand in a death grip, removing the object of my torment from my torso, moving a few more steps away. She's relentless. "I'm taking off, you guys staying?"

JJ smiles as Jada comes up behind him, rubbing his shoulders and her friend sits on his lap again, "Lexi, you give me a ride later?" he asks the double meaning clearly there.

"Of course, or you can stay the night with us," she offers, and I turn to Chandler, over that conversation already.

"I'm good." He shakes his head and waves me off.

Thank Christ, they're my friends, but I'm not in the mood to hear them give me shit over how that all just went down with Kadence. I'm already set to have blue balls from fantasizing about her nearly all damn night last night and then today and can't forget I'll have a tender dick from being chaired. "I'm out."

We say our goodbyes, and I make my way to my truck, brushing Jada off one last time and nearly tell her to just straight fuck off. I didn't do it, but I sure wanted to. She can't take the hint at all that I'm not interested in her—period.

So, Kadence is my little assailant's name...I like it. The name's unique like she seems to be. Her no-nonsense vibe I get is intriguing too. Not many can brush off the Owens charm, and it seems as if it doesn't faze her in the slightest. I need to figure out what makes her tick, why she's so different from the others, and why she doesn't appear the least bit interested in getting to know me.

Loading up, I turn on some Kurt Vile, *Pretty Pimpin*, and lower my truck windows. The Alabama night air feels fantastic after sitting in the overly-cool cafeteria. The humidity warms me just enough to be comfortable, and the cross breeze makes it all pretty damn perfect.

The football house I share with the guys isn't too far away, just a few streets down from campus. I could've walked today, and a lot of times we do, but I wasn't sure what we'd all end up doing for food. Besides, my body's still sore from the rough practices Coach ran us through today preparing for this weekend. You can only ice a body part so much before you just suck it up and deal with the ache.

Two figures on the sidewalk draw my attention. As I get near, I can make out Brianne and Kadence. She's dressed in jeans and a t-shirt like yesterday. I love it; she looks normal—not all dressed up trying to show off for anyone.

I like it when a woman can be herself and still be beautiful. The fakes stuff gets too over-the-top sometimes, and when you go swimming or take a shower, and all the fake comes off, it's like being with an entirely different person. And sometimes the other person looks pretty scary. That sounds dickish, but it's the truth. Too much black on your eyebrows or under your eyes is really a curse, not a benefit. Don't ask what it is with me noticing eyebrows, but I always have for some reason.

Pulling over beside them, their pace increases, clearly thinking I'm a creeper or something. Turning down the radio, I shout through the open passenger side window, "Kadence! Brianne! Come here."

At their names they stop power walking and turn toward me, Brianne shielding her eyes from the headlights. "Ty?" she asks, squinting.

"Yeah, get over here! Both of you."

Freight Train

I can't believe they're walking in the dark. At least there are two of them in case someone were to bother them. They approach the passenger window. Kadence stands back a little bit, while Brianne leans on the window sill, smiling. "What's up, Ty?"

"Hey, stranger; you guys hop on in, and I'll give you a ride."

"Okay, thanks. Come on, Kay," Brianne calls.

"No, I'm fine. Thanks, though." Kadence starts to walk off.

Brianne turns to me, "She's not going to let you give us a lift, she's stubborn like that. Thanks, though."

"No, wait. I'll get her. You get in, and I'll put her through the driver side."

"You're actually going to carry her over here?" Her eyes grow wide, and I grin mischievously as the vision of her holding onto me like I'm her prince fills my mind. She's small enough I could lift her no problem, and I'll probably get bonus points when she sees how strong I am. She has no idea all the fun we could have together. These muscles aren't just fluff.

"Why not?" I shrug. "She bumped into me yesterday, after all. I think me carrying her around is probably the next step in our physical introduction."

She giggles, full of excitement at our plan. "She's going to kill you. It's going to be hilarious, go for it! Oh and be careful; I'm pretty sure she knows self-defense. She may throw a kick or two."

Brianne's acquainted with me well enough to know that I wouldn't hurt her friend, just mess with her a little. When I open my door and sprint after Kadence, Brianne jumps into the passenger side, quickly closing the door. I can hear her excited laughter float out of the open window as she watches us.

I snatch Kadence around the waist, lifting her up before she even knows what's happening. Then take off running back toward my truck, jiggling her around like a sack of potatoes. She's small enough that I could tote her around all day I imagine.

"Ho-ly s-hi-t! Put me do-wn!" she yells, making me chuckle louder as her voice dips and rises with each of my bumpy strides.

"Nope, you got me yesterday in the hall. Now it's my turn." Getting back to my still-open truck door, I practically launch her petite body inside. Then I jump in beside her before she can escape, slamming my door closed in a flash.

"Stealing me is payback for accidently bumping into you? It wasn't even that hard!" She huffs while Brianne laughs, tears trailing down her face as she giggles at Kadence being manhandled.

"Nah, if I were stealing you, then I wouldn't be dropping you off at your dorm. I'd just keep you, and I'm pretty sure there'd be a rope or handcuffs of some sort."

"Well, that's not creepy at all."

I wink, smiling at her. "I'm assuming you stay in one of the dorms over here or do you belong to one of the sorority houses?" I doubt that she's in a sorority, but ask anyway. I don't want to offend her by ruling it out right away.

"We're in Charleston Hall." Kadence sends me a sideways glance.

"You're even closer to me, then."

She leans forward, turning up my radio and restarts the song after she hears what's on.

"Please, help yourself to the radio."

Freight Train

"Hey, you stuck me in here, so technically it's your fault. Just be thankful a good song's on, or I'd be dj-ing for you." Grinning at her, she returns it with a soft smile and pink cheeks.

Moments later, we pull into her dorm's parking area. "See, no kidnapping charges to be filed. If anything I may have just saved you from some unnecessary foot blisters. You really should be thanking me."

"Gee, you're so thoughtful."

Brianne opens her door, waving, "Thanks, Ty."

"No problem, see you Wednesday." I wave back, as she steps out and my gaze lands on Kadence again.

"Unless you want to be kidnapped?" I ask. "I could work something out. I do have an empty room and a loud radio to drown out any noises you decide to make."

"You're really not making yourself sound good; I just want you to know that."

"We could go for a drive." It's full of innuendo, but she ignores it.

"And where would you take me?"

"Well, where would you want to go?" I'd take her wherever she let me as long as we'd get to be alone. I want to know everything there is to know about her, including the color of her panties.

"I guess you'll never know, Tyler Owens." Smirking, she climbs out, closing the door behind her.

"Hey!" I call as she turns to walk away.

"Yes?" Her eyes sparkle with our easy banter.

"You should probably give me your number."

"It's like that destination we were just discussing; you'll 'probably' never know it." She winks and walks towards Brianne.

Cute.

She's got jokes, and it makes her even more fascinating. Now not only do I want to kiss her sassy little mouth but I also want to smack her on her sweet round ass. Christ, this is exactly what I needed after that fight last weekend and then having to sit out of the last game—a good ole-fashioned distraction. A fun one at that, I can already tell.

Waiting, I make sure they get inside the building safely, and the entire time, I'm thinking of our exchange. I can't get over the excited feeling in my stomach and the way that my heart's beating fast. She's a damn tease, and I love that shit. It makes me want to discover each inch of her body and get to know her in every other possible way as well.

Since when have I wanted to waste time on a chick like this? It doesn't matter; I want to now. There's one thing I'm good at besides football, and that's winning. I'll get that number, just wait and see.

KADENCE

"He likes you," Brianne announces loudly, nearly singing the words as we walk through the corridor toward our shared dorm room.

Exactly what I didn't want to happen. But secretly inside, I'm flattered, but that man spells trouble, no doubt.

"No, he doesn't; that was just flirting. That's all guys like him do. They play with the 'me types' and date the 'Jada types.' I'm way too boring for a man like that."

"Oh gross." She waves me off. "Jada's such a tramp. When she came up to him at the table, I swear his skin crawled. Ty's friendly with pretty much everyone, but I see him in class twice a week. He doesn't flirt with all the girls like you two were doing in the truck just now. He'll tease sometimes, but it'll be for like two seconds until the girl gives in and hands over her number or whatever." She unlocks our door, and I follow her into our room.

Like that's any better. "You're so not helping his case with that one."

"I'm not trying to, just wanting you to see the point that I'm trying to make. I'm not going to lie to you about him to try and make him look good or anything. You'll see the kind of person he is on your own, and I have a feeling you'll like him back."

"I see he's a flirt and if I want him to stop, then I should just cough up my number, is that right?"

At least that's what I'm getting from her defending him anyway. She seems to think he actually likes me and is thrilled with that prospect. Me—not so much. Ty is all trouble with a capital T. I noticed it from the first time I laid my eyes on him, and I don't have any time for that!

"No...Well, shit. That did sound kind of bad, I guess. So, umm Ty sleeps with girls, lots of them. But he's also mega popular around here. You saw how those females in the cafeteria acted with the football players tonight. Girls just throw themselves at the guys. It doesn't mean that he's a bad person or that he'd be the same way if he actually liked someone. That someone being you."

"Why do you care about this, anyhow? You get absolutely nothing out of me liking him except putting up with my bitch fest about him. I'm not like you; ice cream doesn't solve my problems when it comes to guys. If anything it makes my issues worse because my butt gets bigger."

"Ugh, I don't know, essentially I'd get nothing, but this isn't about me. It would just be nice to see you with someone like him. I think you'd sort of balance each other out or something. Especially with what happened at last week's game. He needs someone who won't bring any drama around. And by the way, I love ice cream, thank you very much."

I know she does, I'm the one who gets stuck eating it with her.

"I have no idea what went down at his game, you know I only watch the NFL."

"Well to get straight to it; he ripped a guy's helmet clean off his head and was sitting on top of him, throwing punches. He knocked the other player's tooth out and everything. It was pretty awesome after watching the asshole ram into Ty during almost the entire game."

Jesus, she's not helping his case at all.

"Oh, God. See, he has violent tendencies. Exactly why I need to stay away from him and you just let him carry me around. I see who's side you're on."

"Whatever! You're being dramatic, and I'm the dramatic friend, remember? And uh, good luck with staying away from him, because you're definitely on *his* radar." She beams a smile, and I roll my eyes at her for the twentieth time today. She's used to it. Over the years it's become my go-to response with her whenever she comes up with her next scheme.

    That's fine. I'm sure I'll be back off his radar just as quickly as I popped on it. Guys like him can't stay devoted to liking or being interested in one person, so I'm not worried in the slightest bit. Tyler Owens is exactly like all the rest of the jocks in college. One thing on his mind and when he doesn't get it from me, he'll forget I even existed.

Sapphire Knight

Freight Train

It's hard to beat a person who never gives up.

-Babe Ruth

Game five-

One week later and three hours until game time...

"That cheeky fucker." Mumbling the words, I close our dorm door once the delivery guy walks off. The hall was littered with nosey students, probably wanting to know why we were getting a delivery that didn't consist of take out.

"Who was it?" Brianne mumbles, taking a big bite of pepperoni pizza. I swear this chick could live off the stuff and she stays looking like a twig too.

"Delivery guy. He dropped off tickets to the home game today."

"No way! You ordered us tickets?" She asks around chewing a big bite of food, clearly excited to go and cheer for our school's football team. Alabama students pretty much eat, sleep, and breathe football during the season.

Facing her, I hold up the number twelve football jersey—a Tyler Owen's replica jersey that was just dropped off with the envelope full of game tickets. She bursts out laughing, and I follow with my own giggles. She knows I didn't order it, that's for sure.

"How is he being cheeky? I think it's very sweet." She chuckles around another bite of pizza. "Plus, that means we'll get to go early and tailgate!"

"Yeah, no. And because he's automatically assuming I want to watch *him* play football, and wear his jersey at that. I should show up wearing a jersey with another team member's number for that one."

"But you love football."

"Wrong. I love NFL football, one team in particular, actually, and you know I don't do the tailgating. Those guys end up trashed before the game and half the time in a fight. I've seen the news about it and have read the campus paper about having a good time but being responsible on school property."

"They do get pretty wild with the partying." She nods. "You've never even seen Ty play before though, he's good."

"So? Neither have you." I shrug, and she grins, guiltily. "Wait, you've seen him play before? How do I not know this? You've been holding out on me a lot."

"You were visiting your dad in Texas and my date at the time took me. Ty ended up scoring two touchdowns."

"My best friend, and yet you leave out vital information."

"Nah, that date turned out to be a dipshit. Now get dressed; we have a football game to go watch!"

"I'm not going. Maybe I'll see if one of the skanks down the hallway wants the tickets, lord knows they were nosey enough when the guy dropped the envelope and jersey off."

"Hell no! Remember what he did when you wouldn't let him give you a ride?"

My thoughts flash to him carrying me, his muscles hard against my soft body. They felt delicious, way better than they should have, that's for sure. "You're right." I nod, "We can show up to the game for a while, but once it gets boring, we're leaving, or at least I'm leaving."

"He sent more than one ticket? And trust me, it won't be boring. College football's not what you think it is."

"If you say so, and yeah, he sent five."

"Holy shit!" She jumps up and runs to her closet. "I have the perfect shirt to wear too."

"Why am I not surprised?"

"Do you want to invite anyone else?"

"No, we'll get all that space...Plus I don't really have anyone else I'd want to spend that much time with," I reply bluntly, and she laughs.

Brianne turns into this excited maniac, rummaging through both of our closets to find her outfit and some shorts to go with my newly-acquired jersey. I have to admit, seeing him in those tight football pants does have me a little excited.

Tyler

"You sent *five* tickets? Five, bro?" JJ looks at me like I'm crazy.

"And a jersey." I shrug, and he bursts out laughing.

"Oh man, and you haven't even hit it yet. She's going to have you whipped at this rate."

"I will though just wait, and it'll be ten times better than what you've been dipping into." A few of the guys around me snicker, knowing I'm talking about Jada and her slutty friends. Kay is prime meat, no doubt in my mind, but none of these idiots take the extra two seconds to see it.

"I don't know bro; you send her tickets, buy her a shirt...Now you're talking about her pussy being better." He looks behind me. "Watch out, Chandler; our pussy magnet may be getting spoken for."

Huffing, I slam my locker closed. "I'm having some fun; it's not like we're falling in love or any of that crazy shit."

"Mmhmm," Chandler pipes in from behind. "So where are you planning on taking her after the game?"

"Back to my bedroom if the tickets work like I want."

Laughing, JJ bumps my forearm with his, giving me props.

"Hey, Niner, check this out, Owens sent some chick five tickets for the game today."

"His eyes widen. "Does she have hot friends?"

Freight Train

I shrug. Brianne's not bad looking, but I don't know about any other friends of hers.

He busts out laughing and makes a few 'whipping' sounds causing the other guys to chuckle with him.

Nosey asses.

Ignoring them, I grab my receiving gloves and check myself over again, to make sure I'm all set for today's game. I'll take Kadence out any day if she'll let me. I'm not admitting that to my boys, though, and besides, right now she's playing hard to get. It's all good. I love the chase—makes things way more entertaining.

She's the best type of distraction for me right now, too, with the fight happening two weeks ago and Clyde not letting me or Nate help him out at home. I need something to get my mind off it all, and she's perfect. Besides, once I do finally get her, it'll be that much more satisfying.

"Come on twelve!" Coach shouts so I'll get to the front of the team with Kash our QB and lead everyone out. Grabbing my helmet, I get in my position. "Defense and offense team captains?"

"Yes, Coach!" Kash and I both yell together as our teammates start stomping their cleats against the concrete floor, getting pumped up. Between stomps they smack their hands against their thighs, making loud clapping sounds. The locker room begins to sound like a giant rumble, and it causes my heart rate to speed up.

I play both sides; offense and defense. I'm actually slotted for four different positions but play wherever the team needs me at the most. Plus, it allows me to be a team captain for the defense. I'm close to a lot of the guys, including our quarterback on offense because of it.

"We ready to show them how Alabama football gets played in *our* house?"

"Hell yes!" The entire team shouts back, making the locker room sound like more of a thunderous echo. It's the stomping and chanting that always gets my adrenaline going, then when we run out and hear the fans doing the same, it does insane things to my stomach. I always feel a huge burst of energy and excitement come over me.

"Then send them back home!" Coach hollers and the team goes crazy.

The guys stay in line, jogging behind Kash and me as we make our way out the hall and onto the field. The stadium's full today, with fans standing and screaming to greet us. I'm grateful for all of the support, every single one of them cheering us on, but my gaze immediately scopes out one section in particular.

Kadence is easy to spot, and I damn near stumble as I take her in. She looks nothing—and I mean *nothing*—like the nerdy, sweet girl I've gotten used to seeing. The one that I've started looking forward to seeing every day in passing. I may even silently hope she'll run into me again in the hallways just so I can feel her up against me.

Kash grips my forearm, his brow wrinkling, "You okay, brah?"

Meeting his eyes, I chuckle. "Yep, never been better." And it's the truth. Kadence has evolved into one hell of a swan, that's for sure. I already thought she was beautiful before, but hello sexy college girl.

Releasing my arm, Kash grins and bumps my knuckles once he notices exactly what's caught my eye.

Freight Train

Jogging toward my spot, I give Kadence a small wave with a few of my fingers. Her beaming smile is enough to make me swallow roughly. If my cup weren't on so damn tight, I'd need to adjust it. I hope my dick doesn't decide to grow with her bouncing around like that. It'd hurt pretty fucking bad to get throttled with my cock full in the middle of the game. Not to mention a little embarrassing too.

JJ comes up beside me, staring at my reserved seats as well. "No fucking way."

"Yep," I smirk, knowing he's referencing Kadence in her sexy as hell outfit. I wonder why she didn't invite anyone else with her. That fucker I paid to deliver her stuff better not have kept the other tickets.

JJ and I check Kadence out the best we can from this far away. She's dressed in tiny white shorts, cropped jersey, and a ponytail. She's got my number painted on one cheek, and her glasses are missing. I guess she owns contacts or only needs them for reading and stuff.

JJ's most likely choking over his words right now from teasing me in the locker room about her earlier. Jesus, I thought she was pretty before, but now she's fucking smoking hot. I don't know if it's because she's clad in my number or what, but I've never been this breathless checking out a woman wearing clothes. If this was Brianne's doing, I owe her big time.

She's definitely going back to my bedroom with me if I have anything to say about it. I want to peel off each layer she's got on and discover the rest of that tight body she's been keeping hidden. Just call me Christopher Columbus, and I'll happily make her body sail.

KADENCE

"I told you it would work!" Brianne laughs happily after we watch Ty nearly fall over his own two feet. He looked up, and his mouth dropped. It was pretty epic; I wish we'd gotten a picture of it.

So, I was completely against her idea of this outfit and fought her on it, but she obviously knew what she was talking about. "I'll admit it; I'm happy I wore it now. Just wish these shorts were a little bit longer. I feel like my ass cheeks are hanging out and my name should be changed to College Barbie."

"Kay, you've been beautiful your entire life, let loose a little. This *is* college, so have some actual fun. And your butt is not hanging out; you're covered, I swear. *College Barbie.*" She winks, and I stick my tongue out at her.

"I like my normal clothes. And besides, I'm here and in this ridiculous outfit, aren't I? I'm going to have some fun. I got nachos, didn't I?"

"Yep, you definitely are, you crazy partier." Her tone's sarcastic as she digs out her phone. "And I'm posting this shit on Facebook." She smiles and snaps a picture of me with her smartphone. "Hashtag—at the game with 'The Freight Train's new girl,'" she mumbles while she types.

Oh, God. She didn't really say that, right? "Holy shit. You didn't really put that, did you?"

"Yep." She nods and shows me the screen after it's already been posted to her feed.

A few guys behind me cheer. "We're by his girl! Check her out; she's hot."

"Oh shit, don't hate me." Brianne gapes, staring down at her phone as comments begin to pour onto her post and her notifications begin to ping like crazy.

She glances up, her eyes growing wide, eyebrows nearly to her hairline.

"What did you do?"

She shakes her head, pointing up and behind me.

Turning, I face the jumbo screen that currently has her Facebook post on it. It's massive in size so everyone can see the picture of me all dolled up and read her hashtags easily:

#AtTheGameWithFreightTrainsNewGirl #12SentHerTicketsAndHisJersey #AlabamaFootball #CuteCouple #PictureTheBabys #KayAndTy #12 #Owens #AU

"Oh, my gawd! Brianne!" It comes out shriller than I had intended, but she gets the point.

"How was I supposed to know they'd monitor his hashtags?" She shrugs, appearing guilty while women around us start shooting me death glares like I just cursed their mother or ate the last damn Oreo.

"Just great, fan-freaking-tastic! You've unleashed the piranhas." Resting my hand on my face, I pretend to hide, wanting a small hole to sink into, even for only two seconds.

"It'll all be fine, relax."

But it won't....Nothing is going to be the same after this. Bad enough *I'm a football star's daughter*, but now, apparently, I'm one's girl as well. My dad was able to keep my privacy intact for the most part, but there's no way this will just up and disappear, not now and not anytime soon. With social media, everyone knows everything in college. Nothing's secret or sacred anymore and I've just become the highlight, or lowlight in some cases, of AU today.

Fuck. My. Life. My dad's going to flip when he finds out about this.

Now I feel like a giant circus freak as people smile and wave at me or send me dirty looks. There's really no middle; it's either they love me for supposedly being the girlfriend of one of their favorite players or they hate me for it.

I can't believe Brianne didn't consider any of the consequences a post like that could have on Ty or me. She's known me nearly my whole life and should also know by now that I like my privacy.

Now if we supposedly 'break-up' all of Tyler's fans will end up all hating me even more. I need to pray to God that he plays well or next I'll be branded as bad luck and fans will boot me out of the stadium. This is the south. Football is serious, like basically its own religion down here.

I was really enjoying it that very few people here had any idea about who I am. I was fortunate to have a father who loved me and had a successful career while I was growing up, but it came with its own negative side effects. At least he wasn't ever like any of the celebrity parents I see online now. They're always boasting about their kids and trying to make money off them somehow. Thank God he was never into any of those reality shows or anything.

My father was gone a lot, always training or traveling to games. I grew up with my Nan outside of Boston, who was my live-in nanny until I was fifteen. Dad's career was over then, and Nan moved back to England to be with her family. Dad declared he was 'sick of fucking snow, that we're southerners' and moved us to our summer house in Texas, right off the Gulf.

Living those last couple years with my dad was interesting. He was always loving and good to me. He still is, but he's changed so much. I was grateful when it came time for me to head off to college. Dad made a big fuss, but I know he was happy about it too. Now I fly to Texas to visit him, or he'll come here sometimes, just depends on what's going on at the time.

My father never told me much about my mom, and eventually, I stopped asking. If I ever brought her up, he'd close up and then change the subject.

Dad's family's from Ireland. I've gotten to meet them a few times over the years when he's flown us over to visit. He has a sister. I'm not close with her, though; she's not fond of America and never visits.

Dad was sent to live with his aunt who lived in Alabama when he was eight, so he grew up in the states and even played college ball before the NFL. It's one of the main reasons why I chose to attend Alabama for college. It has history in our family, and I respect that. I'm in a football-crazed college, and I'm the daughter of a football-crazed man, so I fit perfectly.

The game goes by quicker than expected and is far better than I ever would have imagined. Ty plays like a man possessed, and I can easily see why the masses love him. After witnessing my dad play for so many years and being submerged in the football life, I know by watching Ty play today, that he has 'it.' He's talented enough to play for the NFL if he wants to and be successful at it for a really long time. Some people get out on that field, and it's like they can finally breathe, as if they're free.

It's exciting because I know that if *I* can sense it about him, then no doubt there are teams looking at him and he most likely has no idea yet. We're both starting our third year in school next semester (yes, I broke down and googled him), and I wouldn't be surprised at all if he's picked up in this next draft. I wonder what team he'll eventually go to and what teams he follows.

"What did you think?" Brianne turns to me, full of enthusiasm now that the game's over and Alabama took home a big win. I honestly can't believe it went by so fast.

"I totally loved it. I can't believe I haven't come to these games sooner. I should've given college ball a chance."

"So you want to start watching them then?"

"Yes, but thankfully next time we'll know to get our own seats so people won't be staring at me the entire time and I'm definitely wearing a hat or something."

"Are you nuts? These seats are unbelievable! I was literally able to see everything. I feel like I could reach out and touch them, they're so close."

We are set up in the prime location, and I shouldn't be complaining, but I have a feeling Tyler's not going to be thrilled when he sees what's all over Facebook now. I'll probably be kidnapped by hordes of angry football groupies begging me to give them his cock details, and I'm not actually dating the guy. I don't think I have any more football tickets to look forward to from him in my near future, that's for sure.

We're exiting our row as one of the team's water guys stops next to us. "Hey, are you Kadence Winters?"

"Yes, that's me." I raise my eyebrow in question and scoot to the side so people can go around me to leave. It was a packed house all the way up until the end.

"Okay great. I'm Rob, and I'm on the team." He points to the field. "I mean, I help with the team. But that's not the point. I'm here because Owens asked me to see if you'd like to come and wait for him."

Interesting. Did he already see the jumbotron and know about the Facebook post?

"And if we say no and decide to just leave?"

"Well, then I'll walk you to your vehicle or dorm, wherever you need to go, so you don't have to do it alone."

"But it's broad daylight," Brianne argues.

He shrugs his shoulders, appearing nervous. "Look I'm just doing what Owens asked. He's a pretty nice guy, and many of them aren't, so please let me do this for you guys? You obviously mean something to him, if he sent me up here. Plus I saw the jumbotron and the Facebook posts. If it's true and you are his girl, then I definitely need to make sure no one bothers you."

Gritting my teeth, I glare at Brianne for the mess she's created and drug me into. This sounds like the pushy Tyler that I've caught a glimpse of the past few run-ins we've had.

"Fine. Rob, you can take us to meet up with Tyler. I don't want you to have to walk all the way to our dorm for no reason. Thank you for being a loyal friend to Ty."

He blushes when I say he's a friend to Tyler and nods. "Okay, thanks, follow me, please. We can use the field entrance and bypass the crowd."

"What about security?" Brianne pipes up, pointing toward the big guys in black and yellow security shirts. They should at least make them wear black and maroon, so they go with the school colors. Add a few stripes to their shirts, and they'll look like bumblebees on steroids.

Nathan holds up his badge hanging from his lanyard. "No worries, I can get us through. Regardless, they all saw the jumbotron too, so they already know to let you through to see Owens."

"Oh God," I mutter, wiping my brow again, wanting to punch my best friend as I follow along. This is all her doing, and I'm going to have to live through it at least until the semester's over and everyone finds something new to gossip over.

Brianne and I have to practically hop down the stairs, our short legs trying to keep up with Rob's long, quick strides. The guy's like six foot four and a total beanpole. He seems friendly, though, so I can see why they'd let him help out with the team. He strikes me as more of a basketball guy, though.

We stop at the field entrance where two security guards check over Rob's badge, then smile and nod at me like we're acquaintances or something. The trek over the green seems to take forever, but Rob's right, it probably just saved us thirty minutes from trying to get through everyone leaving. I'm pretty excited too, being able to walk out on the field. You don't get that chance often; they guard the field here like its sacred ground.

There's a bench outside the locker rooms in the hall where we stop. "You ladies have a seat, and once they're finished, everyone will come out. Did you want me to get you a soda or something while you wait?" Rob asks politely.

"Actually, I'd like..." Brianne starts to order, but I cut her off.

"No, we're good. Thanks for coming to get us," I respond politely, and he smiles.

"Okay, see you later." He takes off toward a door labeled 'Office,'

"Bye!" We both call and then get quiet.

"This is neat." She looks around, noticing the painted murals and such on the concrete walls.

"You're still in the doghouse," I grumble, and she sighs.

I swear we wait for twenty minutes before the door finally opens and a group of beefy guys carrying big duffel bags full of gear come pouring out, tired but happy. They're freaking huge too. I mean I know how big football players are from my dad, but it's not every day you're right beside an entire team of them. It's a bit intimidating and also sort of a turn on.

These guys look like they come from the south as if they were fed well and trained by pushing tractor tires around or something. No wonder Coach Stratton barely loses a game from what I hear. Supposedly, he only works with the elite when it comes to his own team.

I just saw how good Tyler is, so obviously, the rumors are true, and he's the prime pick for his position.

Speaking of the game, I wonder if my dad was watching. *I can only imagine the call I'll get if he saw the jumbotron and Brianne's Facebook post.*

So awesome, I think and roll my eyes to myself.

There's only two things you can do
when someone says you're not good enough:
you can prove them right, or you can prove them wrong.

- Julian Edelman

Tyler

I sent Rob to get Kadence from the stands for me and jumped into the shower as quickly as possible, skirting around all of the locker room celebrating going on. Then, of course, Coach wanted to talk, and the guys wanted to discuss the after party. Everyone's pumped up to celebrate our win.

I tried getting them to party tomorrow instead, but I was shut down. No one wants to practice on Monday being hungover. I get it;

I'd be the same way if I weren't in a hurry to get to Kadence. I want to spend time with her alone, away from the guys. However, it doesn't look like that's going to happen anytime soon. One of the many downfalls of sharing a house with a group of guys is the lack of privacy whenever you want it.

We get everything settled, and I throw on some fresh basketball shorts, a tank top, and a pair of Jordan slide sandals, and then head out to greet her. I know I look like a total bum, but I'm exhausted after playing my ass off today. Everyone still has energy because they didn't play as much, whereas I was in nearly the entire game. I think I even ran faster than usual today. Could I have been showing off for her and not even realized it?

At this point, I just want to eat three steaks, have wild monkey sex, then take a damn nap and in that order if possible.

I was thinking of the best way to get Kadence to come over to the house without coming off as some desperate douchebag, so I suggested we have a barbecue instead of just a kegger. I have a feeling she's not the typical party girl, so this may give me some room to get her to give in and come too. My dumb ass even agreed to do the initial grilling. The shit you'll do to get time with a chick you want is freaking crazy.

JJ and Chandler follow me out of the locker rooms, planning to ride with me back to our place. Kash is driving his car over now as well, to help get stuff set up. Everyone else is supposed to be bringing alcohol, the food, and any other supplies needed for the night.

One step into the hallway and I'm reminded exactly what Kadence was wearing for the game. So help me, if I wasn't beyond exhausted my dick would already be tenting my shorts, hard as granite for her. She's a stunning sight and to know that she's waiting for me is even more exciting. I don't know what it is about this chick that has me so sprung. Maybe because she acts as though she couldn't care less about me? Whatever it is, she's driving me crazy inside.

"Hey! Great game, you guys!" Brianne jumps to her feet and cheers, giving Chandler and JJ hugs. JJ introduces her to Kash, and for once, Brianne acts a little bashful towards a guy, growing quiet while staring wide-eyed at him. Chicks always stare at Kash like he's hung the moon. Wish Kadence would look at me that way too.

"Hey, Pretty," I greet as Kadence gets to her feet. It's become my nickname for her from when I didn't know her name. I called her Pretty to the guys, and they thought it was hilarious.

Jackasses.

"Hi, Tyler." She stands and glances at the ground like she's tongue-tied herself. Something's clearly on her mind. I want to pull her to my body and kiss her until her own turns to putty in my hands. I could fix that tongue-tied issue really quickly.

She's not usually like this around me; she's spunkier. I hope she doesn't change just because of seeing me play football today. One thing I like about her is that she acts like me being a football player is completely normal to her. She doesn't make a big fuss or try to coddle me. It really isn't a big deal to her or else she just doesn't care. Fingers crossed that it's the latter.

Chicks who try to show me off all because of me being a football player do nothing but turn me off. Kadence, on the other hand, has me damn near chasing and panting after her. I'm enjoying it too. It'll make it that much sweeter when I finally get her right where I want her.

She's so fucking gorgeous up close too. Her shorts hug her body, while the cropped jersey shows off about two inches of smooth, creamy skin on her stomach, and best of all, her cheek has my number painted on it in maroon—big and bold. I fucking love that cheek.

Not being able to stop myself from touching her any longer, I reach out, sticking two fingers into the super tight pocket and pull her closer to me.

She steps forward, still looking at the ground while she plays with her bottom lip, lightly biting it between her teeth. If only she had any idea how innocent and sexy it makes her look. My brain's on total overload when it comes to her and all the things I want to do to her. Delicious images plague me, imagining her naked body underneath mine undulating while she pants my name. Where has this girl been the past few years? I don't get it how I could've missed her until now. She's stunning.

With my other hand, I lightly push her chin up until her luscious chocolate and gold-speckled irises meet mine. "You okay, sweetheart?"

"Yes," she answers quickly, glancing away for a brief second before meeting my gaze again. Softer, she finishes, "But did you see the Facebook post?"

"No, not yet, I haven't checked my phone. Why what's up?"

She pulls her own phone free from her back pocket, tapping a few times until she can show me a post that Brianne had made earlier. It has five hundred fifty-two likes already and two hundred thirty-seven comments underneath.

Freight Train

Closing out the screen, I hand it back to her, without paying much attention to it. I'm too worn out to care at the moment if I'm being honest. "We can talk about it later?"

"Are you sure? I mean, I understand if you don't want me to come to any more of your games." Her mood lightens some, and one of her eyebrows rises. She's adorable, every new little quirk she shows me, I swear it's my favorite. I can only imagine how much I'll enjoy seeing her head back, moaning in bliss.

"Of course, I'm sure. No worries about whatever's going on, I want you to be here. There's stuff on social media constantly; I ignore the majority of it." Caressing her jaw lightly with my thumb, her cheeks tint under the crimson-colored numbers, and I drop my hand, grabbing hers. "Come on; everybody's waiting on us. I'm driving everyone, well excluding Kash. He's going to meet us at the house. We're having a barbecue to celebrate the amazing win, and you need to join us," I say matter-of-factly. There's no room for argument; I want her there. Especially after seeing her looking like this, she's my own personal prize for kicking ass today.

"I don't know if that's such a good idea. I have to go to our room and wash this war paint off and change my clothes." She points to my favorite cheek. One look at her and I can tell she's full of anxiety, probably over the party and all the people that'll be there, but I'm not letting her out of it.

It's not the answer I wanted from her, but I roll with it for a minute and think of how to get her to the house. Pulling her lightly we start walking to the parking lot. Most of the other players have taken off in a rush to get supplies for the party, ready to get their drink on and stuff their faces after our easy win.

We get to my truck where JJ, Chandler, and I, all throw our bags into the open back. Kash climbs in his car parked a few spots over, waiting for us. The guys load up in the back seat while Brianne takes the front passenger seat. Opening the driver's door, I let Kadence climb into the middle like before when I gave them a ride home. I like having her right beside me; she fits in that spot perfectly.

"Fine, but after you wash up, you have to come," I mumble, trying again and starting the truck up. We head toward the back road that'll let me pass up any lingering traffic so I can get them back to the dorm safely and quickly. "And I love the war paint, by the way. Especially because of what number it is."

"Oh yeah? It is a pretty good number, I suppose," she teases. "Why do I have to stop by? Won't you be busy with everyone else? I don't want to take you away from visiting with your friends."

"Well, because I'm doing the cooking and I want you there, and no, I don't care about anyone else. I want to spend some time with you." My response brings a small smile to her face, and my chest grows warm inside seeing it.

"So, like cooking-cooking or just ordering food and then pretending that you've been cooking?"

Chuckling, I reach for the radio and hit a different channel while lightly brushing over the smooth skin of her knee. "I'm grilling all of the meat. What do you like to eat and I'll make it for you." Chicks love it when you cook for them.

"Wow, you surprise me, Mr. Owens. Let's see, could you do some chicken kabobs if I were to show up after all?" Her eyes sparkle and I decide that I may have to send someone to the store if necessary to get me the right stuff. It'll be worth it, though, just to show her that yes, I can, in fact, cook like a damn pro as well as play football. I have many talents, and if she'll let me, I'll share them all with her.

"Just promise me that you'll be there, and I'll have them for you."

"I guess we could stop over since you're offering food and all. It'd be rude to turn down a meal, and I'm sure Brianne would like to go. Besides, she owes me now."

"Well, don't let me put you out or anything." I grin as we pull into her dorm parking lot, the drive entirely too short for my liking.

"I'll hang out for a little while with you and eat. I don't drink, though."

"You a chicken to let me see you have some fun, Pretty little Kadence?"

"No, but I've heard the rumors. They've been whispered all over campus about one of the football player's videoing women. And, I'm not little, I'm actually five-foot-five, you're just ginormous."

Her declaration sends me on edge even with her being cute about the size thing. I know exactly who the fucker is that she's talking about when it comes to the rumors. For the first time, other than my family and team, I feel protective over someone else—her. I don't know why I feel like that, but I'll be damned if anyone hurts her or makes her uncomfortable around me. She's too sweet of a person to have to deal with anybody's shit around here.

"Listen to me, Kadence." I face toward her, speaking lowly. My hand rests on her knee, so she's leaning toward me as the truck completely comes to a stop. "You never have to worry about anything like that happening to you. Do you hear me? And if at some point you end up having any issue at all about something, I don't care if it's with my best friend. You tell me about it, and I'll sort it out, okay?"

"Okay." She easily agrees, not taking me very seriously, "I will."

Staring deeper into her eyes, I sternly demand, "Promise me, Kadence. It's important." She has to take me more seriously and know inside that I mean what I say. I want her to trust me.

"You really don't have to do this. I know I'll be fine. It's just that my dad drills it into me about needing to be careful, especially around guys and not to go anywhere by myself."

"I said, promise me." I need her word on this one. I won't tolerate her being hurt in any way on my watch.

Blinking a few times, another soft smile overtakes her mouth, and she nods, finally getting it. "Okay, Ty...I promise you that I'll speak up if anything makes me uncomfortable."

"Good. Now go wash your face, but keep these sexy short-shorts on and get your ass over to my house. This game day outfit you have on right now has to be my favorite set of clothes you own." Chuckling, I open my door and climb out, then hold my hand to her so I can help her step down.

"Geez, you're pretty bossy today, you know that?"

"You haven't seen bossy yet, Pretty." Grinning, I grip her hip, squeezing it just enough to show her that I definitely want her right now and not being able to hold myself back from touching her in some way again. I want to slam her against my truck and own her mouth before letting her out of my sight. I stop myself from doing it but damned if it won't happen in the future.

"Bye, Tyler Owens." She winks, setting my heart fluttering like I'm fifteen years old and fuck if I don't love the small rush.

"Later, Pretty little Kadence Winters," I reply, teasing her about the size thing again and then wait outside my truck, watching as she walks inside with Brianne. I hate to see her leave, but boy do I love to watch her go in those shorts. She needs a pair to wear every single day.

Loading up, I mumble, "Fuck, those shorts," and adjust my own pair that has grown a bit tighter after watching her ass sway back and forth. It's loud enough that the guys razz me about her the entire way home. The crazy thing is that I couldn't care less. They're right, I do want her, and I'm going to do whatever I can to get my way.

KADENCE

As much as I pretend not to be rushing around to leave sooner, I really am. Thankfully, Brianne doesn't notice, excited herself and helps me again with my wardrobe by letting me borrow more of her clothes. I have nothing at all that's similar to what I was wearing today, and for some weird reason, I want to look sexy. I have shorts and everything, but they're three inches longer, and none of my jerseys are cropped. They're my size, but cover me completely, and no way in hell am I cutting up signed NFL jerseys just to impress a man, even if he is undeniably hot. And Christ, Tyler Owens is scorching hot. To the point that I forget how to talk sometimes when he's around.

By the time we're ready, I'm in a pair of tiny, dark-wash blue jean shorts and a burgundy with lace halter top. I've never dressed this way for a guy, and frankly, I don't know why I'm suddenly okay with doing it now. Maybe it's because of the type of guy Tyler is? He's insanely popular and well-liked by everyone that maybe I'm dressing to sort of 'go' with him?

Regardless of what I'm wearing today, I'll be back to my normal attire of jeans and comfy t-shirts tomorrow. But, the burgundy color does sort of match the team colors, so hopefully, that'll make him happy.

Finding his house was easy. He lives nearby, and it took us ten minutes to walk here. Not to mention the music coming from the backyard and the twenty vehicles parked out front were a dead giveaway. I wonder if the cops get called on them a lot for this sort of thing. I imagine they party a lot though and everyone around here's most likely used to all the noise by now.

One of his teammates answers the door. The guy's practically the same size of a mountain. If I remember correctly, his name's Niner and he plays on defense. He also kicked butt today, getting two quarterback sacks.

"'Sup, ladies?" He smiles, flashing a deep, perfect dimple. The type you want to stick your finger in, or tongue, whatever.

"Hey, good job today," I mumble following him inside.

"Thanks." He flashes a grin, telling me that he knows he kicked ass. "I'll show you where Owens is." I nod gratefully, even though he doesn't catch it. I'm impressed he knows I'm here for Tyler too.

How does everyone know who I am, anyway? Oh God, probably that damn post earlier at the game and from the jumbotron.

Freight Train

Niner leads us toward the open dining area where a bunch of guys are sitting around an eight-person table, playing cards. It's one of those ugly, plain white, plastic, buffet type tables you buy for events and it makes this place scream 'man house.' He takes a seat, picking up his cards, basically forgetting that we're following behind him.

I want to say something so badly, but stay quiet instead, just staring at them all like the dork that I normally am. I don't talk to people like them regularly, so what in the hell do I say to them, and where's Tyler? And why didn't he ask if we wanted to play? I may not know how to, but I'd bet my left tit that Brianne does.

Brianne and I stand there for about two seconds before Tyler's beside me, thank God. I felt incredibly awkward standing beside a table full of huge-ass men that I have no idea who they are. You can only look around at the bare walls so many times before the hulky figures catch you staring at them too.

His nose trails up the side of my neck, breathing me in and causing me to close my eyes at the sensations blossoming in my stomach. He's so close to giving me goose bumps, and I can't help but hold my breath in anticipation. I don't think the shock last week was from static. I've increased my dryer sheets, and he still makes me feel something inside each time he touches me.

"There you are, Pretty. It took you long enough." Tyler draws me toward his body, placing his mouth next to my earlobe. "Fuck, you look good. *So good,* in fact, I could eat you," he murmurs, nipping lightly at the spot just behind my ear. His deep voice along with the light scrape of his teeth have me turning my head toward him, as my nipples grow hard, wanting him to bite me like that all over. I don't date guys like him or even mess with them. He's bold and smells divine like peppermint mouthwash and Old Spice deodorant. I love it. He smells clean and completely edible himself. I wonder what he'd taste like if I ran my tongue up his neck next.

"Ty." Breathily, his name escapes my lips as I part my eyes, in a blissful daze, meeting his. "Do you even know my name?" I ask, thinking of him calling me Pretty all the time. I love it; don't get me wrong, it's original. He could've gone with the generic 'baby' or something, but he decided to be different, and I appreciate it.

"Of course I do. You're just beautiful, so I prefer to call you something that shows it. Come here," he mumbles, grabbing my hand and pulling me through the kitchen. He's good…no, he's better than good, all that keeps running through my mind as we walk, is that I'm so done for already, and I've barely arrived.

"I'll be right back!" I call out to Brianne, following Ty through a doorway to find us in a laundry room. "What are we doing in here?" I can imagine things like me licking him and using my tongue to play connect the dots with his phenomenal bone structure, but it's not the time or place to be doing that. Not yet, anyhow. I'm not a slut by any means, but this man does something to my mind and body that has me completely spinning and wanting to peel my clothes off. It's dangerous. He's dangerous to me and my well-being. He could seriously cause some damage to my heart if I let him get too close, but it seems like each time I try to talk myself away from him, I want him even more.

Five minutes beside him and I'm already picturing us naked.

"I wanted to get you away from everyone for a minute," he tells me truthfully and pulls me closer to him. His large hands, just a bit rough on his palms, warm my biceps as he lightly holds them in his strong grip. His tenderness makes me feel dainty like I'm special to him and he wants me to be comfortable.

"Okay, why?"

"To do this." He gazes at my mouth, licking his lips as one of his hands lightly caresses my cheek, making me tilt my head toward it slightly. "Fuck, you're *so damn pretty*, Kadence." He shakes his head, the words coming out in awe, as he stares down at me as if I'm something precious and uncommon, causing my cheeks to heat up. He finally said my name, too, and I swear it's never sounded better coming from anyone else before. I want to beg him to say it over and over again.

"I'm just me, nothing special." It comes out with a nervous chuckle as I gaze up at him through my lashes. His head finally dips toward mine, and my heart speeds up, knowing what's coming. His hand goes to my neck where he was biting earlier, pulling my face to his, the rest of the way.

On my tippy-toes and holding my breath, I wait for his lips to land on mine. Sweetly, Ty sucks my bottom lip between his, coaxing my mouth to open for him. His soft nibbles have my eyes rolling back and my body humming.

"I've wanted to kiss you for so long now," he murmurs, his voice raspy against my lips. "You're so much more than special. I can't hold myself back from you any longer. I've tried all week, and still, you tempt me."

"Then don't," I whisper, giving him my full permission, and loving the moment that his lips fully meet mine.

It's tender, slow, and soft in the beginning, as our tongues collide and embrace for the first time. The velvety smoothness of his mouth is intoxicating, easily morphing from something almost innocent, to purely sinful. I was wrong. Completely and utterly wrong, to think that I had even the slightest clue of what was coming when he finally kissed me.

God, the man knows how to freaking kiss too.

A tantalizing dance of sorts begins, as our tongues become acquainted with each other. It wasn't mint that I smelled earlier as in mouthwash. No, I think he was just some eating candy before I arrived. His tongue tastes of chocolate and mint mixed together, an alluring combination, making me want to suck on it until I get my fill.

Tyler moves in, his body setting mine a blaze as he pushes me up against the wall. His solid form molds to mine, his strength becoming more pronounced as I'm able to feel the dips and cuts of his muscles. His tongue morphs into a provocative tool—demanding, lustful, and no longer exploring or playing, but stroking mine on an erotic mission.

I want him.

I swear I can feel him licking me the same way in *other* places, making me wet and his lips haven't even left mine. His mouth has me conjuring up blissful images of where else I'd like it to be, of where I'd love to feel it licking and stroking.

Almost as if he senses my very thoughts, his hands move to my thighs, running over them until his thumbs stop about two inches away from my pussy. It's like he's already teasing it, making me clench wantonly. Each brush of his tongue has my body purring, desperately craving his touch.

Moments later, his palms move around to the outsides, where he's no longer caressing, but lifting me higher. His strong grip parts my legs so he can rest his hardness against my center. He lifts me so easily, and images overtake my mind of him holding me just like this, right now, but completely naked.

"Ty." Moaning breathlessly, my body aches for him. His name flutters over my lips, leaving me and interrupting our kiss. It's like magic, coaxing his hips to rotate right where I need him the most. The pressure from his cock floods my core deliciously, nearly to the point of making me beg him to take it even further. I want to feel him enter me right now, long and hard.

"Oh." I let loose in a quiet whimper of bliss right before Brianne has us pulling apart.

"Kadence? You back here, hon? The guys asked me to come find y'all so Ty can start grilling the food."

"Damn it," he mutters and pushes into me again, rubbing his cock deliciously against me in all the right spots.

"*Oh!*" I groan deeper into his shirt, as I clutch it tightly in my fists, holding on for dear life at the same time as I'm silently begging him not to stop.

Brianne finally figures out where we are. "Sorry guys." She glances sheepishly at both of us. "Ty, you're up," she says, and then giggles at the double meaning.

His cheeks are flushed as he clears his throat and nods, not setting me down until she turns back toward the kitchen.

Backing up a few paces, he adjusts himself and clears his throat again, having a difficult time reining in his control. "I'm kind of kicking myself for not doing that sooner."

I nod, chuckling "I'm...Uh, glad it happened too." My brain is mush right now. I'm lucky that I conjured up that much in response and my voice even sounded somewhat normal. I don't feel normal, not in the least bit. More like a cat going through their first heat, begging for some attention. I feel more like a hussy, and frankly, I couldn't give two shits about it at the moment.

"Good. Can I add to it a little later?" His arm goes around my waist as he places a few chaste kisses over my lips, nose, and then forehead. He went from burning inferno to sweetness overload. I think my ovaries may be carrying pickets with his name on them at this point.

"Yes." I don't know what I'm agreeing to exactly, but that little sample has my body reeling for anything that's more at the moment.

Smiling, he kisses me once more before taking my hand again and leading me back out to the kitchen. Brianne sits down at the table full of football players in the dining area and starts playing cards, looking like she totally belongs there. I stick by Ty to help him start seasoning trays full of meat.

"This is a crap ton of food, how much do you guys eat?" I give in and ask by the fourth cookie sheet full of burgers we've seasoned.

"Well, it's not just us in here. It'll be anyone on the team that wants to stop over and then if they bring dates or friends, whatever. The team's always a little crazy after a win at home, and everyone's always convinced that they're starving to death. The only thing we ask is that they all pitch in and bring food to cook or give us money to help out with the cost of it all."

"I see. So, is this home for you? I think I read that you're from Alabama, right?" Shit, I basically just admitted to his face that he's been Googled by me.

"Yep, born and raised here. I love everything about the state. What about you?"

"I grew up right outside Boston for most of my life and then lived in Texas for a few years. My dad lived near here when he was younger and went to college here, so it seemed like a good choice for me."

He nods, grinning, "I'm certainly benefitting from it." I want to straight up lay a big kiss on him after earlier. I don't, though, instead playing it off by rolling my eyes. Tyler's a never-ending flirt. I doubt it's only with me, though, He's probably like that with everyone. "Shit!" He grabs a hand towel as the steak marinade splashes all over his tank top.

Kash chuckles from the dining area. "You can catch anything I throw at you, but every time you cook or eat, you spill or drop shit. How is that possible, brah?"

"Hell if I know. You think I like not being able to wear white?" he honestly admits and all the guys laugh. I think his answer is sort of adorable, though.

Tyler's mischievous gaze meets mine, staring at me full of purpose the entire time he peels the fitted tank off, revealing his shredded physique. I don't think I've ever seen washboard abs in real life and I have to bite my tongue to stop from groaning out loud. Definitely trouble with a capital T. He knows damn well what he's doing to me.

Brianne glances over and mutters, "Oh Lord." She pretty much read my mind with that comment.

He tosses the shirt into the trash bin; his solid form is rippling at the movements and suddenly making me feel weak. His mouth hikes up on one side in a cocky grin. He knows what his body looks like and is damn sure enjoying being ogled by us. "You, uh, don't mind, do you?" Tyler's gaze flicks down toward his stomach, causing mine to follow along dutifully.

Stupid Kadence, don't look! Totally just fell for his trap and did exactly what he wanted.

Quickly, I grab another baking sheet, distracting my mind away from imagining my tongue running over each delicious ridge of his abdomen. "It's your house." Shrugging, I pretend not to be affected, when inside I'm doing fist pumps and roundhouse kicks at the thought of seeing this man cook with his naked torso on full display. That would be one cooking show all women would watch. Not sure we'd pay attention to the recipes, but it'd get some good ratings.

It's like having dinner and a show for free, and I didn't have to do the cooking.

Opening a drawer, he pulls out an apron with abs airbrushed on the front, causing me to giggle at the ridiculousness of it. "Yeah, like you need that," slips out before I can hold myself back and his grin grows into a bright smile.

"I don't know…Why don't you double check?" He steps closer, taking my hand and running it over his hard stomach.

Holy. Shit. This man is naughty in all the right…no…I mean, all the wrong ways. At this rate, I'll be visiting the church on Sunday to pray for strength against him completely owning me by next week.

"They're good." It comes out in a cross between gasp and mumble, my mouth suddenly dry as my fingertips run over his smooth skin.

Freight Train

"You sure?" He cocks his eyebrow like he doesn't believe me and runs my fingers over them again. If he sticks my finger in his mouth next, I will hit the floor, I swear it.

"Uh-huh," comes out even breathier. Thankfully we're interrupted again—this time by JJ—before I can maul Ty on the kitchen floor.

"Hey, lovebirds, how's it coming in here?" JJ moseys in, stopping next to Ty, nosing over everything we've prepared so far. "Damn, you guys are actually getting stuff done. With the way you were dressed at the game, Kadence, I would've thought you couldn't peel this man off of you."

"I wouldn't have her laid out on the counter, bro," Tyler grumbles, not pleased that JJ clearly approved of my outfit earlier.

"Why not? Sounds like a lot of fun to me. I think it's time we take a break for a shot, don't you? Kadence is wearing the perfect shirt for belly shots too." Oh, he's even worse than his buddy number twelve, here.

The guys around the table stand, agreeing. "Hell yeah." A few respond, quickly joining us. They make the kitchen seem tiny, the space shrinking as I'm enclosed by a group of massive men, all wanting to drink liquor off my body. It could be much worse; the football players for Alabama are pretty good looking and stacked with muscles from their vigorous training at practice.

Ty takes a step closer to me. "Nice try. None of you assholes are putting your mouths anywhere near her body." His eyes meet mine, and I hope he can see how truly grateful I am at this very moment. "But, it doesn't mean that I can't." He smirks, and I could punch him in his pearly whites.

JJ laughs, digging through a cabinet until he comes back with a brand new bottle of Jose Cuervo. "Counter, Winters," he orders me, calling me by my last name like they do with the other teammates and nods over to the cleared-off bar top that's separating the kitchen and dining area.

Unsure, I glance toward Brianne, only to see her mouth at me, "Have some fun!"

Of course, that'd be her response. She's the outgoing one; I'm the one who keeps to myself. I enjoy the quiet and simplicity of my everyday life, despite what she may think sometimes. But, this is college, and she's hounded me many times before to step outside my bubble and let go of my comfort zone. I like Ty, and these guys seem to be a decent group, so when in Rome and all that.

Taking a deep breath, I draw on my inner bad girl....the one I don't have inside and decide that I'm going to just go with it. Fun is fun, right? No harm in a little body shot, taken by a guy you think is insanely hot and sweet. At least it's not beer pong they're trying to get me to play. I don't want to drink, and that'll let me participate and remain sober.

"Okay, but only Ty and only one."

He nods happily, as I hop up on the hard surface and the guys surround the bar to watch and cheer us on.

Lying back, I rest on my elbows with my chest sticking out. Tyler stands over me with his excited gaze running all over my body. Tenderly, he pushes me down until I'm lying flat against the cool surface and lifts away the lacy halter, adjusting it until the thin material sits right underneath my breasts, muttering an eager, "Fuck yes."

Freight Train

JJ brings everything over, laying it down beside me while calling loudly, "Salt her up!" He's making this into more of an event to witness, getting the guys pumped up over what was supposed to be a quick shot.

Chanting silently over and over, *'it's better than placing it between my boobs,'* helps me remain calm.

Tyler's head dips closer, his warm tongue gliding over my rib area. When he steps back, JJ sprinkles salt in the same spot, wearing a devilish grin. "Ready, you two?" He sets the shaker down, and rubs his hands together, excited.

Nope. I take a deep breath.

"Yep," Ty replies, and I nod, giving in while staring at my pale stomach, waiting for him to fill my belly button with a dash of tequila.

"Woops," JJ says nonchalantly, clearly full of shit as he pours the liquid from underneath my breasts, down to the line of my shorts until a few stray splashes trickle a trail running underneath the waistband toward my panties. "Guess it was fuller than I thought. Got to get it all up, Owens!"

Tyler's head quickly lowers to my stomach, licking and slurping the liquor. He moves fast, getting as much up as he can so it doesn't run over the sides. Each spot where his tongue slides across, the air conditioner follows in his wake, sparking goose bumps to overtake my flesh.

He pauses briefly, just enough to meet my stunned gaze. I wasn't expecting the cold air to make my nipples hard as diamonds and in front of everyone at that. I also wasn't counting on getting so damn turned on by it all. Tyler has my body on complete overload ever since I stepped into this house.

He tenderly unclasps the shorts button and pushes them down a bit, brushing his tongue completely across my abdomen from one side to the other. The movement forces my breathing to kick up a notch as a new burst of goose bumps decorate my skin from the wetness. How does anyone handle this? If there weren't a crowd around us, I'd be pulling him on top of me already.

Once he's finished, he eases back. His cheeks flushed a shade of crimson as he stares me down, his gaze full of undeniable hunger and need. I know he wants me, hell everyone can see it so clearly from the determined fire burning in his irises.

Not even a peep can break free from me before his mouth's on mine. The kiss is ruthless. Completely demanding and full of control, his lips divulging what he wants and then attempting to take it. I barely know him, yet my body seems to think it's known him forever. I'm drawn to him, no matter how I fight it. Oh hell, who am I kidding, I'm not even fighting anymore.

His movements become urgent like he can't hold himself back from me. It's so freaking hot, knowing he's wanting and feeling everything that I am as well. Returning each sinful twist of his tongue with just as much fervor, my hands start to shake, wanting to pull him fully on top of me so I can feel his skin against my own.

It's so easy to get sucked in and forget that we're in a room full of people, but none of it matters, only him, only this…right now.

The guys hoot and holler in the background, but I barely hear them for a few brief seconds as Tyler's lips sweep me away, making everything else disappear but him. My body heats all over; we have too many clothes on for a kiss like this. We should be taking them all off and sampling more of each other. I want to taste and pet him in all the best places.

We continue, taking, playing and consuming for what feels like hours before he finally pulls away. When ending one of the best fucking kisses ever, he does something so uncharacteristically sweet for his type; he tenderly bumps his nose with mine before stepping away. The movement is so perfect, it squeezes my heart, making me see him as something other than just another hot football player.

That's not the way he's supposed to end it. He just made it into more than it needed to be, damn it.

When my eyes finally open, we're still in the kitchen, but now completely alone. No one's in the room or dining area anymore, and the house is silent. The shot was beyond what I would've imagined, and now I don't want to move from this spot.

I've been kissed many times, but that...that was different. It can't possibly be called something as simple as a kiss. To me, it was overwhelming in the best sort of way and to me—with the right man involved—it could be my future.

But overall the kiss was heartbreaking. Because I know it was only a bit of fun for him, and after this, I need to pull myself back when inside, I want to open up and give him everything.

Wins and losses come a dime a dozen.

But effort? Nobody can judge that.

Because Effort is between you and you.

-Ray Lewis

Tyler

"Hey Owens, the grill's hot, bro." JJ breaks the spell that was consuming the majority of my thoughts. Kadence has me so wrapped up in her, I'd forgotten about everything else I'd been doing. We'll be fortunate if I don't end up burning all the food tonight at this rate.

"Thanks, man, I'll be right there."

He nods and closes the back door while I swiftly turn around to grab some of the meat trays we'd prepared. I can't look at Kadence right now without possibly attacking her. One small kiss and it's like I can't get enough of her.

I do the smart thing for a bit of self-preservation and clear my throat. Noticeably adjusting the hardness currently making my normally loose-fitting basketball shorts tent out like a man possessed and wet my heated cheeks with the cold tap. Once my heart rate has slowed down a bit, I wash my hands, tossing the dish towel over my bare shoulder and grab up one of the trays.

Kadence hops off the counter, fixing her own shirt and then grabs some of the food as well. We both remain silent as she follows me out the back door. Pretty confident that we're both stunned and thinking about what just happened. She's not like others that I've kissed. For some reason, it's like I can't control myself when it comes to her.

Did she feel it like I did? Or was it just another kiss to her? Jesus Christ, that was something else in there. I'm turning into a chick feeling like this.

"Thanks," I comment, and it comes out gruffer than I had anticipated as she hands me her tray filled with hamburger patties. I need to get them all loaded on the grill before my teammates start giving me grief. It's a shitty propane grill, but I can feed about twenty people at once.

"Look, Tyler, about inside—" she begins, and I effectively cut her off before she can say something either one of us may end up regretting.

"It was just a little fun. Relax, okay? I won't let anything bad happen; you know that right?"

She nods, staring at the grill, not meeting my eyes. "Yeah, I do. I had fun too."

"I'm glad; we can have fun like that more often if you'd like." I wink, and she blushes. "I'll cook your kabobs in just a second when this heats up some more. Why don't you have a drink while you wait? I made sure the guys got some sodas for you."

I'm shutting her out, pushing her away after a mere kiss, but it was more than that. More than just a brief moment of fun shared between two people who don't know each other that well yet. I could feel it like she's some kind of special and I'm going to lose myself over her.

It freaks me out inside, knowing that she may not have felt it all like I had. I'm not looking to meet someone that can hurt me, and I have a feeling that enough time with Kadence and she could do significant damage if she wanted.

My stomach twists as she smiles and replies, "Great, thank you."

Good, I think she gets it that I don't want to discuss anything that happened. I got sucked in way too quickly with her. What the hell was I thinking, practically calling her mine in front of the guys when it came to doing the body shot? I should've just let them do it. Well, if she wanted them to anyway. I swear she looked scared about the idea until I'd announced that I was the only one touching her. And just the thought of the other guys touching her body anywhere had me wanting to rip someone's hands off.

I don't understand why I did the shot in the first place or why I felt so damn possessive like that. Seeing her clam up in there had something protective coming out of me though, and before I realized it, I was practically growling to show them that she's mine.

I need to chill out when it comes to her, or she'll get the wrong idea. I'm not that guy—the one who has a girlfriend and doesn't want anyone touching her and she's *not* mine. Maybe I'll try chanting it: she's not mine, she's not mine, she's *not* mine.

Fuck, her small smile makes me want to kiss those lips even more.

"You got it, Pretty," replying absently, still chanting inwardly to myself.

I steal her little flirty move and wink, which ends up making her laugh quietly as she walks toward the ice chests. At least she doesn't seem hurt with me shutting her down like that. I'm in another trance, ignoring my grilling duties and most likely turning our dinner into charred black bits while watching her ass sway sexily with each step when Chandler comes up beside me.

"I had no idea she was hiding all that under her jeans and glasses," he admits, cocking an eyebrow as he stares at Kadence.

I did. I saw through her little facade the first day she ran into me in the hallway. I knew then that she was stunning and each time I see her, she only proves me more right.

Inhale and exhale...Don't rip his head off for noticing the woman of your current fantasies; he's your best friend.

Even after the lecture I just had with myself, I still want to karate chop him in the dick for seeing her like I do. "Dude, she's gorgeous; even in her nerd girl clothes, she sports on the regular. I love that shit." *God, I do too.* Not sure when that happened either. She's completely different than the usual, and it makes her sexy as fuck.

"The Game of Thrones t-shirts and black frames do it for you, huh?" He smirks.

How the fuck does he know what she wears exactly? Don't growl at him, take another deep breath and be cool, damn it.

"It must work for you too, if you're paying that close of attention to her attire." It sounds jealous, and it is, damn it. I brought her here for me, not anyone else and knowing that other guys are checking her out as well, has my guard rising.

Shrugging, he swallows down a large gulp from his longneck bottle, hitting me with a dose of reality. "They've always been more of my type. She's my type."

Right, because he's the smart one, always reading and doing papers and stuff. JJ's the big time partier, and I'm right in the middle, I guess. "So, you're saying I should step aside and let you make a move on the girl I have my sights on, even if I don't do the whole relationship thing like you do?"

Startled at my bluntness, he backtracks. "No man, I wasn't saying that at all. If anything, I was leaning toward the opposite. I like her, but for you. She's not one of those trashy bimbos you're used to sleeping with, and it's refreshing. Kadence is just...Well, she's girlfriend material, you said it, relationship type. That's her, whether you like it or not."

"I don't do girlfriends. Everyone knows this, she probably even knows this."

"I know, and you're right, that's why it won't work."

"You think I should cut her loose then and let just anyone have her? Someone like you, maybe?"

"Not exactly. Look, Ty; I'll always have your back. I just think she'll end up getting hurt and chicks like her aren't used to that shit. They get hurt, and it fucks with them for a long time. Trust me, I've learned from my sister, you know this. What do you think you should do? Not what you want, but what's fair to her? She'd be loyal to you, and you'd just toy with her like a plaything."

I don't reply, thinking over everything he just said. He's right. She's the perfect distraction to take some of the stress off my back, especially with the draft coming up this next year. Most players that're going pro get picked up in their third year. The really good ones do anyhow. My plan to go to the NFL never included taking a woman along with me.

Could it work? I couldn't imagine toying her along like he said, though. For some reason, I like her a little too much. I'm not sure if it's because she's been making me work my ass off just to get around her long enough to kiss her, or what.

Usually, a chick gives me her number when we first meet and later that night I'm fucking her. It sounds harsh, but it's the truth. Kadence, however, hasn't been like that at all. If anything, she's standoffish and making me want her even more. It's like drinking for the first time. You don't know your limit and then, bam, you're drunk and thinking it's the greatest thing ever. Kadence is my drink of choice at the moment, and I haven't reached my limit yet.

She's also what I need to keep my mind off my brothers and my parents' ranch. The last thing I should be worrying about is Clyde getting popped by the cops discovering his secret business venture on our land or the tax lady harassing him. I need that big contract to make sure they're set up financially, besides taking care of myself.

Then there's the huge fact that I don't have 'girlfriends.' *Ever.* I haven't had one since my freshman year in high school, and my parents passed away. They're usually drama and a headache that I don't want or need.

When I really think about it, I rarely even date anyone. And, it's not from being heartbroken by some chick or becoming emotionally scarred in some other way. We usually fuck, and that's the end of it. They leave happy and satisfied, and I've had a chance to relax with some female company; there's no reason to drag it out. I'm up front with them too. They know what it is; I never lie or promise them anything.

My parents' death screwed me up in ways that it made me become more focused and determined on my future—not women. That's a major part in why there hasn't been a serious relationship for me. I've worked too hard, and my family has sacrificed enough for me already. My drive and determination need to stay intact; a girlfriend could easily screw it all up.

"I hear what you're saying, and I like her, but I don't know about taking it to that level."

"I figured that's how you'd feel, that's why I told you she deserves more. You're both not in the right place to get involved like that anyhow."

"So you don't think I could do it? Have an actual girlfriend, one woman all the time?" Is he seriously telling me this? He knows that's challenging me to prove him wrong.

"Nope, I don't. You never commit to anything that's not football. I wouldn't be surprised if you held off on getting serious until you're forty and retired from playing ball. Well, unless you find someone to string along, on the way."

He's being honest—not condescending—and he's completely right. That reality makes me shaky inside. Could I be setting myself up to be alone for the rest of my life? Many athletes have multiple marriages or girlfriends. Do I want that in my life? No. And besides Chan doesn't think I can do it. I'm always up for a little hardball.

Challenge accepted.

Glancing at Chandler, I take a leap and seal my fate. "You know what? I don't want to just fuck her. I think I want to keep her."

"Dude," he deadpans, "you've had too much of JJ's tequila, you'll be backtracking first thing in the morning."

Chandler doesn't think I can do it. I bet JJ doesn't think so either. Bastards! They're supposed to be my closest friends too. I'll prove them wrong and get a good girl by my side.

"Nope, I'm doing it."

His eyes grow wide. "Seriously? Are you sure? One pussy and all that other bullshit the guys spew?"

Nodding, I flip her chicken skewers over, checking to see if they're cooked enough. The decision's been made. I'm going to have a girlfriend for the first time in who knows how long. Instead of it freaking me out, I'm a little excited over the thought, especially if she uses that skillful tongue like that on the rest of my body.

"Then you better get on your game, because a lot's going to change. Plus you have to convince her that you're even worth giving the chance to."

"No shit, Sherlock, but how hard can it be? I'm Tyler motherfuckin' Freight Train Owens. Women love me, and you saw how hot she got on the counter inside." Never mind how turned on she had me. I could've given someone a black eye with how stiff my dick was.

He laughs and shakes his head. "This is going to be so much fun to watch. Owens' falling all over a chick."

"She's not just any chick, now shut up and take my future woman her chicken, since I'm charged with manning the grill." I dish up her kabobs on a paper plate along with some grilled corn on the cob and red potatoes. Feeding her is step one. My mom always said a way to a man's heart is through his stomach. I guess a woman's gotta be the same and I just so happen to know how to cook. Too easy.

"My pleasure." He laughs. "I'm going to go flirt it up with her and make it even harder for you to get laid. I'll turn on the Chandler charm."

"By that you mean you're going to let her know which action figures you still have stuffed under your bed? She won't want it, bro," I counter, and he shoots me the bird as he takes the plate of food to her.

Kadence thanks him, as he hands her the food. She beams a grateful smile my way, and it's official, I'm fucking toast.

Two weeks later...

I think my balls will permanently have a blue tint to them for the remainder of my lifetime. The thought runs through my head as we all sit in the cafeteria having lunch, per our new routine. I thought she'd be easy to get and this whole 'mission to make her my girlfriend' would take no time at all.

Boy was I wrong. I haven't even made it underneath her shirt, let alone into her pants or gotten her to make it official with me. If anything I'm feeling more 'friend-zoned' than ever and it's driving me crazy. I'm pretty lost when it comes to what to do at this point, so I'm taking it one day at a time.

Chandler, JJ, Niner, Kash, Kadence, Brianne, and I have formed our own group over the past two weeks that we've all been hanging out together in our free time. It's usually just lunch and sometimes dinner that we can get together like this; otherwise, it'll mainly be Kadence and me and one or two other people around. She's made it damn near impossible for the two of us to be alone, always inviting our friends to join in with whatever we're doing.

Jada attempted to take the one open chair when we first switched tables but was turned away, as we declared its use for all of our belongings. She and her crew of groupies sat directly behind us, throwing a small fit that she wasn't included in our new seating arrangement. They were pretty pissed that the guys had booted them off their laps too, but it was like cutting off an abscess finally getting rid of them. We became happier and lighter.

I've dealt with her group over the past two years, and now that they've been gone for a while, I can see that they were all over us all the time. It was like they thought that we belonged to them or something. The guys have even started meeting new chicks. I'd never noticed it before, but come to find out, Jada and her monkeys were often ugly toward any other females trying to come around.

However, these past two weeks have been a new kind of hell for me, from trying to keep my hands off Kadence. She's backed off some since we had our heated kitchen kiss and the body shot fun, but not completely. I've been able to get a few chaste kisses out of her, but they've been brief, almost like she's skittish. It hasn't deterred me, though. I'm stubborn when it comes to getting what I want. I always have been, and it's partially why I'm so good at playing football.

Freight Train

"Take a bite," I order and hold the large, chocolate-covered strawberry close to Kadence's soft lips. I found out they were her favorite, so I've brought them for her twice so far—once last week and then again today.

"You don't have to do this, Tyler," she whispers.

"I want to; it's why I get them for you."

The guys have learned to ignore me fawning over her, although I hear about it when we're at the house away from her. I've been feeding her for a week now, and the guys think I'm stupid, but I'm determined. It's been driving her crazy to have the attention bestowed on her alone, but I'm slowly proving to her that I can be the doting type.

I can tell it's working, and it's starting to chip away at her wall. She pretends to hate it, but I know she secretly enjoys each minute I fawn over her. Brianne keeps reassuring me that it's working and that Kadence talks about me constantly when she's not around me. The woman has me completely sprung too. I can't go for a full hour without wondering what she's doing or picturing that strip of smooth skin along her stomach that I got to lick when doing that amazing body shot not too long ago.

After Chandler and I had spoken at the barbecue, it was like a lightbulb went off. Out of nowhere, I knew what I wanted with her no matter how much I told myself not to go after her. Now, I can't seem to stop thinking about Kadence and the future that we could have together. It sounds ridiculous; we've only known each other for a short time, but that's exactly how it happened for my parents. My mom used to tell my brothers and me all the time that falling in love was easy. The staying in love part is what took work.

It's too soon for *love* surely, but it could definitely happen with her.

"I'm full already," she protests, turning back to listen to Kash as he explains the differences of throwing times based on the current wind speed to Niner.

I hate being ignored. Yes, I'm a bit egocentric at times, but it's been forever since a woman's paid attention to me. Well, one that wasn't obsessed with me being on the football team anyhow.

Kadence is like that, not giving two ticks that I play ball. There's a decent chance that she knows more about football than everyone at this table. We've talked a lot, and she knows her shit. I know her dad used to play college ball, so I guess he taught her everything she knows. Her mom wasn't around much, which is most likely why she's been this little tomboyish book nerd her entire life. I bet her dad was clueless on what to do with a little girl, but who knows; she doesn't talk about them much.

"Come on, Kadence, one more for me," I coax, loving her perfect lips. I never see her eat enough.

Her mouth parts slightly and I watch her hungrily as her white teeth sink into the juicy fruit, her perfect peach, glossed lips closing as she chews. *Fuck, it makes me hard.* Chocolate bits break over her lips and saliva rushes into my own mouth at the sight.

Witnessing her bite down like that makes me imagine her biting onto my shoulder. I can almost fucking feel it, her teeth pushing into my flesh while I drive deep inside her. She has me feeling like some sex-crazed maniac. I've been using my hand so much I got a cramp in class the other day taking notes. I was so fucking embarrassed. I didn't think that it was possible to jack off too much. What if I end up with carpel tunnel syndrome over this shit?

"What's up for this weekend?" JJ interrupts, causing me to blink as he sits back in his chair, finished with his food. "With it being another home game, we should get some ideas going around for the after party."

"I need to head to the ranch after the game." I place the green leafs from the strawberry on my plate.

"What about you, Kadence?" JJ nods toward her. "Do you have any plans or are you going to party with us, even though Owens will be going back home?"

"Brianne and I will probably stop by to congratulate you guys. Y'all are going to kill OC!"

"Hell yeah we are," he agrees, and it irritates me, knowing she'll be with all the guys, around *my* friends and I won't be there.

They better not fuck with her.

Damn it; I know it'll happen. Someone will try something. I'll come back to school with a bunch of stupid-as rumors floating around since everyone already believes that she's my girlfriend. And I can't forget about Briggs with his screwed up hobbies of recording drunk, naked chicks.

We didn't discuss the infamous Facebook post that landed us in this position to begin with. I think we should keep up the charade, especially now, since I want her to really be mine. If anyone asks, I tell them she's my woman. Kadence on the other hand, when she's asked, just rolls her eyes and walks off.

Every single time.

"How about we do a bonfire at the ranch?" I offer, not thoroughly thinking it over before opening my mouth. Clyde's going to kill me for this... But it'd be the best way for me to keep an eye on her, plus there's a good chance I could talk Kadence into staying over. She could even meet my brothers.

I want her to meet my family?

Shit. I do.

Chandler shakes his head. "Clyde freaked out the last time we had a party. I'm not going to be there for it to happen again."

He sure as hell did. I'll never forget it. "That was different. We were screwing around while we were underage and the state could've taken Nate and me away from him. We're all over twenty-one now. He won't care." I'll talk him into it if I have to. This may be the best time for me to get Kadence by herself. I swear if I don't kiss her lips sometime in the next century, I'm going to explode or end up screwing some random chick to hold me over, and that's the last thing I want to do at this point.

JJ glances at Chandler uneasily, and then at me. "Maybe you should call him first. I remember him flipping out too; he's crazy when he's pissed."

God do I know. He's shoot-you-in-the-ass type of crazy. I grew up with him, they have no idea.

"The ranch is partially mine too. It belongs to all of us. If I want to throw a party, then I will." That's a lie. Well, it is partially mine, but I definitely have to get permission first.

"All right bro, it's your ass." JJ shrugs "Sounds good to me anyhow." He easily gives in while Chandler keeps whatever he's pondering to himself, clearly not buying it a hundred percent.

I understand their hesitation. The last time we planned something, we invited a bunch of girls over to the pond on my family's land. We all wanted to swim, drink, and hook up back in high school. Then Clyde showed up flipping out, and the chicks bailed on us. It sucked, and I was pissed at the time, but I get it now. I'm glad he was like that; it kept us living with him and safe.

Leaning into Kadence, I speak lowly, so the others don't overhear everything. "Come stay with me this weekend."

"What about Brianne?"

"You can leave with me right after the game and Brianna can catch a ride out with Kash later on if they decide to come out."

"If I stayed over, where exactly would I sleep?" She meets my gaze, the gold in her chocolate irises sparkling. She already knows the answer to that question, but if she wants me to say it out loud, I will.

Running my finger along her jawline, I can't suppress the grin as I think of her softness lying next to me. "In my bed, Pretty, right where I want you."

"And what about you? Where'd you sleep?"

"I'd be right there next to you. I wouldn't want you to get cold or anything."

"It'd be like that for the entire weekend?"

"Yep." Staring at her mouth, I tip her chin up a little, wanting a sample. "Saturday we drive there after the game." Leaning a bit closer to her, my breath tickles her lips as I mumble, "We party and sleep together Saturday night, and then hang out Sunday."

Brushing a soft peck against her bottom lip, she draws in a breath, and I continue. "We sleep together again Sunday night, and then I can bring us back to school on Monday morning." Planting a tender kiss on the corner of her mouth, I finish. "I promise to keep you in one piece, too." Sucking her bottom lip into my mouth, I take every bit that I want from her. Not giving her the time to think or argue, just kissing her passionately until I feel her start to pull away.

She nods slightly, answering breathily, "Okay. But on one condition."

"What's that?"

"You get the floor, and I get the bed."

A chuckle escapes me before I can hold it back, causing one of her eyebrows to raise up in curiosity. "I can agree, but you know I'd be lying to you about it. If you're in my bed, I'm there with you."

"What if I just kick you off?"

"You can try, Pretty, but look how big I am. I could just lie on top of you and *make* you stay next to me." Resting my arm across the back of her chair, I practically engulf her with my size.

"You're too sweet to squish me." She smirks, looking all too pleased with herself, thinking that she'll get her way.

Bending close enough that my lips nearly touch her ear, I rest my other hand on her leg and grumble, "Not when it comes to having you in my bed. I'll be anything *but* sweet. I promise you that too."

At my words, scarlet flushes over her cheeks and chest, her breathing quickening as her breasts heave slightly. With a strong squeeze to her thigh, I sit back in my seat and wait for her to argue, already feeling as if I've won.

Damn it; I want her something fierce. I can't remember the last time—or if ever—that I've felt like I actually *needed* to sink my dick in someone. With Kadence, it's like my cock weighs ten pounds resting between my thighs—constantly. Thanks to this brilliant bonfire plan, I'm finally getting the chance to spend some real time alone with her. None of this group outings bull we've been doing. It'll be me and her—alone—in my bed.

Fuck yes!

Sapphire Knight

Tom Brady:

Making football relevant to women since 1996.

-Awesome Meme

KADENCE

What on earth did I just agree to? I can barely tell him no and push him off when we're surrounded by people, and now my ass goes and agrees to spend an entire weekend with him? Just the kisses and quick touches he does when we're around each other have me wanting to rip his damn clothes off.

Tyler's amazing, not just because of his toned body, but because he's caring and kind and funny. He literally feeds me every day if I let him. He's done nothing but spoil me rotten and pay tons of attention to me.

Me. Kadence Winters being doted on by Alabama's Golden Boy.

I don't get it. Does he have some sort of a motive? I'm freaking boring and plain compared to him. I'm the average everyday bookworm who does great on her English essays, and he's this popular, beautiful jock with a heart dipped in freaking gold. He can't really be that perfect, can he?

Don't get me wrong; he's not a saint by any means. I can tell he has some naughty shit running through his mind every time he looks at me, but when it comes to helping people—listening to others and being genuine—that's just the type of man he seems to be. I could do worse I suppose. I could pick a total loser to have some hopeless crush on; instead, I've somehow chosen him. Did I choose him? It feels like it may be the other way around like he decided on me and I'm just along for the ride, and despite me trying to hold back, I'm enjoying it so far.

God what a ride already. I'm going to be so screwed if I get in any deeper with him. He's going to end up breaking my damn heart, I know it. Even with those thoughts running through my mind often, I can't stop myself, nor do I want to, from feeling his energy around me.

Being with Ty is like riding your favorite ride at a theme park. You get the thrill, the excitement, the enjoyment—all of it. I'm not looking forward to the feeling of the ride being over with, though. I'll most likely go into a carb coma trying to make up for it. Sugar's great, but in the end, it doesn't even come close to comparing to the natural high he gives me.

Then there are his friends—whom I actually like—by the way. Surprising, considering I had it in my mind that ninety percent of jocks are douchebags. I seriously doubt I was just lucky enough to meet the ten percent in our school who aren't. I need to stop being so shallow, especially when it comes to football. The game's practically in my blood.

I wasn't so sure about JJ at first. He came off as a bit of a pretentious asshole, but once he lets his guard down some, he's actually not that bad. He's protective over his small group of friends, and I respect that a great deal.

Chandler's pretty much the opposite. He's so nice and calm, just going with the flow of things. Oh, and he's super smart, which is a huge bonus by giving me someone else to talk to who knows what I'm saying when I bring up certain subjects.

I'm waiting for Brianne to confess she's in love with one of them. Once that happens, I may as well say goodbye to Tyler, because she's a train wreck when it comes to relationships. Like I have room to talk. I've never really put much effort into any of my past relationships.

She has the habit of picking dirtbags, though. She ends up with the guys that drink excessively and party all the time, cheating on her with random girls and what not. I end up being the one to help pick up the pieces, which usually involve face masks, peanut butter M&M's, and excessive amounts of Red Bull. Weird combination, but that's what makes her start to feel better.

"Ready?" Tyler stands, along with everyone else, so naturally, I scoot my chair out too quickly and damn near fall forward. Ty's hand shoots out like a rocket, keeping me seated. He's so freaking strong with reflexes like a cat.

"Thanks," I breathe, wide-eyed. He releases me but holds his palm out to take mine, reminding me of the first time I ran into him. That one collision has changed so much in my life already.

Placing my small hand in his, he holds on tightly, offering me stability. It's ridiculous how clumsy I am sometimes, and the fact he notices is embarrassing. At least he's sweet enough not to tease me about it, but instead, offers to help. It's weird, but I feel like he makes me stronger in a sense.

"Sorry about that," I mumble as we walk toward the door leading outside into the large courtyard full of grass and stone benches.

"You have nothing to apologize for," he responds, pulling me closer so he can place a chaste kiss on top of my head and wrap his arm around my shoulders. It's sweet and done so naturally, that a girl could easily get used to it. Day after day his gestures wear me down. Eventually, I'll no longer have my heart; it'll belong to him.

Nearly everyone we pass greets the guys in some way, whether it be football related or just an excited hello. I don't get it how they can be 'on' all the time like this. I'm only around them sometimes, and it's exhausting for me. My father's the same way as me; he likes it quiet. The guys act like it's normal, though, and with how well they each play, I guess life for them has been in the spotlight for quite a while. Even when they're being fawned over by their fans, they never make me feel like I don't belong, and I love that.

Brianne stops next to Tyler's truck, smiling at Kash like he's hung the moon.

Great.

Freight Train

I'd suspected that she liked Kash and possibly JJ or Chandler as well. It seems more and more that I'm right. At least with it being Kash, it's not one of his best friends. If she goes out with him, it could be a little awkward, but not as bad as if it were JJ or Chandler.

Instead of opening the door so I can hop in like Tyler normally does, he cages me in, both of his arms level with my shoulders. The corded muscles of his biceps are nearly the size of my thighs; it should be intimidating, but it makes me grow warm all over instead.

"I'm serious about the ranch. You pack up some stuff, and after the game, you're all mine."

He's so sure like he's waiting for me to argue with him. What he doesn't get, is that I want to go. I want to be with him, even if it is a little overwhelming. "I mean it. I'll go with you, but you better keep your hands to yourself and stay out of the bed."

He chuckles, amused at my demand. "You keep saying that, Pretty, but trust me, you'll want these palms all over you, rubbing you and keeping you warm at night." He raises his large paws in front of my face, before running them over my arms, making me feel dainty compared to him.

"Don't hold your breath," I retort and roll my eyes.

He smirks, brushing his nose against my cheek before taking a step back. Each time he does little things like the nose brush, it makes my insides melt to utter mush. I keep being defiant and trying to push him away, but he won't budge. He's just as stubborn as I am, if not more.

"Get in."

"Only because I don't feel like walking today." Winking, I climb into his big pickup.

"Christ, you're tenacious. My brothers are going to get a kick out of you," he mumbles as I scoot into the middle seat and he climbs in after me.

"You think they'll be around?" Now I have more guys that look like him to worry about like one isn't enough to get my blood heated. I'm going to need those cold nights he keeps mentioning, to be able to get some sleep.

"Yeah, I know they will be. Clyde won't let anyone have a party without being nosey, and Nate will want to drink the free beer."

"Do your brothers, um, look like you?"

The truck swerves a little as he swallows, his brow wrinkling as he glances over at me. "Yeah, I guess so, why?"

"Oh no reason, just curious if I'd be able to pick them out or if they'd blend in with everyone else." Or because Tyler's smoking hot and I don't think I can handle being around two more versions of him. I may abandon my clothes and scream for them to all just take me, right there out in the open. I can imagine the school's newspaper headline and the call I'd get from my father.

Slut.

Shaking my head, I stare straight ahead and thank God Tyler can't read my mind.

We get halfway through a song by Twenty One Pilots, and we're already at the entrance to my dorms. I've gotten pretty comfortable with him driving me around. It gives me time to really take him in, without him being able to distract me. I feel safe next to him.

"Thanks for the ride," I mumble, using the same line I've used every day. I start to scoot out the passenger side when he grabs my arm.

"Pack tonight, so we can get your bag and leave right away."

"Bossy much?"

"Always, sweetheart." He grins.

"Why tonight?"

"Because, the game's tomorrow, remember?"

My stomach drops. I was thinking of this weekend, as in really being next weekend, not tomorrow! "Of course, I do. I was just checking if you were paying attention." God that sounded dumb, even to my own ears.

He chuckles, and I feel my cheeks heat. I'm not used to the sort of attention he's giving me. He's everywhere when we're around each other.

"That explains the light lunch you had today," I say out loud, thinking about the fruit he was feeding me. *Duh, he eats light the day before his games, only clean eating, so he'll feel one hundred percent. Shit.*

"Yes, ma'am. Glad you noticed. So, I'll see you tomorrow." He plants a soft kiss on my lips.

"Bye, Ty." It comes out in a whisper, but it's loud enough for him to hear.

"See ya, Pretty."

Brianne waits patiently with the truck door open as I climb out through the passenger side. We both send Tyler a quick wave and head inside. I've noticed he never says goodbye. It's usually 'see ya' or 'catch ya later.' Just another little unique quirk I've picked up about him.

"I can't believe you said yes! I'm so proud of you!" Brianne damn near squeals when the entry door to the building fully closes.

"Oh God, why? I'm such a slut."

She laughs at me and hits the button to the elevator. "Give me a break; you are not! He's one guy, Kay, one. Have some fun; it's not like y'all are going to fall in love. Besides, this is college." She shrugs like that one meager sentence is enough to excuse any irrational behavior. She's always telling me that.

"Trust me; I'm trying *not* to fall in love. Hence the lack of dates I agree to go on with him."

"That's only because you're always reading those books about the perfect guys. It's okay for you to like a guy that's not secretly a knight in shining armor or a surprise billionaire with a heart of gold. Ty's real, and you need a 'real' type of guy."

"He's real?" I utter, laughing humorlessly. "Uh, hello, Brianne. Tyler Owens is the star football player for the University of Alabama. He's the Freight Train, aka the Golden Boy or Mr. Popular. How is that anywhere near even being remotely close to real?" I argue as we enter our room.

"You look at him like he's perfect, but none of us see him like that. You're already gone for him, woman. Ty's normal. Trust me and open your eyes."

"I am not." I turn my back to her and toe off my shoes into the minuscule closet. I may be sorta gone for him, though; I'm just too stubborn to admit it out loud. I figured when this would finally start happening to me I'd see fireworks or something crazy. I did get a spark when we met, but was that because it was fate stepping in or because I needed to use more dryer sheets in my laundry?

"Deny it all you want to Kadence, but it's happening whether you want it to or not. And he is real; he's emotional, overbearing, protective, and smart. The best part out of all of it is that he's only that way when it comes to you. I have him in classes, and I'm telling you, he doesn't treat other females the way he does you. And especially *now*, he doesn't pay anyone two cents of attention."

"Huh?" That last sentence has my mind spinning, so I turn to her. "What do you mean by 'now'?"

She shrugs, wearing a smirk. "This past week in class, he wouldn't even speak to anyone that had boobs, let alone look at them. There were so many pissed off, scanty tantrums thrown and cleavage put in front of him, it was hilarious. He was like a rock; they couldn't get his attention no matter what they tried. Kash says it's because of you because Tyler tells everyone that you're his girlfriend. And that would make you the *only* girlfriend he's had since he's started college. Think about it, Kay."

"That's absurd." Huffing, I pull out my notebook to go over my notes from earlier because this conversation is officially over. No way do I want to believe that he could be that way all because of me. It's been two weeks—two freaking weeks—since this all started! That's no time for him to act as if I'm his girlfriend as if I'm the only one he cares for.

"Think what you will, but I saw it with my own eyes," she finishes and closes the bathroom door.

Whatever.

No way can she give me credit for all of that. It does make me all warm inside to hear her say it out loud, though, knowing he was ignoring the usual skanks.

Stupid bitches.

"And stop talking to Kash about me!" I yell moments later, thinking over everything she said, as I put my earbuds in. Classic Aerosmith blares through the mini speakers, and I hunker down to get some much needed studying out of the way since I'll be out at the ranch all weekend surrounded by not only one Owens, but by three of them. No way in hell can a woman expect to be able to think around all of those muscles and testosterone.

Tyler

Game day...

Defense stops another play from happening and Coach shouts for the offense to get ready to go back onto the field. Chandler leans over to find out what's going on as JJ comes over, appearing pissed about something.

"What's the issue?" My gaze automatically shoots toward the seats I reserved for Kadence and Brianne, but they're fine, laughing and talking to each other.

"Fucking Briggs, bro. Have you guys heard him yet today?"

Chandler shakes his head, watching Coach carefully for instructions, so we don't get our asses chewed for not paying attention.

"No, why?"

"He's talking about spiking multiple bottles of liquor, so all the chicks at the after party take their clothes off. He wants to get them all recorded."

"What a sick piece of shit," Chandler murmurs.

"No way am I letting that happen to anyone at the ranch."

He blows out a frustrated breath. "Yeah, but how do we stop him?"

Coach catches our gaze, screaming, "Offense! Now! You're on!"

We take off in a jog, each getting into our positions. I have to focus on the game, but it's difficult not to be distracted when all I can picture in my mind is Kadence getting drugged, recorded, and possibly raped by asshole Briggs.

Center snaps the ball to Kash, and like a rocket, I'm gone. Pumping my legs, I run the play that's been drilled into my memory. Left twelve steps, back two, and cut for a quick right.

Kash lets the ball fly free, and she falls into my hands effortlessly, just like we've done hundreds of times before at practice. Juking the guy next to me, I take off for the end zone.

There's nothing like holding that piece of pigskin and letting your legs become lightning, tearing down the vast green field. The guys chasing me are grunting and grumbling, trying to catch me, but there's a reason why I'm 'The Freight Train.' I get going, and I'm gone; I'll plow through people like a powerful force then give them hell trying to keep up with me.

Each stripe I cross, it's like a miniature boost, encouraging me on, to run faster. My mind chants to go harder and the closer I get to the sunny yellow field goal pole, the more focused I become on it.

It's mine. Just like Kadence.

The end zone nears as I'm going full speed and moments later my feet cross over the touchdown line. No matter how many times it happens, the feeling never gets old. It's exhilarating! The safety that was running after me slows down, eventually stopping and resting his hands on his hips as he pants. No way was he ever going to catch me.

There's only one person I'm thinking of sharing my victory with at this moment.

Pointing the ball toward Kadence in the stands, the entire section of fans scream and wave all around her, but the only person I really see is *her*.

For you, Pretty.

KADENCE

Tyler's ridiculously fast as he charges down the field for a touchdown. It reminds me of watching my father run the ball when he played. Excitement fills me to the brim, causing me to jump up and scream the closer he gets.

Within seconds he's made the touchdown, the entire stadium erupting in excited chaos, celebrating the six points added to the board in our favor. In the midst of Brianne and me jumping around like a bunch of dorks, Ty does something he's never done before.

Freight Train

The football is pointed in our direction as he mouths something. I have no idea what he says, but it's enough to make me swoon, just knowing that he was clearly thinking of me at that moment.

My heart fades from my chest a little more as he steadily consumes more and more of it.

About ten different hands pat my back and arms, jostling me around as they excitedly celebrate. They must've seen Ty pointing toward us. I wonder if someone recorded it. I'd love to know what it was that he'd said when he pointed the ball our way.

"I told you he's crazy about you!" My best friend declares happily.

It's hard to hear her over everyone else's cheering and talking. All I can do is laugh and shake my head at her. I have no idea what on earth to say to that or to what he just did. I'm not even his real girlfriend, and he points me out after a touchdown. I haven't seen anyone else do that with their girlfriends, so I'm spazzing out a bit inside with flutters filling me to the brim and my heart beating so quickly it feels as if it may burst.

"Girl you're on the jumbotron again. Smile and wave. Hurry!"

Glancing toward the screen, sure enough, I'm there, appearing shell-shocked. *F.M.L. Really?*

"Smile, Kay!"

Grinning a brief, flirty smile toward the field and where the cameras are coming from, I throw in a little finger wave, thinking of Tyler's touchdown he just made and a bunch of guys start hooting and hollering.

Great. I was supposed to wear a hat to avoid this. Next time I won't forget.

My painted cheek is pretty cute on the big screen. Surprisingly, I look like a normal college chick rooting for her guy, and it's also fairly clear who I am. That's not exactly what I was going for though. I was hoping to look a little bit sexy for Tyler while covering my face with some paint since he loved it so much the last time.

Hopefully, he knows that my smile and wave were for him and most of the college guys have drunk too much to remember who I am in class. I just want a quiet college life, nothing crazy with people knowing me as the football star's girlfriend. That sounds pretty shitty, but it's true. I like blending into the background at school.

"Perfect! You have them going crazy. You're exactly what Ty needs in a girlfriend to represent him," Brianna says animatedly, her hands moving with excitement as she gabbers on.

Meeting her gaze, my smile falls away. "But I'm not his girlfriend." The truth slams into me like a tackle, effectively hitting me in my heart, where Ty's been slowly rooting himself.

"Do you want to be?" Her eyebrow goes up as the crowd quiets down some and we all sit in our seats again.

"I think I do," I honestly reply, tired of not being official with him, especially after seeing him take time out of his favorite thing in the world to acknowledge me. I must really mean something to him, and that's special to me.

"Then you are," she says simply, shrugging her shoulders.

"What? No, I'm not. He hasn't actually asked me to be his girlfriend. Even if he does tell people that I am, he's never spoken to me about it directly." She's lost her mind. You don't just decide to be someone's girlfriend and then suddenly you are. It doesn't work that way unless you're a little cray-cray in the head.

"He's already told everyone that you're his girlfriend, Kadence, so you agreeing with it all just means that it's true. It doesn't actually bother you knowing he says that about you, does it?"

I shake my head. It doesn't. I actually like it, when I admit my real feelings about it all.

She nods knowingly and faces towards the group of excited fans behind us. "Hey guys, you all know who this is, right?" She points her thumb toward me, and they all answer her with variations of 'yes.'

"Who is she then?" she asks, her smile beaming widely as they each respond that I'm Ty's girlfriend and that they appreciate me keeping him happy, so he continues to play well.

No pressure there. Geez.

I can't help but laugh at them thinking I have anything at all to do with the way Tyler plays. Hopefully, he keeps playing the way he is, or they could end up being assholes to me if that's how they think. Thanks to the jumbotron, everyone knows what I look like now too.

Tyler doesn't even know about my father playing football; I prefer to keep that to myself. I hate being bombarded with a ton of questions and fake friends because of who my dad is. Ty might realize just how much I know about football if I admitted the truth to him. I hope I don't get berated with crap from people now, knowing that I obviously mean something to Tyler.

"See, told you." Brianne leans in shrugging, and I roll my eyes in response.

"Okay, you have a point, but I'm not saying it's official or anything until I talk to him about it—really talk to him—in person first."

"Like this weekend?"

"Yeah, I'll bring it up after he's had a chance to relax. I don't want him to think I'm nagging him about it or anything."

"Oh please," she responds, and I shoot her a glare. "All right fine, but I think you're wasting your time. I already know he's crazy about you and thinks of you as his girlfriend, as does the entire school. I'm glad you'll finally be making it official, though."

Cringing a little, I mutter, "I hope your right about him and not right about the school."

"I am." She grins. "Just wait and see for yourself!"

And if she's wrong, I'll look like a pathetic, fangirl loser. But no one's paying attention anyhow. *Well, besides everyone in the entire school according to her, that is.*

Just freaking great. Why'd I have to fall for the Freight Train of all guys?

Playing football with your feet is one thing,

but playing football with your heart

is another.

- baby-g-swag Tumblr

Tyler

The game's over in no time it seems, and before I know it, we've arrived at my parents' beloved ranch. This'll be the first time I've brought home a woman that I really like to meet my brothers. I was fine with it before, but now I'm a little nervous. Not with anything to do with her, but with my brothers. What if they decide to be assholes or they don't like her? I've never cared in the past about what they've thought when they've met any chicks I was dating, but I wasn't serious then, either.

With Kadence, it's all different and weird. I want them to like her, and I want her to like them, but not too much. Not more than she likes me anyhow. Am I really jealous of my brothers? We haven't been the type to compare ourselves outside of our athletic abilities. My brothers and I all sort of resemble each other, along with my mom and dad, so I guess they're considered good-looking.

Shit, I hope she doesn't think they're hotter than me. Didn't think that'd ever be something I'd say to myself, that's for sure.

Both of my brothers haven't had trouble with being lonely in the past. Should I be worried about them liking Kadence too much? No, I think I can relax about it. Nate might feed me some shit just to try and get me going, but Clyde won't go there. He'll most likely lecture me about staying focused and the importance of not getting in too deep with a woman, especially this close to the draft. He doesn't have to worry about that, though. I'm staying focused. If anything, even more so, because she seems to keep me on my toes.

I hope she's not bored. Shit, it didn't even cross my mind when I invited Kadence out to the ranch. I sound like an idiot, all this second-guessing. I'm supposed to be the confident one in everything. If it's meant to be, then she'll be happy out here, and everyone will be just fine. And if they don't care for her, then it's their loss, because I do.

Simple.

God, I wish my mom was here to meet her. Do I like her that much to seek my parents' approval of her? Yes, in fact, I do. I would want them to love her, just like I'm beginning to. I think she'd be the type of woman that they'd want me to end up with in my life.

Freight Train

Kadence isn't superficial like most of the other women around. She's kind and caring. And one of my favorite things about her is that she loves football, maybe even as much as I do.

Fuck, I can't believe I'm beginning to actually fall in love with her. I'm way too young to be experiencing this. It's supposed to be all about having some harmless fun right now. Who knew my good time would run right smack into me—literally?

"Who's this?" Nate perks up from his faded red folding chair on the front porch. I swear he must live in that seat when I'm not here.

"This is my girlfriend, Kadence." Did I just say that out loud, in front of her, no less? I mean, I always tell people at school that she's my girl, but this is different, and she's right beside me.

Surprisingly, she just smiles and waves hello to my brother instead of arguing that she's not my girlfriend. I hope she doesn't say anything like that in front of my brothers this weekend; I'd never live it down from them and I know they'd tell my cousin so he'd give me grief over it too. I should talk to her about it.

"Girlfriend, huh?" Nate stares at me for a few beats, almost like he's trying to figure out if I'm messing with him or telling him the truth. Eventually, he stands to his full height, which happens to be one inch shorter than me and holds his hand out to her. "Hi, I'm Nate."

She steps forward a pace, placing her palm in his, "Nice to meet you."

"Yeah, you too."

I know he has a million questions running through his mind right now, the main one being when in the hell did I get a girlfriend, but he keeps them to himself. I'll be getting a phone call from him and Clyde asking me to explain the minute I hit campus.

He releases Kadence's hand, and I wrap hers in my own. "Where's Clyde?"

"He's inside. Did he, uh, know you were bringing company?" His eyes flick to Kadence briefly then back to mine.

"No, why?"

"Just curious." He shrugs. "But I'm going in the house with you so I can see his reaction," he mutters, and I chuckle. He's always a shit stirrer when it doesn't involve him directly.

"Cool, you can carry my stuff then." Grinning, I toss my duffle bag at him, per our weekly routine. Which he catches and launches it off the porch into the yard. "Dick," I mutter and pull Kadence into the house to meet my other brother.

We find Clyde in the kitchen marinating some meat. "Nice game, glad you refrained from punching people this time," he rumbles, with his back toward us. I swear he has eyes in the back of his head but most likely he heard us pull up.

"Thanks."

"But what in the hell were you pointing at with the football? I thought you had some dumb, slow walk or something for your touchdown celebration?" he asks, still facing the counter. My brothers love to give me shit over my football walk too—well just about anything they can find. My mom used to tell me that it's what brothers do. They tease each other, but they're always there for one another.

"Yeah, I do, but I was pointing at her," I reply, and he spins around quickly, his gaze glancing over my surprise guest.

"Hi." Kadence smiles and waves the same as she did with Nate.

"Who's she?" Clyde asks, nodding toward Kadence and ignoring her greeting like a jerk.

"This is his *girlfriend*," Nate butts in with eyes full of mischief. Clearly, he's all too amused with this introduction.

"Girlfriend, hmmm?" Clyde mutters, washing his hands before he approaches us. "This is the first time I'm hearing about you."

Nice and subtle. Dickface. I keep the thought to myself, but can't help it from crossing my mind.

"Well that makes me feel special, thanks," Kadence mumbles sarcastically conveying my thoughts as well, making Clyde's mouth tip up in an easy grin.

"I didn't mean it like that." His smile grows. "I'm Clyde."

"And I'm Kadence, nice to meet you."

"And you," he replies, eyeing me suspiciously. Probably wondering why he's never heard of her and yet I'm bringing her home for them to meet. "How long have you two been seeing each other?"

"For a while," I answer, shrugging and turn to her, still holding her hand. "How about I show you my room, and we can put your bag in there."

"Her bag?" both my brothers ask at the same time.

"Yep, she's here to spend the weekend with us."

They stay quiet, shocked at the unexpected guest. It's not like me to just show up with someone. I learned a long time ago to call and ask permission first. I get it that Clyde's anal about his side business and I'll be careful to help keep it a secret, but I'm done acting like I'm twelve. I want to bring my woman home, and I will. I want to have friends over to celebrate kicking ass at the game, and I will.

This ranch was split equally into three when my parents passed away. Clyde needs a reminder that it's as much mine and Nate's as it is his.

"And, I'm also having a party to celebrate the win."

That gets Clyde going. "The fuck you are." I knew it was coming, so I'm not surprised to see his cheeks tint a darker shade as he gets aggravated. The color always stands out more on him since his hair's lighter than mine and Nate's.

"Yep, I am. I'll have everyone out at the burn pit."

He's quiet for a minute, hoping I'll back off and change my plans. Eventually, he huffs out a breath and grumbles, "You better make sure everyone stays accounted for. None of those college assholes better go wandering off, or you'll have shit to deal with. Got it?"

I'm very aware that everyone needs to stay close by. I've been working this ranch my entire life. "It'll be fine. They'll drink too much, pass out in their vehicles, and drive home in the morning."

"It better go that way. You need to stay sober and keep watch. Anything goes awry, and I'll chase them off with my shotgun if needed." I hope he never has daughters with the way he wields his shotgun, not the least bit worried about threatening people.

"It's not just me anyhow. JJ and Chandler will be here to help keep everyone in line. You're getting all wound up over nothing. It's only the team and their dates."

"Good."

Nate smiles. "Nice! Free beer tonight."

"Yep, and while you're drinking our beer, you can help out with the watch."

Clyde rolls his eyes and turns away, grumbling about who knows what as he finishes marinating the food.

"Come on, Pretty." Tugging Kadence's hand again, I pull her lightly, so she'll follow me upstairs to my room. Probably not a good idea to be alone with her and a bed in the same room when we're expecting people to show up, but I can't stop myself. I'm giddy inside like I'm about to see my first pair of tits on a woman. Christ, she's beautiful. I can't wait to touch her everywhere and look my fill.

Opening my bedroom door, I let her into my world a little more. It's remained the same as when I was in high school. My mom had decorated it, and I haven't wanted to erase that part of her. My brothers have pretty much left theirs alone too, same for the barn. Nate hasn't touched a thing in there except to clean it up a bit here and there.

Taking Kadence's bag, I set it on my tall black dresser. "Do you need to hang anything up?"

"No, but...We need to talk if you don't mind." She gestures to my bed and then sits down on it. Those words are usually loaded coming from the opposite sex. If it's bad news, I wish she would've said whatever before we drove all the way out here.

It's probably about her meeting my brothers; I knew I'd hear about it, introducing her as my girlfriend. At least she waited to say something in private and away from Nate and Clyde. It would've been slightly embarrassing to get shot down in front of them. I hope they aren't being nosey in the hall and hear her get upset with me.

"Okay, let's hear it." Sitting down next to her, I automatically reach for her hand. It's become a habit like she's supposed to be attached to me somehow at all times when we're near each other. I love touching her any way that I can.

Surprisingly she lies backward until she's resting on her back and gives me a light tug to follow her down. No need to ask me twice to lie next to her. Placing my arm under my head as a pillow, I lay on my side, just watching her.

She's stunning. Before I thought she had this innocent, nerdy look, but now I know it's so much more when it comes to Kadence. Her hair's the softest I've ever felt before, and it's shiny every single time I see her. She needs glasses to read but has them off the majority of the time we're together, and I can always see her gold-speckled irises. Never in my life did I think eyes would matter to me, but no one in the past even came close to comparing to hers.

"What's up, Kay?" I like calling her by the nickname that I've given her, but I have a feeling this conversation is going to be serious for her and I want to show her the respect she deserves, by dropping the pet name right now.

"I...Uhh, well, I wanted to talk to you about this whole girlfriend thing."

"Look, I apologize okay? I know it bothers you, I just—"

"No," she interrupts me. "That's just it. You calling me your girlfriend doesn't bug me at all. I was going to wait until later to talk to you about it after you'd had a chance to relax, but then with your brothers asking about me and everything, well I didn't want to wait any longer. I don't want to pretend."

"So what exactly are you saying? You actually want to be my girlfriend, or you don't want to act like it in front of them?"

Closing her eyes, she remains quiet for a few seconds, weighing over her words. "No, the first one. I want to be your girlfriend."

"You do? Really?"

Her eyes part as she turns her head to look at me and nods. "Yes, Ty, I want to be your *real* girlfriend, as in make it official, to us and everyone."

A huge smile overtakes my face, and I hop over her, straddling my muscular legs on each side of her feminine body, making her giggle in surprise. I love the sound of her happiness. "This is the best thing to happen all day!"

Laughing she quirks her brow. "What about winning your game and scoring a touchdown in front of a ton of people?"

"Nope, this is way better. I can score touchdowns weekly if I want to; I can only make you mine once in my lifetime."

"Oh really, why only once?" Her smile falters, falling from her lips as she becomes serious again.

"Because that's all it'll take until you're mine—always."

Her cheeks grow pink, and I swear it makes her even more adorable. Pressing a chaste kiss to her mouth, I pull back, still excited at 'our talk.' "So, you're my girlfriend in public now? You won't argue with me in front of people at school anymore?" She's been protesting for the past few weeks, so I need to make sure she understands what all this entails. I plan to shout it from the parking lot if she lets me.

Her skin grows redder. "I'm really your girlfriend, Ty, and I promise not to argue with you about it. I'm sorry if it embarrassed you before."

"Oh, baby, it didn't. You just made me want you even more." So badly in fact that I thought my cock was going to fall off from having such a shit case of blue balls.

She laughs again, and I cut her off by placing my lips on hers gently. Without hesitation, her mouth opens, welcoming me inside. I'm definitely falling for her, but it's too soon to admit it out loud to her. I don't want to scare her off or make my brothers flip out, thinking I'm trying to build her a house and knock her up already. Although that's a very nice thought for our future maybe.

Her hands find their way beneath my shirt and the soft touch of her fingertips has my groin ready to pound into her like a body possessed. After watching her eat every day, I've had so many fantasies of just her mouth, let alone the rest of her body.

The craving to have more of Kadence is too strong to stop now. I wedge one leg between hers getting her to open them for me. Once she's spread them out far enough, I slip my other leg in between and slowly lower my body, putting pressure on her slim frame until my cock's resting against the juncture between her thighs.

A hushed moan escaping from her lips on contact is a direct hit to my groin. My hips rotate, pushing my hardness against her, wanting more. The room begins to feel too hot for clothes. Breaking our passionate kiss, I yank my t-shirt over my head quickly, sending it sailing through the air. *I need to have her all.*

Her teeth lightly bite her bottom lip, and it has to be the sexiest thing on her as she watches me. Not slowing down, I shove her tank top up. She lifts her body up a little until I can shimmy it completely off of her. The creamy skin from her stomach's on full display, as are the tops of her breasts that I've fantasized about night after night. I've dreamed of this moment with her.

She's encased in a lilac colored lace bra with very little padding. The sexy material is see-through just enough that I can appreciate the stiff peaks of her nipples, begging for some attention of their own. I've never seen a woman look so perfectly underneath me before, and she's not even naked yet.

Bending back over, I thrust my hardness against her softness, nipping and sucking on her nipples through the bra. She has me so wound up that my body automatically grinds against hers, seeking pleasure. It's the most amazing combination and has her body squirming underneath me, full of her own need.

"Tyler, oh God!" Kadence gasps, as I suck her breast into my mouth again, stronger this time, not getting enough to satisfy the pent up desires she's inflicted in me for so long.

She has me so unbelievably turned on that my hips rock against her over and over until she's panting and moaning, begging me not to stop doing it. Within minutes and two powerful thrusts later, she's crying out.

Her sultry voice calling my name is enough to cause me to explode inside my pants. The hot wetness coats my stomach and underwear as I rock gently against her, letting her ride out her own wave of bliss, catching her breathy pants with my own mouth. She's intoxicating, making me forget anything and everything all at once when I'm like this with her.

I don't know whether I should be embarrassed for going off so easily in front of her the first time we get a little hot and heavy or impressed. I can't remember the last time that happened to me, past the age of fifteen.

Slowing our kisses, I brace myself on top of her, panting, making my body stop before my dick gets a friction burn from my clothes.

My forehead rests against hers as I mumble. "I wasn't expecting that to happen—at all. You're amazing; you know that?"

"Thank you." Her hand runs down my spine. "Me either. I guess our talk was good then if that was the outcome?" She smiles against my cheek, sparking a grin from me.

"I'll say. Jesus, I can only imagine how fast I'll go with the real thing. I promise I'm not usually so..."

"Quick?" She supplies cheekily, and I tickle her sides in response until she shoves me off.

"I have to clean up. Give me a few?"

"Or we could take a shower," she suggests wagging her eyebrows, and I about fall over.

"Together? No way, we'd never make it to the party."

"Why not?"

"Because, Pretty, I'd end up fucking you all day, well into the night."

"That really doesn't sound bad to me."

"I'm waiting to do that when we aren't expecting people over here, but rest assured, it'll happen and soon."

She sends me a bright smile, and I head to the bathroom, wishing the entire time that I hadn't invited anyone over.

Sapphire Knight

It's not about being the best.

It's about being better than you were yesterday.

- Unknown

KADENCE

  Meeting Tyler's brothers wasn't so bad after all. I was a little star-struck, though, I guess you'd call it. They not only act alike with their broodiness, but they're each incredibly good-looking in their own way too. I feel like they belong on their own reality TV show for beautiful people or something, or maybe a magazine spread on men 'a cut above the standard.' And their voices; Lord have mercy. Those guys have southern accents thick enough to give you goose bumps and make you wet. I wouldn't be surprised if old ladies made the sign of the cross when listening to them speak.

I also liked it that they were blunt when asking who I was and admitting that they hadn't heard of me. Honesty can be a hard trait to find in some people, especially when you first meet someone. Growing up with my dad it seemed like there were always fake people around since he was an NFL star. Ty's brothers are like a breath of fresh air. You know exactly what you're getting with them, and I couldn't be happier with that fact.

I'm freaking out inside a little bit, though. I hope his brothers didn't hear us in his room. That's definitely not the sort of first impressions I want to make on his family. I know about his parents dying, the school and everyone else around has published articles on it, so his brothers' opinions probably mean a great deal to him. Ty's friends at school seem to like me, and I can only hope that his brothers will end up feeling the same way as well.

"Are you ready to do this?" Ty asks as we finish lining the rock path with plastic, solar-powered lanterns to lead all the party people in the right direction to the bonfire. He's already brought out a bunch of wire hangers with a cooler full of hot dogs and marshmallows for everyone, along with some folding chairs for us two.

"I'm not much of a partier if you haven't noticed, so I suppose I'm as ready as I can be. I'm glad we're not far from the house, so if I get tired, I can just go to bed and not worry about getting kidnapped walking back to the dorms."

Jesus, I sound so boring to my own ears. But I've never claimed to be a partier, and I'm not going to pretend to be someone that I'm not. I've already changed up my wardrobe here and there for

Ty. Granted, he doesn't know that I've done that for him, and I don't want him to, but I did. He's so gorgeous, and I was starting to feel frumpy around him sometimes, so now I alternate. One day I dress in Brianne's cuter outfits and then the next I wear a pair of jeans and one of my super soft t-shirts. The funny thing is that Tyler compliments me whenever I'm wearing either type of outfit. It makes me feel like he does like me no matter what I wear, but with all the piranhas circling him, I need to wear something sexy occasionally.

"No one will bother you out here. You have me, JJ, Chandler, and my brothers. None of us will let anything happen to you, I promise. Is Brianne still coming with Kash?"

"Thank you; I've just never been a big people person when it comes to crowds. I forget what to talk about and just clam up. People think I'm rude, but I just don't know what to say. Umm, I don't know about Brianne, she wasn't sure what they were going to do today, but I hope so."

"Well, tonight will only be the football team and their girlfriends, maybe a few of their good friends or siblings, kind of like the party at the house. You had a decent time at that one, right?"

"I about came when you did the body shot," I reply bluntly, causing his mouth to pop open in surprise. It's true, though; he had my body humming, pent up with lust over him.

"Trust me, babe so did I." He chuckles and opens a folding chair for me once we get next to the big fire pit. "How about you take a seat and I'll get a hot dog ready for you to roast. You're probably getting hungry by now?"

"That sounds perfect, thank you."

I know not to argue. This man is always trying to feed me. I'm just going to accept that it's the way he is. I'm assuming food must be on his mind a lot with all the exercise he gets, so he probably thinks I get hungry as much as he does. The man could eat an entire cow and then want dessert. No way I'll ever be able to keep up.

Tyler and his brother Nate get the fire going with a decent sized flame to keep everyone warm as the night air cools down. He greets people here and there as they all start to show up and then makes sure that I'm all situated with food and drinks.

After a little while, he takes his seat beside me, relaxing, drinking a few beers and watching the fire as everyone visits and has a good time. No matter who approaches us, he never leaves me out. Introducing me to everyone that I don't know and including me in his conversations. He's done that before when we've hung out, but now he proudly tells everyone that I'm his girlfriend and it's adorable like he's genuinely pleased to have me alongside him.

Surprisingly, the night passes by quickly, and I end up having fun. Niner pulled up a seat next to me early on and had me laughing a good portion of the evening with his and Ty's easy banter. I wasn't expecting to enjoy myself around a bunch of people that I don't really know, but I did.

I get a decent look at why the football team's so close and works together well as a unit. They practice together, eat together, celebrate together, and win together. It's like a giant family away from your immediate family. No wonder why Ty engrossed himself into the sport so much. It was helping him cope with the loss of his parents by adding in another sense of family.

I'm so glad I decided to take a chance and come out here with Tyler. It's turned out to be an awesome day.

Freight Train

Tyler

The night's going pretty smoothly, minus Clyde flipping out anytime someone walks two steps away to take a piss. He doesn't want anyone wandering off and stumbling upon his business. I get it, but shit it's annoying after a while. He needs to learn how to relax just a bit.

Tipping my beer back to finish it off, Chandler and JJ appear, their faces grim.

"What's up you two?" I get straight to the point, thinking one of my brothers is being a jerk to someone or they caught a partier snooping around.

JJ grumbles something, and Chandler speaks up. "We busted Briggs trying to slip something in a chick's drink over by the keg a few minutes ago."

"Are you fucking with me right now?"

"Nope." He shakes his head.

JJ glances at Kadence for a brief second, and I can tell he's not sure what he should say in front of her. "Talk to me, bro," I demand, low enough so she can't overhear everything. I don't want her getting upset over anything. She's been happy all day, and I want her to stay that way.

"I pulled him away. Chan got Nate, and we kicked the shit out of Briggs. Nate sent him packin' but not before I got his phone first. Fucker's sick."

"Where is it?"

"I threw that shit in the fire."

"I can't believe I didn't see anything. My bad, you guys, damn it."

"It's no biggie; we took care of it while you kept everyone else distracted. Besides, Nate had fun helping us and Clyde'll be happy nothing went down that anyone could've seen. You should've heard Nate with the threats he was making while he stuffed Briggs into his car. That part was funny as shit. Your brother's not so bad." He shrugs.

"Yeah, you've also been around when Nate's stolen our beer and then our clothes when we were at the pool. Don't get too comfortable around him. And we can't let Clyde find out about this either. He'd never let anyone on the property again."

I don't miss those days, trying to hide our plans. Anytime we'd gotten some type of alcohol, just being dumbass teens, my brother would show up. It's like Nate had a nose for it and he'd either take it from us or make us share. If we didn't, then he threatened us he'd get Clyde, and that was the last thing we wanted. Clyde would've made us stop hanging out together, and there was no way we were letting that happen.

"How the fuck does he get away with this shit and not ever get in trouble for it?" JJ grumbles, and I shrug.

"Hell, I don't know, but something needs to be done. He shouldn't be allowed at the college around all those women. If he didn't play football, I'm betting he would've gotten busted a long time ago. I'm sure someone out there besides the women he's messed with knows what he's all about."

Freight Train

"We need to figure out a way to get him busted by the dean," Chandler supplies and we both nod.

"Do you have any suggestions?" I ask, and they both shake their heads, annoyed. "Me either. At least you guys got him out of here. This week we need to try to come up with a plan. Even if it's not him getting in trouble for the stuff he does to chicks, it needs to be something that'll get him kicked off the campus."

"Sounds good," Chandler agrees. "I'm pretty sure I know a few of the women he's done it to. I skimmed over some pictures he had on his phone before JJ chunked it. At least two of the chicks are in my classes."

"I'm down; I want him gone. I probably should've kept his phone for evidence. I was just pissed and didn't want him having it," JJ grumbles, his buzz officially gone with all the drama going on.

"Don't worry about it; we'll figure something out."

Kadence leans over, holding another marshmallow. "Hey, it's three a.m., and I've eaten nearly an entire bag of marshmallows. I think I'm going to bed pretty soon."

"Okay, I'm ready too."

JJ's eyes grow wide. "Bro, we usually stay up till at least five a.m. when we do bonfires."

"Nope, not tonight. Nearly everyone's gone and passed out anyhow. The die-hard drinkers can finish the night off by sitting on the back of their tailgates without the fire going."

"Already pussy whipped." He shakes his head, and I shoot him a glare. I don't want him saying shit like that in front of Kadence. I don't care if people think I'm 'whipped' or not, I just don't want her to feel uncomfortable or disrespected. She doesn't deserve that treatment or those remarks.

"Come on, Pretty." I hold my hand out. She grabs it and stands up, stretching her legs out. "Sore from sitting?"

"Yeah, a little. It's been a long day."

"It sure has. Give me a sec. I need to tell Nate to put the fire out, and then we'll head to the house."

"Okay." She smiles tiredly, and I signal for my brother.

KADENCE

I thought he was going to ravage my body the first chance he got last night when we went back to his room after the party. Instead, he lay on the bed in only a pair of boxer briefs and passed completely out while I went to the bathroom.

Now, it's morning, and I'm lying here in his bed, watching him sleep peacefully. He's insanely beautiful as he rests, long lashes shadowing underneath his eyes as he sleeps deeply. He's nearly always wearing some grin or a smirk during the day and to witness him so relaxed, is like watching a piece of sculpted art. He's got a thin white scar above his eyebrow, probably from a rough practice or maybe a quarrel with one of his brothers, and it's taking all of my self-control not to run my finger over the small mark or anywhere else on his body.

Freight Train

Tyler's bare chest is purely enticing as it rises and falls in rhythm with his deep breaths. It's practically beckoning me to stare my fill and to just reach over and pet it. God, I want to, ever since we were alone in here yesterday, I can't get the image of him on top of me out of my mind. I wanted him to go further, even though I know we should slow down and take our time. All I want to do is rush.

What happened yesterday still has me reeling; I can't believe I was that noisy and right after we first arrived too. Thankfully neither one of his brothers said anything about it to me, so hopefully, it means they didn't hear me after all. If he can get me that stirred up inside with my clothes on, I can only imagine what the real deal must be like with him. I don't think a man's ever had me so sexually frustrated and wound up inside before.

Tyler's door creaks open, with Clyde's head peeking in. "You want some breakfast?"

What is it with these guys and food? And thank God I'm in clothes and covered by blankets, or that could've been awkward.

"Ummm...Sure."

"May as well, Ty sleeps till noon on the weekends. It's the only time the kid gets to recharge." Clyde can't be but maybe five years older than Tyler, but just now he made me feel like we're incredibly younger than he is.

"Okay, I'll ah, be down in just a few minutes."

He nods and closes the door softly. Not a man of many words I take it.

Well shit, looks like I'm about to be grilled by the oldest. Maybe I'll get lucky, and Nate will be like Ty when it comes to the sleeping late habit? What if he asks about us fooling around in here yesterday? I know we're all adults, but that would be pretty mortifying if he ends up being pissed about it. You know how it goes when you meet family for the first time; you just want them to like you. It makes the relationship easier on everyone.

I have on my sleep tank and pajama shorts, but I need something to give me a little more confidence when facing down an Owens sibling. Glancing around at Tyler's stuff, I decide to lose my thin tank and yank on one of Ty's big t-shirts.

The material smells like him still and easily swallows me up. He doesn't seem so big around all his friends and the other players, probably because they're all large-sized men, but to me, he's huge.

Perfect. I nod, continuing my search.

Going a step further, I pull on a pair of his long socks. I probably look like a huge dork, but I couldn't care less. They're comfy, and since he's officially my boyfriend, it gives me free rein to wearing his clothes. If we're still dating come winter, I'm living in his hoodies. I'm already laying claim to them...

Wait, if we're together? Of course, we will be, there's no reason not to be. It's only been one day, and already I'm worrying about losing him. I need to stop all the negativity and have hope.

Digging through my bag that's still in the same spot as yesterday, on top of Ty's dresser, I grab my toothbrush and a hair tie. I quickly throw my hair up in a messy bun and brush my teeth before I head downstairs. I won't win anyone over with bad breath and Medusa hair.

The kitchen's quiet as I come down the stairs and head for the table. My steps are light, as my stomach knots up, nervous about being alone with Clyde for the first time.

Freight Train

"Coffee?" he asks, without turning around. He has that 'eyes in the back of his head' gift that parents often have. It's impressive and a little freaky.

"No thanks, I'll just have a glass of OJ."

"Help yourself," he offers, and I grab the pitcher in the center of the table, filling a small glass tumbler in one of the places that's already been set.

After a moment he brings over a plate loaded down with heaps of bacon and another overfilled with pancakes.

"This looks amazing. Do you enjoy cooking?"

"I don't mind it," he replies, shrugging and sitting to the left of me.

"Do all of you cook?"

"Pretty much, but on the weekends my brothers sleep late, so I make breakfast. Usually, pancakes or French toast so they can microwave it whenever they decide to get up."

"That's nice of you. Tyler's grilled me chicken kabobs. They were delicious."

Clyde glances at me briefly, placing six pieces of bacon on his plate along with four large-sized pancakes. "Eat up." He gestures to the food, so I take a few of each. "Let's get the awkwardness out of the way, Kadence. I'm not your enemy when it comes to my brother. You obviously mean a lot to him, or you wouldn't be here. I can't remember the last time he had a girlfriend or one he cared to introduce us to. I'm happy for you both. That being said, I will always watch out for my brothers' best interest. If I catch you bringing him down in any way, you'll hear it from me immediately. Those boys have become more to me than just my younger brothers. They're my heart and not to replace my own parents, but in a way, they're mine. You understand me?"

"Yes, sir. I respect that," I reply the same way I would if it were a father saying it, as I know that's what my own dad would expect.

"Good, I'm glad that's out of the way. Now make yourself at home and relax. We're family. If Ty bringing you home is his indication on how he feels about you, then you'll eventually be a part of this family down the road."

I have to hold the tears from falling at his declaration. It's said with such sincerity; it makes me *want* to be in this family, surrounded by these brothers. It may be too soon for me to declare my love for Ty, but I can see it happening quickly if this is any indication how he and his family will treat me.

"Thank you." I smile graciously and dig into the best pancakes I've had since my nan cooked for me.

Later that afternoon...

"I thought you were going to sleep forever!" I tease Ty as we walk to the swimming hole on the ranch that he's told me all about back at school.

"Oh come on, my brothers weren't so bad, were they?"

"Nope, not at all, but you should've warned me you like to sleep all day on Sunday."

Freight Train

"Just until noon, then usually football's on, and we eat bad while we watch whoever's playing."

"Especially the Patriots?"

"Hell yeah, them and the Saints for sure."

"So where's this swimming hole at, exactly?" In the afternoon warmth, it feels like we've been walking longer than we really have.

"Right over this small hill." He smiles, and we trek up the short climb. Sure enough, there's a giant, uneven oval that's full of water, with a small dock leading out nearly to the middle.

"Oh my God, this is awesome!" The area's surrounded by various established trees, giving it the perfect amount of shade and privacy. We set our towels down, and I take it all in.

"See, I told you."

"You weren't kidding. No wonder you guys lived out here during the summers. I would've too."

"When I was younger, my dad wouldn't let us near it. He said it was for the animals only, drove us crazy as kids."

"So who built the dock then?"

"He did. Once we learned how to swim, my dad couldn't keep us out of it. He gave in eventually." Ty chuckles, reminiscing over the happy memory.

"Your dad must've been one amazing guy to have run this entire place and deal with three boys."

"Oh he was, but it was my mom who took on my brothers and me. To put it lightly, she was a force to be reckoned with. My father provided for our family, and my mom held the fort down, so to speak."

"They both sound very strong. I wish I would've had a mom like that. But you already know that mine was never around. Luckily my dad and my Nan was there for me, though. Clyde seems a lot like I'd imagine your father to have been."

"He is. It's like they should've been brothers or something. He's more like my father than Nate and me."

"He loves you very much," I reply softly, and he nods.

"Enough with all the serious talk, it's time for you to strip."

"What? Who said I was stripping?"

"It's called skinny dipping!"

Nate comes over the hill. "Yes, this is what I like to hear!"

"Not a chance," Ty hollers at him. "Go back to the house!"

"Screw you. If she's going to get naked, I'm staying."

Laughing, I argue, "Well rest assured, it's not going to happen." Pulling my shirt over my head, I slip my flip-flops off and push my stretchy shorts down until I'm left in my bra and panties. Both guys stand staring as I take off in a dash, running over the dock and jump straight into the middle of the pond.

Seconds later two loud splashes follow, bringing a cheesy smile to my face. It must have been so much fun growing up here, with siblings around all the time to do things with like swimming. Looking back, my life was sort of lonely growing up. I was loved, don't get me wrong, but today so far has shown me an entirely new look at what family is. Could I be so lucky to have Ty and his brothers in my life for the future? And if Ty and I had a family, they would have a chance to grow up in what was pretty much a dream life to me when I was younger. I could see us here, with a family of our own, teaching them things.

Okay so Ty, Nate, and Clyde would teach them, along with me. I'm more of a city person, but I would definitely show them all the love a person has to give. It's crazy to be picturing this when Ty and I are such a new couple. It's merely been weeks, and we have to get through the part where he eventually meets my father. I still haven't even shared with him who my dad is, exactly.

Will he like me more when he finds out? There's a possibility, but then he could also not be happy about me keeping it from him for so long. Usually, when you start a new relationship, you're busy sharing every little detail with each other. All those small pieces of information that mean everything to you, but the other person eventually forgets about.

I've started doing that, shelling out pieces here and there, but I don't think Tyler will be able to grasp what I'm talking about when I tell him those things until he knows just how famous my father was, and in many cases, still is. It's nerve racking, but I hope he'll forgive me for keeping it from him.

Sapphire Knight

If you don't believe in yourself,

why is anyone else going to believe in you?

- Tom Brady

Sitting underneath an old oak tree on a blanket after hours filled with laughter and swimming, I've come to the conclusion that it's been one of the best days I've had in a long time. This wasn't what I was expecting when Ty invited me to come home with him. I'm going to miss this place when we have to go back to campus tomorrow.

"You're so perfect." Ty leans over, tucking a strand of sun-dried hair behind my ear.

"That's a word I don't usually associate myself with."

"Why not? You should."

"Have you seen me?" Chuckling, I pull my shirt back over my head, now that I'm completely dry.

"I have, and every day I can't believe you weren't already spoken for. Men are stupid to not be following you around."

"Thank you, that's sweet of you, but I'm a klutz. Running into you wasn't my first time colliding with someone; it's pretty much a weekly occurrence. And I don't like dressing like the sorority girls, so most guys just look past me, I suppose."

"Is it wrong that I'm happy that they're too dumb to see what's right in front of them? And that I'm grateful, because it means you're mine?" His words make my cheeks heat up; they're heartfelt, and he says them with such honesty in his gaze it makes my heart beat fast.

"Ty, that's very kind of you, but I'm really not that special."

He bends forward until his nose brushes mine softly. "Oh, Kadence, you really have no idea...You're so much *more* than just special." At that, his lips meet mine, softly, not hastily like yesterday's tussle in his room, but tenderly coaxing mine to give in to him.

I think it's at that moment that I completely fall in love with him.

No one's treated me with such a high amount of respect and care that he has. Tyler's always saying exactly what's on his mind, and for it to be something like that, I can't help but melt and fall for him. With a few swipes of his skillful tongue, he owns me, not because he claims me, but because I offer myself freely to him.

Lying back on the blanket and hard ground, I give him not only my heart, but all of me and every movement is beautiful.

Like the way he carefully removes my shirt, taking the extra moment to make sure I'm comfortable, and how he makes sure to nearly kiss every piece of my body, not leaving a spot untouched. His lips and intense gaze make me feel wanted, needed and adored. His hands cherish each of my soft curves, rough palms grazing over me as they leisurely explore.

"Please," I utter, and he complies, peeling off my panties. Lying back, I watch as he pulls free of his light gray boxer briefs, releasing his length—fully aroused and wanting me. It's the perfect size, big enough so that I'll feel everything.

He enters me gradually, letting my body adjust to him, so it doesn't hurt too badly. It's been a while for me, and even though I'm sure he's much more experienced than I am—if the playboy rumors are true—I almost wouldn't believe it. He so careful and attentive, it's like he's been waiting for this moment his whole life. Part of me believes I have been too; it couldn't be more right. It's like a scene out of one of my books, and he has no clue that he's making my dreams come true.

"Jesus, you feel good, Kadence." He mumbles my name, and it's all I need to set a fire ablaze inside.

It's as if he's tuned in to my body, and within moments he has me wanting to come, just like yesterday. Men have had to work for it in the past, but not Tyler. No one even compares to how he feels filling me. Not only does my mind want him, but so does my body, my soul, every piece of my being.

"You do too, just the right fit," I answer as he kisses my neck. Up and down his lips whisper over my throat, pausing exactly where I need them too, each scorching touch of his breath unleashes goose bumps flooding my skin. Every marvelous swipe of his skillful tongue has my core growing wetter and wetter with my excitement.

With a thrust and a nibble on my throat, he grumbles, "You were made for me."

I know what he means. I feel it too. He's right about perfection, but it's not me. It's all him. He's the one who has no idea just how truly special *he* is. He has to be, to capture my heart completely, for me to offer myself up so easily to him.

"Yes," I moan. My core clenches around him tightly, silently begging to keep him inside longer. He's forced me to blossom into this wanton version of myself, ready to hold him in me as long as possible, wanting him to expunge every last drop of his cum.

Tyler's hands stroke my skin, driving my body on further, making it crazier with need for him. His muscles ripple with each thrust, showcasing his strength, making him more gorgeous than before. His body's a thing of pure beauty, carved from hours of hard work and dedication. I feel unbelievably lucky to have him sharing it with me.

His drive speeds up, becoming more urgent and his fingers follow, pulling and softly twisting each of my nipples. The sensations have me hot all over, my body becoming lava as my orgasm climbs inside, nearly ready to burst as my stomach spirals with anticipation.

"More," I demand, his teeth clenching, as his jaw grows tight. He stares straight into my eyes as he thrusts into me with more vigor, blinking but never breaking the spell he's spun. Each strong pump has me panting, sweat lightly sparkling over my skin and coating his.

In one last powerful drive, his mouth slams on mine, pushing himself into me as deeply as possible. It sends my mind and body flying—floating and falling at once—spinning out of control as I cry out at the wonderful sensations zinging through my system.

His warm cum fills my insides, causing my center to throb at the delicious intrusion as he pants beside me, on his own blissful ride. "Fucking perfect," he mumbles beside me.

"It was so much more," I reply, copying his earlier proclamation.

"It was. Fuck, it was." His lips meet my cheek softly, and then my forehead as he peppers chaste kisses all over my face. "I'm so damn sorry I did that. I lost control at the end. I should've had a condom on. I promise I'm not trying to sabotage you in any way."

"It's okay, Ty, I'm on birth control."

"Yeah, but it wasn't safe without you knowing if I'm clean. I'll get checked again for you, I promise."

"Look, I trust you, okay? I know you wouldn't hurt me on purpose, and that's enough for me. It was perfect, I promise."

"Okay good, because it was pure heaven for me, and you're right, I would never let you get hurt in any way."

"Good." I giggle, and he climbs off of me.

"You hungry?"

"Oh, Tyler, how did I know that was going to come out of your mouth?"

"Is that a bad thing?"

"Nope. It drove me crazy at first, but I've come to terms with it, and to answer your question, yes, I'm starving."

"Me too, let's go see if Clyde made lunch."

"You're pretty spoiled for being a grown man; you know that, right?"

"You forget that I had to grow up with him. Trust me; I've paid my dues."

"You poor thing," I tease as I put on my clothes and he folds up the blanket.

"Just wait, once they get used to you, it'll be a whole new ball game." He laughs, and we head back to his family's house.

Tyler

Monday morning comes along way too fast. Ever since we got back on campus, all I can think about is how did I get so lucky to be the one she ran into that day nearly four weeks ago? I can't believe it's been that long since I first laid eyes on her. Time flies when I'm around her, and while I'm happy that we've gotten a chance to know each other, it feels like I can never see her enough. I want to be around her all the time, and it drives me nuts when I can't be.

Is this what it's like when you're in love with someone? Do you want to be near them, even after you've just spent time with them? I wasn't expecting to feel so deeply for her this quickly. I thought it'd all be a fun time, for however long it lasted. Now I feel as if I can't breathe properly if I don't get to see her at least once a day.

Do I seem clingy? Would she mind if I were? I'm a guy. I thought this shit wasn't supposed to happen to me. Isn't it the woman who's supposed to become attached so quickly? I wish my mom were here so I could talk to her about it. If I attempt to speak to my brothers about it, they'll just give me a bunch of shit for acting like a pussy.

There shouldn't be double standards about this shit. If it were her, everyone would be saying how cute it was, but me on the other hand, they'd say I was whipped. Not that I give a shit what other people think; it's just annoying, and I don't want to hear about it.

"Hey bro, you ready for Coach to whip us in practice?" JJ asks as he climbs into my truck, throwing his bag in the back seat.

"Not after the day off I had."

"Ah, the shit with Briggs wasn't so bad since we caught him before he got to anyone."

"I meant my time with Kadence; it was pure fucking heaven. But, I'm beyond pissed about him trying to pull something at my house. That's so messed up. Could you imagine if y'all hadn't caught him and one of those women ended up raped or something? Not only would she be scared for life, but the ranch would be known for that, and it's the last thing Clyde needs right now. An entirely new fucked up shit storm."

"I get it. We were lit too. Nate and I beat the shit out of him. We'll see if he's there today."

"I don't want to look at the scumbag."

"I feel you, trust me. I want to sock him every time he shows his slimy smile."

"Where's Chandler anyhow?"

"He's meeting us there. I guess he met up with a chick yesterday."

"Nice."

He nods as we pull into the parking lot at the football field for practice. After having a day off, this practice will feel even longer than usual.

Yesterday with Kadence has me wanting to sham off practice to go see her. But I can't. This is the test where I need to balance my feelings for her and my love of football. I have to stay dedicated and focused to make it into the draft and be picked up.

I should've talked to her about it yesterday, but I didn't want to ruin our time together with serious talk. Eventually, the conversation must happen, and the sooner, the better. The draft is just a few months away, and she needs to be ready to transfer schools if needed and if she is willing. I hope she does. I want her to come with me if I get drafted. I'm surprised I'm considering that—even more so than thinking I'm falling for her. I want her in my life and in my future. It's scary and exciting all in the same breath.

Gearing up, we head out on the field, ready to warm up and run some plays. The coach was lenient this morning by letting us skip weight training, but it's back to it tomorrow. I used to think that there'd never be anything else in the world that I enjoyed more than playing this game, but after making love to Kadence and swimming the afternoon away, I can add a few more favorites to my list.

Last night she let me have her again and then ended the night by curling up beside me and sleeping with half of her body on my chest. Her little frame kept me the perfect temperature all night, and I slept better than I have in years. I thought she'd be sore today from lying in that position all night, but she was fine. I'm hoping there's more of that in my future.

Freight Train

Kash calls a play, and we break to the line. I'm too busy focusing on what I have to do, to notice when Kadence shows up. People are always watching us, so I've learned to ignore anyone that's not on the field practicing.

Center snaps the ball, and we're off, rushing to get into position. The ball's not coming to me to run it, but I have to do a catch and toss. That's where the quarterback tosses it to me while running, and then I throw it at the intended target to carry out the play. It fakes out the other team so we can gain yards and possibly a touchdown.

The play goes over smooth as butter. I easily catch it from Kash and then fire it yards away to JJ. It's almost too good to be true how well it worked, making it one of my favorites to run.

Coach's whistle sounds and Kash high-fives me as we head for the line to find out what's next from the quarterback coach and Coach Stratton. That's when I notice my sweet woman standing up in the first row of the bleachers, looking more beautiful than I remembered.

Sapphire Knight

Ability is what you're capable of doing.

Motivation determines what you do.

Attitude determines how well you do it.

- Lou Holtz

Seeing *him* touching Kadence, causes something to snap inside. She's the first person I've cared for in a very long time, and he's the last person that should be anywhere near her.

She throws her head back, laughing loudly at something Briggs says to her. He stands on the field below her; while she leans over the rails listening to whatever he's telling her. It's my breaking point. I couldn't stop myself if I tried; I'm too far gone over her.

My feet pound against the ground as I full on charge at him, tossing my helmet behind me, not caring where it lands. Twenty yards is plenty of time for me to gain a decent speed, which when we finally collide, I know he'll be feeling it later.

Briggs' body tumbles to the ground with my impact, and I quickly climb over him, bracing my legs on each side of his body to hold him in place and start raining punches left and right. There's a satisfying crunch as my knuckles connect with his cheek before I'm being yanked in all different directions. I'm pretty much out of it as several arms pull at me. Eventually, they're able to physically drag me away about ten feet from Briggs but not for lack of my trying to charge him again.

Panting, ready to pummel him still, Kadence is a blur in the background. The blood rushing through my body makes it impossible for me to focus on her other than notice tears trickling over her cheeks. It's like an igniter, spurring me on further to hurt him for getting near my woman. The adrenaline's enough to cloud my thoughts, making me believe that he's the one who's caused her to cry—not me.

Eventually breaking free, I charge after him again, only to be blocked by my teammates and physically carried to the locker room by a few of them. The field and hall pass by quickly as they damn near run with me, swiftly getting me into the locker room.

The water's icy, as I'm thrown into one of the shower stalls and the sprayers are pointed down toward me. The water is turned on full blast—dutifully soaking through my practice uniform, pads, and cleats—chilling me enough inside to break me out of my hateful rage. I could've killed him and not even realized it, knowing what he's capable of doing to women. I promised to protect her, and I'll do everything I can to keep that promise.

Freight Train

Meeting my friends' concerned gazes as they peer down at me, sitting on the cold tile floor, has me placing my head in my hands, wondering how badly I just fucked everything up.

"Kadence…Where is she?" I mumble, looking up at them.

Niner glances sideways, not meeting my eyes. "She ugh, I'm pretty sure she took off, man."

"Fuck," I utter quietly, staring down at my knees as my back rests uncomfortably against the shower wall. "Was she alone? Di…did he touch her?"

"No, her friend was with her, no one touched her," he reassures.

Coach Stratton angrily storms into the locker room, shouting, "Where the hell is he?"

"Over here, Coach." Niner gestures to me and then steps away.

"Give me space! Brent, run Thursday's drills again," he orders the assistant coach and the locker room grows silent after everyone piles back outside.

Coach's black Nike 5.0s come into view as he stands in the shower entrance. "After you get cleaned up, you meet me in my office," he orders and walks off, not waiting for a reply.

Just the calmness of his voice is enough to bring tears to my eyes. My college football career is officially over. I just threw my future away because of an anger problem, because of jealousy and fear for someone I care deeply for.

Briggs didn't actually do anything wrong, but it doesn't matter. He shouldn't even speak to her. She's my girl, and he knows that;

she's supposed to be off limits. Just knowing about everything that he's done to other females, I couldn't stand seeing him around Kadence, let alone talking to her.

I think the entire team has seen the videos he's made at some point. Getting the girls all over campus plastered at parties and then recording them having sex or him putting random objects inside them—bottle necks, foods, dildos, that sort. It's all so he can blackmail the chicks later, making them give it up to him whenever he wants or else he'll upload everything online for the entire university to watch. It's sickening, and he shouldn't be able to get away with it. He deserved every punch I gave him.

He's lucky all he got was an ass beating from me and not more. If we were at the ranch, there's a decent chance I'd have a shotgun by my side, and I'd protect her no matter what I'd have to do. My football career is very important, not just to me, but to my family as well. However, when it comes down to it, at this moment right now, Kadence means so much *more* than any of it. My family can hate me, and my school can expel me, but as long as I know she's safe, that's what matters most.

Turning the cold water off, I dry my body, trading the sopping wet gear for some lightweight basketball shorts and a tank top. I slide on my Nike sandals and take a deep breath as I face the consequences of my anger.

The knock is quiet as I rap my knuckles against Coach's door, emotionally drained and not looking forward to what's to come from my family, my coach, or from *her*. Kadence probably thinks I lost my shit for no reason. I can only imagine the thoughts running through her mind. She looked terrified, but, was it of me? God, I hope not. My parents would be so ashamed of me not holding it together better.

Freight Train

"It's open," Coach calls out, and I enter the spacious office. A few trophies and framed awards sit on shelves, proudly displayed behind his desk. I'm in the team photos from the past two years. He has them all the way back to the ten-year mark; then they move to the hallway. The rest of the room is filled with a couch and two leather guest chairs.

"Coach."

"Take a seat, number twelve." He nods to the chair directly in front of him.

"Yes, sir." Sitting, I stare at his oversized football paperweight resting on his solid oak desk while my stomach feels like it's filled with a fifty-pound weight.

"Eye's up here, son."

I meet his light green gaze, full of confusion and concern rather than disappointment.

"You've been the 'golden boy' for Alabama since you first walked through those doors. No one, including myself, could believe you and Clyde were even related with your different personalities, let alone brothers. He was such a hot head around here all the time. Now, all of a sudden, I'm busting up backyard brawls on my damn football field, and the source is another Owens. Is your family just destined to not play pro football?"

Remaining quiet, I pay attention. I know he doesn't really want me to answer; he's making a point. If my mom were here, she'd be telling me to give him the respect he's earned.

"You know I'm going to have to take your captain patch for this, don't you?"

"Yes, Coach."

"If this happens again, kid, you won't be on my field or my team."

"Yes, sir."

"What the hell happened out there, anyhow?"

Clearing my throat, I glance around, remembering everything. There's no way to make this sound better. It was me overreacting and showing my ass. No matter how pissed off I got, I was wrong. I should've held it together and helped find a way to expose him to the dean.

I give him the abridged version, leaving out a lot. "He was talking to my girl. The flirting made me flip out when she started laughing, and all I could think about was hitting him."

"Kadence Winters?"

"Yes. You know her?"

"Her daddy happens to be an old buddy of mine. We played college ball together. You know who her father is, son?"

"No, sir; she hasn't introduced us yet."

He starts chuckling, sitting back in his chair, looking a little too pleased with my admission.

"He was one hell of a linebacker, that's for sure. You better clean your act up real quick if you want to keep seeing her. If he catches wind of Kadence dating you and you're not the good old Tyler Owens, Team Captain of Bama, you'll never see her again." He pauses, drinking his bottled water, then continues. "He got drafted to New England right into our third year. That's what made me decide to coach, hoping to work with him eventually."

Freight Train

"You're telling me Lance Winters; number eighty-seven is her father? Chaos?"

"Yep—Chaos-the man himself. He's probably got two inches and fifty pounds on you, not including a wild streak a mile long. He'll go to jail if you hurt his little girl too. Maybe we'll talk this over and see if we can pretend that today didn't happen after all. I've known Kadence since she was about seven years old, and believe me; she'll punish you enough for today. *But,* I mean it, Owens, you screw up again and not only are you off my team, but I call my good buddy and give him a friendly update on his kid. Understood?"

"Yes, Coach."

"Good. Now get the hell out of my office and run the bleachers until I send someone out there to scrape you off the ground. I need to have the team doc examine Briggs and make sure he doesn't need to go to the hospital."

"Yes, Coach," I answer immediately and head to my locker for my fresh practice gear. This is going to suck so badly, but no way am I going to complain. Hearing him mention Briggs and a hospital in the same sentence brings a tiny bit of satisfaction. I only had a few seconds before we were separated, though, so I doubt he's messed up that badly. One can hope, though.

Tomorrow when I'm sore enough that I can't walk, I have to remember that it could be so much worse. I could be going home for good. And I need to have a chat with my girlfriend. I can't believe she kept this from me about her dad. But so much makes sense now, like her knowledge and love for football, about her attending a college known for its football, about her growing up the way she did. I get it now, but she still has some explaining to do, and I clearly have some groveling to do as well.

KADENCE

It's been days since I last saw Tyler, but after his out-of-control rage, I had no clue what to even say. I asked the guys what happened—practically begged Chandler to tell me what was wrong—and they told me nothing.

The one thing they did say was to stay away and give him some time. I'm so torn; I've never seen Ty act like that toward anyone. He's not been hateful—period. He's always wearing a smile or talking to someone.

He's a friendly person but one look while his teammate was standing near me and you'd think we committed a heinous crime of some sort. I just missed him after what I'd felt was an amazing weekend together. Sure, I had seen him that morning, but I wanted to watch him doing something that he loves. He plays football so graciously, and it's wonderful to see him in action.

Everything happened so fast; I was shocked at first and then confused. People were around me at his party at the ranch, men included and it didn't seem to bother him. It was the same way with his party at their house that they all share. A bunch of guys were teasing us and everything, yet he didn't get angry.

The other day at his practice, it was something else. He was so furious it was scary, and I'd once believed that he wouldn't harm anyone in any way—not maliciously anyway. The way he'd stormed over to his teammate, throwing his helmet to the side and ripping the other guy apart was baffling. His fists flew at him so quickly I couldn't believe it, and when they were torn apart, his teammate had blood running all over his face. I don't know how badly he was hurt, but Ty must've gotten him a few good times.

I've cried to Brianne, but she has nothing. Kash doesn't share a thing with her about what's going on. He just tells her to keep her nose out of it. Whatever *it* is.

I want to call him to make sure he's okay and to get some sort of an explanation, but I'm doing what his two best friends suggested I do and giving him some space. It's killing me inside, though. Tyler and I have been growing so close, and I felt like we'd become even closer over the past weekend.

Part of me wants to call his brothers. I can't help but wonder if they know what happened? Would they tell me to reach out to him or know how to handle the situation at all? Would they even care? After my talk with Clyde, I know they would. I'm sure he must be beside himself with this.

What if Tyler gets kicked off the team? That's what normally happens when someone's in multiple fights, and they play sports. The school could even expel him completely and possibly fine him for fighting on school property. It's one giant clusterfuck, and I'm hanging on by a thread over here, dying to know what's going on.

I almost want to call my father. Coach Stratton would confide in him in a heartbeat and maybe if it came down to it, I could ask my dad to help out. He hates being involved in this type of stuff, but I care for Ty. Hell, I'm falling in love with him, and I only want him to succeed in whatever he wants in life.

Spinning around in our office chair we have crammed in our dorm room; I face Brianne. "Do you think I should call my father?"

"Your dad? Why?"

"It's been two days since I've spoken to Ty and I'm worried."

"I don't know what you should do, honestly. Kash says to wait, but you know Ty in a completely different way than the guys do."

"If it were you and Kash in this situation, what would you do?"

"Well, for starters you know I don't listen to anyone's opinion unless I really want to. That being said, I would've already called him."

"Why didn't you say something sooner?"

"Because, Kay, you're not me, babe."

I'm calling him. Forget this waiting around crap; it's for the birds. I held back from him for long enough before giving in to be his girlfriend. I know inside that he's trying to give me some space, I was pretty freaked out after all and it makes me happy inside to know he's giving me what he thinks I need from him.

But what I could really use is him, not time apart. I don't want a rift to grow between us, and I don't want him to be dealing with whatever's going on alone. He's made it loud and clear that he'll protect me and he's done nothing but try to make sure I'm comfortable all the time. I need to make sure he's okay and show him that I'll be there even when he's dealing with his own lows.

Success isn't owned, it's leased.

And rent is due every day.

-J.J. Watt

Nervously rapping my knuckles against Tyler's front door at the football house, I wait for one of the guys to answer. I was going to call but thought it might be better to have this conversation in person. It's time I tell him about my father and find out what his issue was on the field the other day.

We can't go one like this, separated and not communicating. I miss him already, and it'll only get worse with the more time I waste waiting around for him to pick up the phone. I don't want us to let our chance of being together slip away.

"Kadence?" Niner gazes down at me confused. His brown hair's rumpled like he's been running his hands through it a million times. "Owens didn't say you were coming by or I would've kept the PlayStation volume turned down. I never would've heard you knock if I wasn't fixing a snack real quick."

"It's okay; I wasn't out here long. Ty's playing video games?"

"No," Niner steps back, out of my way so I can come inside. Noticing his wrinkled shirt and basketball shorts he has on, it looks like he's in full on bum mode. "He's in his room. Want me to let him know you're here?"

"No, that's okay. I can just go to his room myself; it's no biggie."

"'Kay, cool, I was waiting for my new game to load so they should be waiting for me by now."

"Are the other guys here playing too?"

"Nope, it's just Owens and me right now. I play online with my little brothers. They're twelve-year-old twins, and I don't get to see them much with me being away at school. Plus, it keeps them busy and gives my mom a few minutes of downtime."

"Oh wow, that's a good idea, and nice of you. I didn't know you had brothers." Which means most of the other guys we hang out with, probably do as well. I need to find out more about these people now that I have actual friendships with them. Sometimes I think I'm a selfish asshole for growing up as an only child, but I don't do it on purpose.

"It's weird being away from them, but what can you do?" He shrugs, grabbing his sandwich from the counter as we walk through the kitchen. He veers off to their designated game room, and I continue down the hallway to the third door on the right. It's Ty's.

My stomach's full of flutters as I knock on his closed door. Two days is the longest we've been apart for nearly three weeks; maybe I should've thought about it a little more before just showing up here uninvited. What if he's not ready to see me? I hope he's missed me as much as I have with him. I haven't stopped thinking of him.

"Just a sec," he yells, and it sounds like he's hopping around. After a few moments, he opens the door, peeking out while shirtless.

"Kadence?" He squints, his voice raspy and hair in every direction.

"Are you sick?" It's the first thing that comes to mind. He looks exhausted.

"No, I was just taking a nap. Come in." He steps to the side and lets me into his dark room, his covers halfway on the floor as if he jumped out of bed in a rush and was tangled in them.

"But it's the afternoon."

"Yeah, I know. But yesterday and today's practice have been sorta rough." He limps over to relax on his bed while I take his desk chair.

"I can imagine."

"Please don't sit so far away from me."

"Okay." I give in and move beside him, sitting on the comfy mattress. "So why are you limping?"

"Again, rough practice," he answers, and I nod.

"They didn't hurt you did they?" Instantly growing concerned for his well-being and ready to visit my dad's friend, good old Coach Stratton, if needed in Tyler's defense.

"Not anything more than what I deserve. You run up and down the stands enough and your calves eventually seize up. I've been soaking them in ice water, but they're still cramped really bad."

Nodding like a bobble head again, I stay quiet. This is a piece of the game I understand well, after watching my dad practice for many years and seeing the other players get reprimanded for screwing up. Physical punishment is readily accepted in the form where they usually burn out your body in some way. In Ty's case, his legs will probably hurt for a week to two weeks if they keep making him run up and down the stairs like that for God knows how long each day. One thing's for sure, though; he won't forget about it.

"Can I get you anything?"

"No. Thanks, though. Why are you being nice to me? You looked horrified the other day."

"We're going to get straight to it, huh?"

"I want to get it out of the way. I hate feeling like this around you," he mutters while staring at the carpet. He hasn't tried to grab my hand yet, and it makes me sad to know our relationship could already be reaching its first hurdle.

"Good idea. Okay, truthfully you did freak me out. I thought you were going to murder your teammate. You were so out of it; they had to lift you off the ground and carry you away. That's not at all the way I'm used to seeing you act. But then I started thinking about the other fight before, and it made me wonder if it's the type of person you really are and if I know you at all."

Freight Train

"You do know the real me, Kadence. I promise." Running his hand over his face, he continues, "There's so much more to that guy than you know about. I hadn't told you because I didn't want you to worry about him. I see now that it was a mistake keeping it from you. I should've spoken to you about everything going on out at the ranch."

"Well, you can tell me now."

He nods. "That guy's name is Briggs. You remember when we first met and you told me that you knew about the rumors floating around?"

"Yeah, I remember."

"Well, he's the cause of them—all of them. Then JJ and Chandler busted him at the party the other night trying to slip something into a chick's drink."

"No way!"

"Yep, they took care of it with Nate's help, but it still infuriated me. And then when I saw him that close to you at practice the other day...I completely lost it. I couldn't stop thinking about him hurting you, and I wasn't going to let that happen."

That explains so much, and I almost feel like an idiot for getting as scared as I did. I should've known he'd have a good reason for his actions.

"And the fight that happened before?"

"He was talking trash about my mother. I can usually block it out, but he was able to break through."

Another answer that I can understand. I would probably freak out, too, if I had a set of amazing parents and they were taken from me, and people thought it was okay to blast it everywhere. This is why it was so important for me to come over, to see with my own eyes that he's telling me the truth. Not that I've doubted his honesty before, it's just growing up with a celebrity as your father; you tend to be quick to mistrust. Tyler doesn't deserve that from me, though, and the next time that there's an issue I have, I'm going to trust he has a valid reason behind it.

"I'm sorry," I admit softly.

"It's not your fault." He reaches for my hand—finally.

"I mean for questioning you about it. I should've trusted that there was a serious reason behind it. You've never given me any reason to think of you as anything other than a good guy."

"I'm glad you feel that way. I have something that I want to discuss with you also."

"Oh, okay."

"Why didn't you tell me who your father is?"

"Who told you?"

"Coach. He said I better get my shit together if I wanted to keep seeing you."

Shaking my head, I apologize again. "I'm sorry for keeping it from you. I was planning on telling you today actually. My dad's not the same person as he used to be. He wasn't that outgoing when he played football, but now he's pretty much gone in the opposite direction. Some people want to get closer to me thinking it'll get them near my dad, so I have to hold back for a while to see if the person is really into me or just wanting to use me."

"Of course, I want you for you. Are you crazy? I'm gone over you."

"I love hearing you say that and knowing you feel the same way I do."

"Why is your dad different now?"

"I don't really know. I'm not sure if something happened that made him decide to retire and move nearly across the country or what. It's like one day he loved nothing besides me and football, then next thing I know, we're moving to Texas, and he's becoming a biker."

"Biker, as in he likes to ride in the marathons or whatever they're called?"

"No, like vroom, vroom—biker gang—equipped with leather jackets and all."

"Holy shit, that's what Stratton meant about Chaos not being afraid to rip through me. Your dad really is a badass."

"Yeah, that's not his football name anymore, but his road name. I trust you; that's the only reason why I'm telling you all of this. Please keep it to yourself."

"Of course, anything you tell me is private. So, that explains why you know more about football than me on some days, huh?"

"Oh, you caught that?"

"I'm pretty sure we all did." He grins, and I smile in return.

"I didn't think I was being so obvious. I figured you guys were used to talking about it all the time so you wouldn't pay attention to me doing it too."

"Baby, you're a beautiful woman discussing the ins and outs of football with a group of guys that breathe football. You have every one of my friends' respect. I think a few of them even believe that you're a goddess at this point."

That makes me snort and then laugh. "So you're not mad at me then for keeping it from you?"

"I was shocked to find out and also surprised that you hadn't said anything, but it filled in a lot of blanks for me when Coach said something. But no, I'm not mad. We need to be up-front in the future, though, both of us."

"I will, I promise you."

"Good, I do too." Pulling me close he presses a few chaste kisses against my lips and then one to my forehead, before sitting back again.

"Why didn't you call or text me the past few days, I felt like I'd done something wrong and you didn't want to talk to me. I know you care for me, but did it not bother you that we didn't speak?"

"Of course, it did, are you kidding? I was going crazy inside not talking to you, but I needed to give you some time to yourself. I didn't want to overwhelm you even more than I did the other day. I knew I had to have scared you and I wanted to give you a little time away from me, so you didn't think I was smothering you especially after seeing me so pissed. I wish you'd never witnessed any of it. Truthfully, I was ashamed that I let you see that side of me. The jealousy and anger, that's not the type of person I want you to think of me as."

"I make you jealous?"

"Knowing what I do about you, I know what I have to lose and what others have to gain. So in a way, I guess yes, my jealousy comes out around you. I try to push it down, but parts of me can't help it, you're amazing, and I don't want anyone else ruining that or taking it away from me. I'm so fucking selfish when it comes to you, Kadence."

"I'm selfish when it comes to you as well, Tyler," I admit. Inside it drives me bonkers thinking of all the females constantly after him. He's mine and just like him, I don't want anyone to take that away from me either.

"You are?" His eyebrows rise, hope appearing in his irises, and I giggle.

"It makes you happy hearing that?"

"Hell yeah, sweetheart. I like knowing that you feel possessive over me, at least a little bit anyhow. It makes me feel important to you."

"You are, Tyler, probably more than you should be already."

A grin overtakes his mouth. Clearly, he likes what I'm saying. I find it mildly amusing that he likes my jealous side rearing its ugly head.

"Now what?" I mumble.

"Well, I want to make love to you like no other, but my entire body hurts every time I move, so we'll have to raincheck it."

Damn it that would be perfect right now. Not only have I missed him, but so has my body. I've tossed and turned at night, thinking about the way he feels against me.

"Maybe you should take a hot bath to help? And we can come back to the making love part."

He presses another kiss to my jaw, a low grumble escaping as his lips meet my skin, "God, I want you. How about instead of the bath, you just lay with me?"

"I think that sounds like a good plan," I agree, and he brushes a soft kiss on my mouth again and edges his way up to the pillows. I would happily lie here all day long and allow him to kiss me all over. I can never get enough of him and that skillful mouth.

Following along, I toe off my flip-flops and try not to jostle him too much as I get comfortable, partially lying on him with my head resting against his chest. The side of his bed's littered with melted ice packs, the poor guy must've hurt too bad to take them to the sink. No worries, I'm here now, and I'll make sure he has everything he needs. I'm not planning on going anywhere. I should've been here the whole time, helping him.

"Want me to turn on the TV?"

"If you want to watch something, then go for it, but I'm fine either way. I just want to lay here and feel you against me."

"You are so much *more*, Kadence," he mumbles making my heart melt a bit more with his meaningful words.

I love him.

"So are you," I whisper and eventually fall asleep, happy once again to be by his side.

Freight Train

"Hey Pumpkin," my dad rumbles through the phone. He called at the perfect time. I ended up staying with Tyler all night long after our talk and I barely made it to the dorm when my phone started ringing. Ty went to practice and came back to bed, all without waking me up. I must've been more tired than I thought, napping the afternoon away on his chest yesterday. We cooked a late dinner together, and then I was out again, oversleeping this morning.

"Hi, Dad."

"So, how's school going?"

"Oh you know, just the usual."

Brianne overhears me reply and yells, "Tell him about Tyler!"

Bitch says it loud enough that my dad no doubt heard her. I've been planning to tell him, just maybe not today, but it looks like that's changing.

He clears his throat, "So who's this Tyler?"

"He's a guy I'm friends with," I answer slowly, and Brianne yells again.

"It's her boyfriend!"

Pulling the phone away, I mouth at her, "Shut up!" And the traitor grins.

"You have a boyfriend? Since when?"

"Well, we've been friends for a while, but it's been official for about a week now."

"And you didn't think you should tell me about it? You haven't mentioned anyone in the past."

"He's a good man, and I like him, a lot."

"Maybe I should plan a trip."

"But you never visit here, how about I come see you on break instead."

"You're right, and I think it's time that changed. I need to visit you more, and that's going to start happening, now."

"I love it that I'll get to see you more, but why now?"

"Because you're at the age where men become significant in your life, and you need another man there to scare them away."

"Dad," I mutter, knowing he wants to come see how far he can push Tyler before he gives up.

"Look Pumpkin, the last time you told me you really liked someone of the opposite gender, it was a ferret that Nan smuggled into your bedroom. This is a big deal, and I need to come check it out for myself."

"Okay fine," I huff. "You win, like always."

"It's what I do kiddo; you know this."

"Yeah, just..."

"What?"

"I like him. I want you to promise me you'll give him a fair chance."

"If he's good to you, then there shouldn't be anything to worry about."

"So when do you plan to visit then?"

"I can be down this weekend."

"Wow, already?"

"Is that a problem?"

Yes. It's way too soon. "No, of course not, just wasn't expecting you to come until one of my school breaks."

"I'm not waiting until Thanksgiving. I need to meet this guy now."

"That's only like a month away."

"Not happening, Kadence. I'll see you this weekend."

"Great, we can go to his game on Saturday."

"Game? He plays football?"

"Why do you automatically assume it's football?"

"Because they play on Saturdays."

"Oh yeah."

"So, he's a football player? I thought that wasn't your type?"

"You know I have a type?"

"The last guy was artsy or something, wasn't he?"

"Holy shit, you knew about him?"

"Of course, I'm your dad."

He says it so surely like I should expect him to know about my past boyfriends.

"Okay, so are you flying?"

"Of course not. I'll be on the bike."

"All right, see you in a few days."

"Sounds good. Love ya, Pumpkin."

"Love you too, Daddy."

We hang up, and I immediately think that I should start calling him Dad. I'm in college. Maybe if I call him Dad instead, he'll realize I'm not some teenager who needs her father as a bodyguard warding off the opposite sex.

"So your dad's visiting?" Brianne asks and takes a bite of her apple.

"Yes, thanks to you blabbing about Tyler."

She starts giggling because even though she knows I love her, she's also evil.

"I'm not amused."

"Oh come on, Kay! He needs to meet Ty. It's been awhile, and you guys are getting all hot and heavy, practically attached at the hip."

"It really hasn't been that long. Plus, what if my dad scares him off?"

"He won't. You've dated boys in the past. Ty's a man and a big one at that. The others would've been scared shitless, but your beau is buff, plus he's an athlete—a good one—and he's smart. The two of them already have something huge in common."

"That's what I'm afraid of. My dad is well aware of how shallow a lot of football players are. He's going to have a preconceived image of Tyler before he even meets him."

"Maybe you should have him watch the game first. Would he be excited about it and go easy on Ty?"

Freight Train

"I don't know. Tyler's so thrilled about eventually meeting my dad. I hope he's not let down because my dad decides to be a jerk to him."

"I'm sure it'll be fine. Give them both a chance, you never know. You were hesitant with Ty in the first place with your own preconceived opinions, and they turned out to be completely wrong, right?"

"Right. Okay. We'll just roll with it and hope it doesn't go too badly."

"Good plan." She winks and tosses the apple core in our small trash bin. "What ended up happening to the guy Ty punched out the other day anyhow?"

"From the brief version he gave me, I guess the guy needed a few stitches and his jaw may be dislocated. Tyler wasn't too sure because they've been keeping them separated."

"Geez, he did all that with just a few hits? I can only imagine what he'd have done given more time."

"Yeah, no kidding. Thank God they were pulled apart. I'd hate it if Tyler got into serious trouble because of some asshole."

"Asshole, huh? So you know why he went after the guy then?"

"His name's Briggs." I shrug, not wanting to tell her all the details of why Ty really lost it. He told me not to say anything about it right now because he didn't want details floating around campus. "Tyler didn't say much about it; I was more concerned about him being sore from practice. He did warn me that Briggs isn't a good person and we need to be careful around him."

"Weird, but good to know."

I nod. There, at least she's warned to watch out for him, but doesn't know the entire story. I kept my promise to Ty and still protected my friend.

"I'm going to lunch with Kash, wanna come with us?"

"No, I don't want to party crash on you two."

"Are you sure? You're always welcome."

"Thanks, but I'm good. I need to reserve a room for my dad for this weekend or else I know he'll forget to. Are you and Kash a thing, now?"

"We're working on it, I think."

"I'm happy for you."

"Thanks, chick. So I'll see you later then?"

"Yep, if I'm not here then I'll be with Tyler. I already missed my class so may as well do the next assignment and find something new to read."

"You work too hard, Kay. Take some time to relax."

"I will. Have fun."

"See you later." She smiles and heads for the door.

"See ya." I smile back and pull on my headphones. If my dad's coming, I want to be ahead on all my schoolwork, so he doesn't think Tyler's had any effect on that as well.

Freight Train

Be strong when you are weak,

brave when you are scared,

and humble when you are

victorious.

-Unknown

Tyler

"Bro, you're meeting her dad? Already?" JJ's eyes grow wide as I tell him about the call I just received from Kadence. The guys don't know her dad's a famous retired NFL player. I've kept that part to myself to respect her privacy.

"Yep, this weekend. It doesn't seem too soon to me. I mean, she did meet my brothers last weekend."

"That's not the same, though. You're not a chick. What if Stratton doesn't even let you play?"

"Not to be a dick, but do you think he's going to bench me? You know he only did it last time because the school and media were having a shit fit over it all."

"You're probably right, but still. Are you nervous?"

"Ummm, a little." More like a lot. Her dad was a football star, plus I really-really like Kadence, to the point that I know I'm going to slip up and say the L-O-V-E word soon.

If Kadence hadn't been the one to tell me that she'd told her dad, I'd almost think it was Coach trying to whip me into better shape. He'd do it if he thought it'd make me play better in any way.

"She stayed here last night, huh?"

"Yep, I sleep awesome when she's in bed with me."

"I bet." He laughs.

"Shut the fuck up, man. You know what I mean."

"You bang her until you're dead to the world."

"You know it." I grin and fist bump him. That shit's so untrue. It's because she's a little heater and she smells good, and I don't know, she just makes me feel comfortable. Last weekend when I found her wearing my socks, though, I thought I was going to rip her clothes off, she looked so fucking sexy. Nate still won't shut up about it.

"Really, you're picking the Patriots again?" he whines as Madden sixteen loads on the TV.

"Don't be jealous because I got the best team in the league."

"Yeah, I call bullshit." More like he's going to shit if he gets to meet Kadence's dad this weekend also.

"What are we going to do about Briggs? We need to come up with something."

"Chandler's friends with a few of the girls that Briggs has messed with. They're going to try and get a copy of the videos he has of them."

"And do what?"

"I think take it to campus police and tell the Dean about it all."

"No way, that easily?"

"Well, they may be hung up on Chandler a little."

"Two chicks at one time? Since when does he see more than one person?"

"When it comes to helping you out." That's real friendship. I've known Chandler for years. He wouldn't do this for just anyone, and he would never possibly hurt a woman's feelings, so this is big.

"Shit. I can't believe he'd do that for me. I know after his sister got screwed over he's been really protective and determined to never be a jerk like that. He needs to know I'm grateful. I wish I could do something."

"Actually, you already did."

"Oh yeah?"

"By having the party at the ranch and Nate being there, we now have an outside witness and then with you laying him out the other day."

"How did that help anything?" It frightened Kadence, got me in a shitload of trouble and made my body hurt from the repercussions. Thankfully, it was a closed incident, so my brothers have no idea about it, or I'd be in a whole other shit storm from those two.

"You've been busy running the stadium, so you haven't heard Stratton down on the field. He's been all over Briggs' ass. He knows something's up and he's trying to break Briggs. We've all been watching, waiting for him to hit the right spot and have Briggs up and leave, but it hasn't happened yet."

"Stratton deserves more credit than we give him; he definitely knows more shit than he lets on."

"I swear he has spies planted around campus. It's the only way he can always know what's going on."

"No telling, but I wouldn't be surprised. Is Chandler coming back tonight?"

"Not sure, he's been splitting up the past few nights. He goes to one chick's place and then to the other's afterward."

"Holy shit. He's pulling the same moves that I used to do."

"I know. It's about time he started living the college life," he proudly beams.

If only he knew that being with one woman, the right one, all the time, is so much *more* than being with fifty random women. He'll learn one day. Until then, though, I hope he enjoys himself and doesn't hurt any women involved.

That's one thing I made sure of before I got serious with Kadence, any woman I spent time with knew exactly what the score was. I never messed with anyone that way. It's fucked up, especially when so many women want to be a little wild in college. You don't *need* to lie to them about your intentions.

The rest of the week flies by, and before I know it, Kadence and I have been together officially for two weeks, even though it feels like longer. To me, it is. I've been thinking of her as my girlfriend long before she agreed with it.

I have to get through this game today, which shouldn't be too difficult. The team's not that talented, and Coach is, of course, letting me play. But he didn't share that with the team or me until he gave me a long-drawn-out speech about how just because I have the skill, it doesn't mean I'm exempt from my actions.

We all know it's bullshit, though. I paid my dues in the beginning, and he wants to win too badly to exclude me from the games. He may run me like a pig at practice, but he wants me in on defense and offense when it's going to count. Thank God for that, because Kadence and her father are expecting to watch me play.

I don't think I've been this nervous since my mom told me about the first scout coming to watch me play. I was only in ninth grade, and it was right before she passed, but I was a wreck inside. I didn't let any of it show, and my mom said the scout was impressed and would be back each year to see me play one game.

After the second year, I got to know him and became less nervous. In return, it was easy for me to shine in front of him. Arthur Macintyre was his name. He was there each year just like he promised, and he's the one who signed me to Alabama. He tried to make it to every game I played here too. Unfortunately, he had a stroke and passed away last year. I'll never forget him. Like my mother, he's someone who believed in me.

I could use that support today when I go out on the field. Not only do I want to play well for myself, but for Kadence as well. I want her to be proud of me. She hasn't given me a reason to think she's not, but it felt so good to point that football in her direction after I landed a touchdown. The beam that lit up across her face at that moment is something I'll never forget. She was utterly breathtaking.

"Ready, bro?" JJ asks me the same question before each game.

"Yep, as I'll ever be. Was your mom able to make it to this one?"

He grew up with a single mom who had to work a lot of hours to support him and his progressing talent in football. She was the mom missing practices and games. Not because she wanted too, but because she was working extra shifts to pay for him to go to camps, have trainers, etc. She couldn't always be there for him in person, but she no doubt loves him beyond measure, always sacrificing so he could do what he loves.

Had my own mother been alive, I think they would've been friends too. JJ's mom, Marie, is a woman who's always welcomed me with open arms and made me feel like family. JJ didn't need a father growing up, Marie made sure that when she could be around, it counted.

"No. She asked for it off, but the lady who was supposed to work ended up quitting."

"Sorry, man."

"Yeah, I just hope I get drafted. I'll make sure my mom's able to be at all of my games, in every city I play in. That woman won't have to work another day in her life if I can help it."

"It'll happen, especially if we run the two pass play we've been practicing. The NFL scouts love those, seeing that we can be versatile in positions."

Chandler steps beside us, looking exhausted. "Hey, guys."

"Fuck, are you sick or something?" JJ asks.

"Yeah, you look terrible."

"Ugh, you guys don't want to know. I'm fine, just tired."

"How can you not get sleep the night before a game, Chandler? I'd never expect this from you of all people." I'm a team captain, so I have every right to be pissed at him. This isn't summer ball' this is college and everyone not giving it one hundred percent affects the entire team.

"Trust me, I know. But Lila wouldn't let me go to bed when I got to her place."

"You were at a chick's? Dude, I get it that you're trying to get these women to help us, but you gotta set some limits."

"I will, I promise. She was just emotional when she called me I thought it'd only take a little while for her to calm down, but she went on all night long."

"You need to get your head on straight. It's game day," I reprimand, disappointed in one of my best friend's choices.

I already have to deal with asshole Briggs still being around and not knowing when or if he'll eventually be kicked off the team, but now Chandler's slipping up. Granted he's not a piece of crap like Briggs and I know he's trying to help me, but he has to put football first when it comes to this stuff. We get one chance to hit the NFL—just one. The shit going on with Briggs is extremely important, but our performance is going to dictate whether this'll be our future careers. I haven't worked for damn near my entire life toward being drafted, for people to start fucking it up when I'm so close.

"Who's ready?" Coach hollers, interrupting everyone chatting and going through their pregame rituals. "I said, who's ready?" he yells even louder. I swear the man's voice can reach decibels I've never heard before. It must be a requirement for coaches or something.

"Alabama, baby!" the team shouts back and stomps.

"Who?" Stratton goes on, pumping everyone up.

"Alabama, baby!" The team grows louder, taking over one of our many chants.

Kash and I line up at the door like usual, ready to lead the team to the field.

"Watch Gomez." He turns to me, looking a little uneasy. Usually, if there's an opposing player he's concerned about, we discuss it ahead of time, so I can get him to chill out and help deal with whoever the threat is on the field.

"It'll be okay, bro."

"No, he was on the injured list, they just released him. I got a text update."

"Okay, no big deal. I got you, turn off your phone and get game ready."

Freight Train

"He's going to try to take out my legs," Kash continues as if I didn't speak at all. Clearly, he's tripping out inside. "He's told a few players that he wants me gone for good. For. Good. Owens."

"Kash, I won't let that happen. If it means I don't run the ball today, then that's fine. I've got your back, always."

He takes a deep breath and nods, relaxing a little. "Good, I appreciate it. I know I can count on you, twelve. Okay, time to go win a football game."

"Let's do it." I smile, and fist bump him, ready to own the field.

I hate it that my QB was right, but this fucker keeps charging Kash, on a mission. My shoulders have taken one hell of a beating, fending Gomez off. I promised him that I'd protect him, though, so no way am I switching spots.

Gomez is built like a goddamn tank. I know he'd ruin Kash if he got the chance, but I'm the Freight Train for a reason. I have speed and strength. He may be a tank, but I'm built to play multiple positions, so where he's all muscle, I have power and quickness that he can't match.

The downside is it's wearing me down to keep fighting him on every play. So now my body's becoming too tired to help my own crew—the defense. The other team is pummeling D without me helping get a few sacks in, but there's nothing I can do. Niner has to step up and work twice as hard for it. Our quarterback's safety is top priority, always. Without him to fire off plays and passes, we don't win at all.

Heading toward the line, Kash shouts 'Nancy.' There's no way I can fend Gomez off and run Nancy. That's our two-toss play that we've been practicing all week long when I haven't been being punished by Coach for losing my temper. As much as I love the play, it won't work for us today.

"Call a time out!" I yell before everyone's in place and Kash shoots his hands up, giving the signal for a timeout to the refs and Coach Stratton.

The whistle blows, and we come together, "What's going on, Owens?" he asks when we hit the huddle.

"No way can I run Nancy and still protect you. I can't be in two places at once, and I won't break my promise about your safety."

"Fine." He thinks for a second then glances at JJ. "We switch it up. Instead of me tossing the ball to JJ and then him throwing it to you, we'll do this…" He trails off changing around the play.

We line back up with a plan and I'm shitting a brick like no other. JJ's in the QB spot, ready to toss the ball to Kash. He counts down, the ball shot gunned to him from the center and quickly tossed to Kash. The defense on the other team scrambles to keep up and charge Kash, but before they get anywhere near him, he rockets the ball in my direction.

I have to leap a little to make the clean catch, but it plays out beautifully, and I'm gone. Holding that tough leather, cradled tightly in my arm, my legs pump ferociously, on fire from being used against Gomez and being abused all week by my coach. One foot in front of the next, running, I watch as I pass my teammates and they throw the other players out of my way, giving me a clear path.

The goal's in sight, that touchdown is nearly close enough that I can taste it. My lungs burn as I force myself to breathe evenly and push my body hard, going as fast as possible. Not skipping a beat, I charge forward, never faltering and cross over the painted line signifying my personal victory.

Thinking of the woman who means the most to me now, I scan the crowd, picking her out and the large man wearing a baseball hat low on his forehead next to her, who no doubt is her father, Chaos. Pointing my ball toward her, a smile overtakes her, lighting up her face as she jumps up and down.

The fans around her go nuts, loving it that I made another public declaration for them to witness. They all start chanting, 'Freight Train!' in response. Everyone close by pats her back or shoulders, telling her that Alabama loves her and they should. Anyone in their right mind who knows Kadence Winters knows she's special.

Tapping my chest, I mouth, "For you."

Some may think it's a little obnoxious, but I couldn't care less about what they believe. I want the world to know she's my woman and I'm her man, heart and soul. She no doubt owns both.

Kadence kisses the palms of her hands and then shows them to me. She's got a number one, and then a number two painted on her palms and once again her thoughtfulness takes me by surprise. It's her response that fills me fuller, knowing that she understood my public display wasn't about any of them, but because I was thinking about sharing my victory with her.

KADENCE

"Nice to meet you, sir." Tyler shakes my dad's hand before he sits down at the table with us. I asked him to meet my father and me for dinner instead of trying to bum-rush him right after the game was over. I figured it'd give him a chance to calm down a bit and take a long shower. Those hits he was taking in the game were no joke, and I know he must be sore.

"Good game, young man."

"I appreciate that." Ty nods and grabs my hand. "I mean no disrespect at your table, but I'm going to kiss my girl hello."

I think his statement catches my father completely off guard and he just nods, watching Tyler lean over to give me a soft, chaste kiss. My dad sits back, probably relieved that the lip lock was brief and respectful. If Ty had tried to slip me some tongue, my father most likely would've flown across the table, and Ty's cheek is already sporting a bruise from the rough game he just finished playing.

"Something to drink, sir?" the server approaches, asking Tyler.

"Water, please."

She nods, placing his menu down before she leaves to get his beverage.

"Tell me, Owens, what's the game plan with my daughter?" He cuts straight to the big question, and I cringe.

Timing Dad, geesh.

"I care about her very much."

"Enough to wrap it up?"

"Dad!" I gasp, astonished at his extremely personal question. We're out at a restaurant for Christ's sake.

The waitress returns, setting the glass down. "Are you ready?"

"I'll have the sirloin please, well done with fries, and ranch....and ummm, a baked potato, loaded," I answer quickly to cut off my dad's probing that I know will be coming any moment.

"I'll have a burger, well done with bacon and barbecue sauce with fries, please." Ty pops off something random without glancing at his menu.

My dad grunts, clearly not happy with Ty ordering nearly the same thing he does whenever we eat out. "I'll have a burger, well done with bacon and an egg on it, over medium with fries also."

"Sounds good, I'll have it right out." The older lady smiles, taking our menus, heading straight for the kiosk.

Ty clears his throat. "To answer your question sir, of course, Kadence's safety and well-being are my top priority when we're together."

"Only when you're together? If she's your girlfriend, shouldn't it be your concern all the time?"

"Yes, I mean when we're intimate."

"Don't say that word to me, twelve," my dad rumbles, clearly forgetting his promise he made me that he'd take it easy on my boyfriend.

"I'm sorry, Tyler," I apologize, embarrassed that my dad's being such a hardass.

"Don't apologize, Kadence." My dad butts in. "I have every right to question him. You're my daughter, and if he wants to date you without any issues, then he'll be up front."

"Excuse me, sir," Ty says, remaining polite even though I can see he's a little irritated. "No disrespect, but no one, not even Kadence's father, will dictate how my life is. I've worked my ass off to get where I am, buried two parents at fifteen and made my way into college. I get good grades and have great recommendations from past teachers. I've helped my brothers take care of a ranch, among other things, and I'll be damned if one person will keep me from someone that I love. Life's too short, and I'm too hardheaded to let that happen."

My dad stays quiet for a few moments, mulling over everything he just heard and then nods.

"So you love my daughter then? From my understanding, it's only been a few weeks."

"You're right about that, we've officially been dating for two weeks, but she's been mine since I first laid eyes on her," he states boldly, my heart thumping so fast in my chest from his admission that he loves me and his bravery for standing up to my father. I can't believe that he loves me, the player who never had a serious girlfriend and did whatever he wanted with whoever he wanted before I came along and bumped into him.

He loves me…ME.

And he said it to my dad of all people. Trust me when I say my father's extremely intimidating, especially now, armed with a leather cut, gun, motorcycle, and being the size of a real-life defensive lineman. Ty may play the same position sometimes, but my dad had years to gain his size and muscle mass. If he wanted to, he could fold Tyler up like a lawn chair.

"You've got balls, son. It's refreshing, and I respect you for it. Make no mistake, though; you hurt my girl, and your ass will no longer have a pair hanging between your legs. Got me?"

"Yes, sir."

"Good. Now stop saying sir and call me Chaos."

"Yes, sir," he replies, then catching himself, "I mean, okay, Chaos."

My dad takes a drink of his orange juice, and the waiter brings us our food. Once all the testosterone calmed down, I had an amazing time, being with the two men in my life that mean the most to me. I can't stop going back to the fact that Ty said he loves me, and to my father no less. He didn't say it directly to me, but at least I know that the feelings are there, that I'm not the only one drowning in affection. Now if I can get my dad to filter himself a little more, I'd really be happy.

"You riding back with me, Pretty?" Ty asks when we're heading toward the restaurant parking lot.

"You don't want to ride the bike?" My dad mumbles, staring at me like a giant kid.

"Well, you're going to the hotel, and Ty lives a few streets away, so it would be smart if I just catch a ride with him."

"I don't mind."

"No, Dad," I reply firmly, with love. He has to see me as an adult from now on, not just his little girl. "Thanks, but I'll go with him and see you tomorrow."

"You got it, Pumpkin. We can have lunch before I head out."

"Wait, you're leaving tomorrow? But you just got here."

"I have some stuff to take care of with the guys, plus Owens here seems to have a good watch on you. I don't think he'd let anything hurt you or anyone male near you, for that matter." He glances at my boyfriend, and Ty nods in agreement.

Damn alpha males.

"All right, text me in the morning once you're up and you've had some coffee. Love you."

"Love you, too, kid." He kisses my forehead and turns back to Ty. "Nice meeting you, son. I'll check in on you occasionally."

"You too, Chaos." Tyler shakes my dad's hand and leads me to his truck as we hear my father's motorcycle come to life behind us.

"Did you have a good dinner?" he asks, opening the truck door so I can climb in. His ball cap's pulled low, his hair curling around it slightly from being put on right after he showered. That worn out hat is so damn sexy, I just want to jump him right here.

"Yes, did you?"

"Yeah. I wish I got his autograph, though. I figured that'd be pushing it."

Laughing, I kiss his lips. "I'll get it for you."

"Seriously?"

"Yes, I promise. He won't mind."

"Thanks, Pretty." He smiles bigger and kisses me again before driving us back to his house where he rewards me all night long.

Sapphire Knight

> When my body gets tired, my mind says,
>
> "This is where winners are made."
>
> When my mind gets tired, my heart says,
>
> "This is where champions are made."
>
> - Baylor Barbee

Weeks pass us by in a blur after that night spent introducing Tyler to my father. Now the phone calls from my dad come more frequently, checking in on me and wishing Ty good luck in some sort of way. I'm happy to hear from him more, too. I'd missed him. I should've known he'd play a hard-ass toward Ty, but in the end, he'd be supportive of us. He's been that way my entire life. I think being away from him made me forget that he only wants what's best for me.

November's fast approaching and with the seasons steadily changing, I'm a little sad that it may be too chilly to go swimming again out at the ranch. We had a great time together before, and I was hoping it'd become a regular occurrence, but traveling for football and classes has kept Ty and me both busy.

He made me promise that we'd go out to the ranch next weekend, and I can't wait to have the country air against my skin again. I feel like I can just breathe out there. No one's rushing to classes and spilling coffee everywhere or letting doors close on you because they're in too much of a hurry to show some kindness.

Not only that but for Ty to be pressed up against me as well. We've been apart a lot lately, more so than we were in the beginning, and it's taking a toll on us. I miss him—his smell, his smile, just having him near me. I want to be able to spend time with him every single day, but I know right now it's just not possible and I have to make myself okay with that. Most days I'll head over to the football field and do my homework in the stands so I can watch him practice and just be at the same place as him.

Thankfully, his teammate, Briggs, hasn't attempted to speak to me again. I guess Tyler's message was loud and clear that I'm off limits and I'm beyond grateful. I can't believe he's remained on the team for this long with all the evil stuff he's pulled. I hope one day he gets caught and all those women affected receive some sort of justice. I'm glad Ty, JJ, and Chandler are keeping an eye on him. A creep like that deserves to go to jail.

"Thinking about Mr. Hot Pants again?" Brianne bumps me with her shoulder as we sit under our favorite tree on the campus lawn.

Freight Train

"When do I stop thinking about him?" Grinning, I pluck some grass and toss them at her.

"Ugh, I know, it's gross." She rolls her eyes and smiles. She's enjoying this teasing me lately, way too much.

"Oh whatever, all I hear about from you is, 'Kash this and Kash that.' You have it bad too. Are you guys ever going to be a couple?" Kash seems like a decent guy; he's full of talent and is very well spoken when he's around. I think he comes from a wealthy family, but Brianne hasn't mentioned anything that personal about him.

"Your guess is as good as mine. I don't know what's holding him back; we're together all the time. He just takes things slow, I guess." She shrugs. Slow isn't normal for her so I know she has to be going nuts inside waiting for him to do something about it.

"As long as you're happy, that's what matters."

"Right." She nods, not as cheerful anymore, confirming my suspicions.

"Hey, it'll happen. They have a full month of games left, then they'll be home all the time, and I'm sure Kash will be ready for more. It's probably too difficult to concentrate on so much going on when you're the Captain of the football team. Mix it with classes and all this traveling; I bet he's exhausted."

"You know what? You're probably right. I think they're all a little nervous with the NFL watching so close right now. Kash and Ty want to be picked up in the draft this year along with most of the other guys, so I understand their focus. It's just, well, it's frustrating. I need to be patient because I like him."

"I know, believe me. I miss Ty like crazy. They need our support and understanding right now."

"What are you going to do if he goes to a team that's far away?"

Shrugging, I bite my lip, worrying about losing him already. "I guess all I can do is just hope that he'll ask me to go with him."

"You'd leave with him? Really? It's so soon, though."

"Well, April's still months away, so I think by then if he asked me, yes, I'd probably go with him."

"Your dad would lose his mind."

"I would've believed that before if I'd brought it up to him, but he's met Tyler, and he knows that we care for each other a lot. I think as long as I was to finish out school wherever we went, then my dad would be okay with it."

"You're lucky; I don't think Kash would ask me to go with him." Tears begin to fill her eyes, and I pull her in for a side hug.

"You're being a dramatic Debbie-downer. Give the guy a chance. I never thought Tyler would be the type of guy to be in a committed relationship, but he is. It was just timing and wanting it bad enough. You like Kash, so give him some time to make those decisions himself."

"A few months ago if you'd have told me that you'd be giving me advice on my love life, I'd never have believed you."

"Ugh, you can be such a snot sometimes," I tease, making her smile again. "I have to get to class, but I'll see you later?"

"You bet. See ya, woman." She waves as I start the trek to my next class.

Tyler

"Did you get the videos yet?" I question Chandler after our afternoon practice.

"Lila's supposed to give them to me tonight and Haley in the morning."

JJ lets out a relieved breath, muttering, "Thank God. It's been three weeks since she said that she'd help. I'm sick of having to see Briggs every day when all I want to do is punch him in the nuts."

"Me too and I can't stand having him on the same field when Kadence is around. I swear if I see him look at her I'm going to go ballistic," I grumble. And I'm also tired of seeing Chandler look so damn broken having to go between two women so we can get the help that we need to bust this scumbag once and for all. It's taking a toll on Chan mentally, and I need him to be completely focused on the games, not this mess.

"I think we should go to the Dean first thing tomorrow with the videos, knock it out before Briggs has a chance to hurt anyone else."

"I agree." JJ nods.

"Sounds good. Should I text Nate to come with us too, or wait? He could be an outside witness for what happened at the ranch."

"Let's wait and see what the Dean wants to do. The girls don't want to get law enforcement involved unless the school presses for it. They just want Briggs banned from campus and the whole thing to disappear."

Shaking my head, I grumble, "That's crazy. He can just go somewhere else and do it again to other women. He should be in jail. And he can still blackmail them not being on campus."

"I get it, trust me," Chandler agrees. "I think he should be locked away as well, but this is what Haley and Lila want. They don't want their families or anyone else finding out about it. We need to respect their wishes since they're the ones helping us out and have the actual proof."

"That's fine," JJ interrupts, "but once he's gone, I'm posting an anonymous message to the school paper. I won't name any female names, but someone needs to let others know."

"Yeah, that's a good idea. A few of us should go on and post them so that way people will take notice and none of the victims will have their names blasted, besides Briggs." JJ bumps my fist lightly, and our plan comes together. "All right, I'm out; I finally get to have dinner with Kay tonight."

"Have fun, bro, Tell her to keep it down tonight; we'll be trying to sleep." JJ teases, and I flip him the bird. He loves giving me shit, especially in the locker room around the other guys.

"I'll text you in the morning." Chandler bumps my fist.

"All right sounds good, later," I reply and nod to Niner and Kash as I head out.

After showering and catching up on some homework, I began chopping veggies and marinating meat for my dinner date with my

Freight Train

Pretty. I checked online how to cut strawberries to look like small flowers, and I've been practicing to show off for her. My mom taught us all how to cook growing up, and I've never been so grateful than coming to college and being able to make more than sandwiches and using it in times like tonight.

I made sure all the guys would be gone for at least two hours this evening too, so that way we could have the house to ourselves and get some alone time. I've missed her, more than seems natural for a dude to miss a woman. I wish she were able to come with me out of town to my games, but it's just not realistic financially or with her class load. One day it'll happen, though. I'll be in the NFL, and she'll be able to go to every single game of mine if she wants.

The grill's fired up and loaded with steaks and kabobs, the delicious aromas of prime beef filling the air when the doorbell chimes, signaling her arrival and upping my enthusiasm inside. Is it weird that I want to cook for her? It's just another way that I can give her a piece of myself. Small touches count, and I want her to know just how special she is to me.

Opening the front door, she has me floored instantly in the sweet pink, baby doll style dress she's rocking. How does she come up with these? First, the short-shorts paired with my jersey, and then there was the halter top and now this.

"No jeans and t-shirt tonight, huh?" Not that I mind one bit, I could stare at her all night long dolled up or not.

"I wanted to look nice for our date," she replies shyly, shrugging her petite shoulders, with a soft blush staining her cheeks and chest as I glance at her from head to toe. She's absolutely stunning and never stops surprising me with her outfit choices.

"Sweetheart, you surpass looking nice when you have on your glasses and comfy clothes. This right here is hotness overload. How do you expect me to be able to cook?" My finger tucks a stray lock of her peek-a-boo red hair behind her ear, and she laughs, rolling those gorgeous eyes of hers. Always a little spice to her and I love it.

"Well I can put on a pair of your sweatpants then until you're finished because I'm starving and whatever you're cooking back there smells awesome out here," she chortles, smacking a loving kiss on my cheek as she comes inside.

"Hell no, you wear my clothes, and I'll never get anything done except peeling them off of you."

"Oh lord, you're full of it tonight!" Her smile lights up, making me want to say whatever I can to keep it there.

Leading her out the sliding glass door to the little white patio table, I wrap an arm around her small waist. I can't refrain myself from touching her again. "I'm just happy to see you."

"Me too, I've missed you."

"Same here, Pretty. I'm glad you're here tonight."

"Thank you for inviting me, now what are we eating? God, it smells delicious."

"Steaks and some chicken kabobs." Heading over to the grill, I flip the propane off and load up our plates.

"Mmm, my favorite."

"And you're my favorite." Winking, I set her plate down and make her blush again.

"Being here," she gestures to the house, landing on me. "It makes me miss you even more lately. Does that make sense at all?"

"Yes, because I feel the same way. It'll calm down next month, though, I promise, and we can spend Christmas together at the ranch."

"That would be amazing, but I'm supposed to visit my dad. He did say he wanted to start coming here more, so maybe I can talk him into spending Christmas in Alabama instead."

"Good idea," I agree, digging into my full plate of food. Not having her around me during the holidays would suck. Hopefully, she can work her magic on him.

KADENCE

I don't know what it is about Tyler being in the kitchen, but it makes him unbelievably sexy, kind of like his tight football pants he wears. He rinses another plate and hands it to me to dry as we clean up our dinner dishes. After I wipe off the last dish and the cutting board, he dips his fingers into the water from the faucet and splashes me. He's done it three times already, but this one was the biggest splash. I've ignored him thus far, but this one has me giving in.

Giggling, my hands quickly wind my towel up and lightly let it loose to pop him with it in the thigh.

"Ouch!" he yells, chuckling, then surprises me by pulling me to him. I know I didn't hit him hard enough to actually hurt him, but it made a decent snap sound to make him jump, and that was pretty satisfying.

"You're in trouble," he growls, trying to sound scary, but it does the opposite. It makes him even sexier if that's possible. Dropping down, he lifts me over his shoulder, taking off out of the kitchen and down the hall toward the bedrooms. Thank God the guys aren't around with me being in this dress, my panties are on full display.

"Ah! Where are you taking me?"

"To show you what happens when you start giving me sass." His southern drawl has me going, and I can't help but let loose a loud giggle at his playful threat. I love it that he's not scared to be silly with me.

Storming into his bedroom, a man on a mission, he locks his door and just when I expect him to toss me onto his bed, he does the unexpected. Tyler pulls me down over his chest, my body sliding against his until he gently lowers me onto his bed, laying his frame over mine.

Bringing his lips to my own, he softly sucks my lower lip into his mouth. It's sweet with just the right amount of sultry to have my body humming inside for him. The flirting and laughing, then this sensual side of him is the perfect combination in a man.

"Pretty?" Whispering, he pulls away just enough so he can speak against my mouth.

"Yeah, Ty?" My voice mumbles, just as softly, while I gaze into those sparkly irises of his.

"I sure do love you." His lips flutter over mine as they speak some of the most meaningful words I've ever heard. He's close enough that I can feel his love for me, with his heart pounding against my breast with excitement. The silliness from before is replaced with tenderness as a happy tear trails down my cheek.

Freight Train

"I love you, too, Tyler Owens, so much." He stares down at me as I respond, his eyes full of raw emotions so sincere that they have my stomach twisting in delightful spins.

At my admission, his fingers find my softness, rubbing delicious circles until my core is aching for him to make love to me. Pulling his lips between my teeth, I nibble and urge him on, wanting all of him.

"Can I have you?" He asks, sweetly rubbing his nose against mine.

"You already do. You have since the first time you helped me up. Please make love to me." Gripping the sides of his shirt, my hands work to free his torso that's fit for a Greek god.

"Is it all right if we leave the dress on? You're incredibly stunning in it. I want to remember you like this—cheeks flushed, sexy dress, telling me that you love me."

"Yes, of course." I grin, happy he loves the outfit that I picked to wear especially for Tyler and knowing that this moment is just as special for him as it is for me.

Eagerly, he pulls my panties down my legs and kisses up my calves. Soft, delicate touches of his lips flutter up the insides of my thighs until they caress where I need him the most. His hands are rough against my skin as they stroke me. Words such as 'perfect, amazing, and magnificent' leave his mouth, making me feel truly beautiful inside and out—and loved. He never stops making me feel loved, even for a moment.

And that's when I know that I want him forever...

Sapphire Knight

Remember, if you are not playing your heart out,
someone else is. And when you meet him,
he will win.

Tyler

"Hey." I fist bump both the guys, greeting them first thing the next day at the dean's building. "Are we ready?"

"Yes," Chandler mumbles, with dark bags under his eyes.

"You all right? You're looking like shit, bro."

"I'm fine. I was up all night trying to get the girls to come with us. Neither of them would budge, and both of them ended up fighting with me the entire time I was at their apartments."

"Fun," JJ grumbles sarcastically at Chandler's admission, causing him to roll his eyes.

Not wanting to get into it again with him about not setting boundaries, we head into the main office and ask the receptionist to let us in. Dean Wilcox had a few meetings, so we had to wait a while before he finally called us in.

"Well hello gentlemen," he greets, wearing a friendly smile. "I didn't know it was some of our football players out here or I would've had Annette cancel my last meeting."

"It's no problem, sir," Chandler replies and shakes the older man's hand. JJ and I follow suit, and then we all take a seat in the leather chairs placed around the front of his desk.

"So what can I do for you three? By the way, nice win last week; we really appreciate your dedication to our program."

"Thanks," we mumble, not looking forward to the news we have to share and the fact that it has to do with a football player at that.

"Well, sir," Chan begins, "we have an issue with a fellow player."

I feel like that's an understatement. My problem with Briggs is huge. I'd let him get mauled a few times by an angry bear if it were up to me. There's no love lost between us either, now that he knows how much I can't stand him.

"Shouldn't you ughmm," he clears his throat, suddenly uncomfortable, "be speaking to your coach about that sort of thing, young man?" His eyebrows rise as he taps his fingers on the large white calendar taking up most his desk top. It's full of scribble writing, no doubt his own. A secretary would be fired with penmanship like that.

"Normally, yes, we would, but this has an illegal aspect that we thought you'd appreciate being brought to your attention."

"Very well then, shoot."

Tightening my lips, I try to hold back the chuckle wanting to break free at his choice of words. It's his belt buckle; it's so big that it's screwing with me not to stare openly at it.

Listening aptly, Dean Wilcox barely breathes as we each tell him different parts about what Briggs has been up to with the females on campus and then about our 'social outing' at my ranch and him trying to drug someone.

"Wow." Sitting back in his chair, he adjusts the overly large buckle at his waist, drawing my eyes back to the ostentatious piece of metal. The Dean's like a citified cowboy or something, always in a brand new Stetson hat and belt to match. "I'm assuming you have a way to prove all of this?"

Sitting beside me, Chandler complies, laying a memory stick on the solid oak desk. "Two women who were victims of Briggs were able to download files from his computer each time that they visited his apartment. We had his phone too, but we destroyed it so no one would see all the filth he had on it."

"So these women, they continued to see him after what they'd been through? You're sure these videos weren't authorized by both parties?"

"Yes sir, they umm...they had to keep seeing him, it was part of the whole scheme. If they tried to stop doing what he wanted, he threatened to post the videos and pictures on the public forums."

Shrugging, Chandler quickly glances to the side at us both, uncomfortable talking about the situation.

"Well, shit." A curse slips free from Dean Wilcox, and it's the first time I've ever seen him lose his professional façade. Sitting forward, he rests his elbows on the edge of the oak desk and places his face in his hands.

JJ glances over at me next, looking freaked out as if we just broke the Dean or something.

"I'm going to call campus security and have them arrest this man after we view everything. Whatever you do, gentlemen, don't speak a word of this to anyone. I don't want him to know what we have up our sleeve before we actually have a chance to get the proper steps in motion."

Chandler interrupts, "Sir, the women who were able to get this don't want anyone to know. They're hoping he'd get expelled and banned from the property."

"And I hope you're kidding. If this all happened like you three are telling me, then this guy needs to be put in jail. Expelling him won't stop him from doing this again and hurting other women. The University of Alabama does not tolerate this sort of behavior from a student—ever."

"I agree," I reply and elaborate on our plan. "But they refuse. JJ and I were thinking about contacting sites and papers anonymously about him, so it spreads, but none of the victims are named."

"They won't print it without some sort of proof, police involvement, and a trial. I'm sorry, but this man has the intent to hurt other students. I have to report this. I applaud you for bringing it to my attention; you did the right thing. Now wash your hands of it and let me take care of it. Understand?" He orders sternly, and we all reply, "Yes, sir."

"I'll be speaking to your coach about this as well, but I won't bring you into it. No one needs to know who gave me the information—just that I have it. If you find out anything else, please don't hesitate to come to my office. Now relax and have a good day. You need to be thinking about football, none of this other stuff anymore. Let the authorities handle it." He smiles, back to being professional.

"Thank you," I respond and stand, the guys following suit.

"Have a good day, gentlemen." Repeating himself, he holds his office door open for us to pass through.

Once we're outside, JJ turns to us, "I figured he would've wanted us to give statements to the cops at least."

Chandler nods, chewing on his bottom lip, obviously something running through his own mind.

"Yeah, but maybe he wants to try and bust him without our names being involved unless it's absolutely necessary. He must think they have enough evidence that he won't need to involve our names in it. Frankly, I'm glad about it. I want Briggs gone, but when the NFL does any looking into me, that's not something I want to pop up. It's better this way, and our names won't be tied to it, even if we were just trying to help."

"Yeah, you're right about that," JJ agrees.

"Now what?" I ask.

"We do what we're good at." Chandler finally flashes a small smile. "We play football."

"Sounds like a plan. Did y'all notice his damn belt buckle?" I ask, and they both chuckle.

Three days later Chandler storms into the locker room, forcibly tossing his gear into his locker, clearly upset about something, ready to lose it.

"What's the matter, bro?" JJ steps beside him.

Chandler, angrier than I can ever remember seeing him, faces us. "That motherfucker is gone, I can't believe it. All that work and for nothing, what a waste," he rambles on.

"Excuse me?" I take a step closer so he can explain without involving the entire team.

"Gone, you guys. Like as in, he packed *his* shit up and got out of there."

You know somethings bad if he's swearing like this. He obviously means Briggs by how pissed off he is.

"How? The cops probably have him." I try to reason, not wanting Coach Stratton to notice the noise coming from our way.

"They don't. Lila saw him packing his things into his car and taking off. I called the campus police and apparently 'he's wanted for questioning.' But they don't have him. And now she's freaking out about it all, thinking that he's going to put out the videos of her on the campus website."

Freight Train

Shaking his head, JJ argues, "No way. Dean Wilcox said he'd take care of it, and I trust him, she's just being dramatic."

"Yeah, I thought so too, so I called him. They weren't able to pick Briggs up. Wilcox actually had the nerve to ask me if we were the ones who warned Briggs to get out of here! Can you believe the nerve of that guy?"

Running my hands through my hair, I let out an irritated grumble, "Shit."

"Yeah, that's not all," Chandler continues, outraged. "I told him to go to hell. I wasn't putting up with those ridiculous accusations."

"Oh God." Squeezing the bridge of my nose, I meet his gaze. "Please tell me you're exaggerating."

"Nope. I told him to go straight to hell, and then I hung up on him." He starts fighting with his shoulder pads, his moves too jerky so that they keep getting caught on one of the sides of the small locker box.

"Jesus Chandler, he can get you benched from games for that shit!"

"He needs to worry about catching a psycho running around campus that's blackmailing women, not an angry football player who was rude for two minutes."

JJ interrupts, whispering, "Shhh!" And then glances around at each of our teammates suiting up to make sure no one overheard us.

"Why should I be quiet? I've already thought it over. If he wants to get me in trouble for any of it, I'll go to the media. I've sat by and waited just like he told us to do three days ago and then he goes and fucks it all up!"

"I get it that you're upset man," I try to reason a little with him. "Hell, we all are, but you need to calm down." Stratton will have his pants in a wad if he gets wind that we're caught up in this mess, so close to the bowl.

"Seriously, Owens?" Chan growls. "I've spent nearly every waking moment that I'm not at practice with these two women, and now they're terrified that he's going to come for them or post the videos all over the place. It's my fault for getting them to steal the stuff in the first place. I should've turned that phone in to the police when I had the chance, and then they'd already have him."

"I'm sorry they're freaking out, and I can see that you've clearly started to care for them, both of them, but this is their fight, not yours. It may make me sound like a dick, but you're already doing enough by being around to protect them and help them stand up to Briggs. You should be proud man, not beating yourself up about it all. You did the right thing, we all did."

JJ claps him on the back. "You need to let the cops do their job, C."

With a few deep breaths, Chandler nods. "I'll try to calm down, but it's all wrong. Practice should help, I hope anyway. I don't like feeling as if I'm helpless and right now I'm basically twirling my thumbs like an asshole."

"I know man, I know. You can tackle some of the second strings to help get it all out."

It's the only way that I know how to help him. I've never dealt with this sort of thing before, but I also know that it's not good for Chandler to be losing his shit after he's done nothing but support the chicks and try to get some sort of justice. We have at least five games left, and I need him one hundred percent in all of them.

Freight Train

Pulling my phone free, I send a text to Kadence.

Me: Don't forget to pack your bags for tomorrow.

Pretty Girl: Are we leaving right after the game again?

Me: Yes.

Pretty Girl: I can't wait. I love you.

Me: I love you.

At least one good thing came from today—the knowledge that I'll be with Kadence tomorrow.

KADENCE

Pulling up to the ranch, I'm so happy to be here again and that the guys won their home game today. Last weekend they lost, and their coach made them practice all weekend as punishment. I only got to see Tyler twice this past week and alone time with him is much needed at this point. I get it that football takes commitment, but I want a chance to be selfish with him and have him be all mine. I can handle sharing him with his brothers for a bit, but the rest is me being glued to his hip.

With his admission this past week of him telling me that he loves me, it's seemed like the longest few days ever, waiting for him to have time off. People think football players show up for practice and play a game each weekend, But I've learned that it's usually a cardio session in the morning, practice in the afternoon where they run plays, and weight training in the evenings. It's complete dedication and discipline.

It's crazy and overwhelms me when I don't even play for the team. Occasionally they won't have such a busy day, and that's when Tyler and I will sneak in a date or lunch or a movie, anything. Then there's also travel time for them if they have away games. One week, Tyler was gone for the entire week between traveling and two different games. It's amazing that he keeps up with a full schedule and manages to get good grades while he's at it.

"You ready, Pretty?" Tyler asks as he turns his truck off, parked in front of the large, old white house he calls home.

"Yes, I'm excited."

"Good."

"Why did you make me promise you so many times to come, though? I loved our visit out here last time."

"You're trying to get it out of the way, huh? Never patient." He chuckles.

"So there *is* another reason you brought me then?"

"Yes, but I was hoping to at least unload the truck before we got into it."

"Oh, is it *bad?*"

"Why do people always assume it's something negative and then asks that?"

"I don't know because those words usually mean bad news of some sort."

Freight Train

"No Kay, you don't have to worry about it being anything bad whenever I need to talk to you. We've been apart a lot lately, and we need to get caught up."

"Okay, that makes me feel so much better then."

"Come on, goof." He kisses my hand before he hops out, stepping aside so I can scoot out of his side as well.

"Hey, it's the sexy one and my asshole brother!" Nate calls from his perch on the porch. He's going to wear a hole into that chair if he doesn't stop sitting there so much.

"Don't you ever work?" Tyler yells, grabbing our bags out of the back.

"I work. We're not all pretty boy football players you know," Nate taunts him, and Ty tosses his bag at Nate's head.

"Hey!" His brother protests, grabbing the flying object quickly.

"Don't hate me because I'm the pretty one *and* the talented one out of us three," Ty taunts.

Laughing at them both, I hug Nate, "Hey Trouble." It comes out more like a squeak as he squeezes me tightly, trying to egg on his brother by holding me tighter than needed. He'll pay for it later. I know Tyler will mix a ton of pepper in his food or let all the air out of his truck tire. I've learned that he's all for pulling pranks on his older brothers, and I love every minute of it. I can only imagine how they were when they were younger; I bet their mom was always after them for something.

Rolling his eyes, Ty frogs Nate in the shoulder and takes off inside. Nate's mouth drops open, and he lunges at him, releasing me just like Ty wanted.

Giggling at them fooling around, I follow them into the house. Tyler takes off out the back door with Nate hot on his heels as Clyde appears.

"Hey, Clyde." I smile, shaking my head at his two younger brothers being silly, still acting like a bunch of kids.

"Kadence." His big arms pull me into a side hug, making me feel welcome. "Was the drive all right?"

"Yep, it was fine, just had to listen to your brother sing the entire way here."

His eyes squint like he's remembering a certain time. "Ah, yeah, after a while he sounds more like a wallowing cat."

Grinning, I hold back my laugh. "That's not exactly what I was going for, but I can see it."

"You hungry? I'm about to fire up the grill."

"I swear, all you guys do is eat. Tyler's constantly trying to feed me and every time I'm here, you're cooking."

He just shrugs, waiting for me to answer his initial question.

"I could eat."

"Good, I'll fix some potatoes too."

"Oh, are they *broken*?"

"That depends..."

"On what?"

"If you keep being a smartass, and I need to toss one at you."

"Gah, force-feeding *and* violent with the food." The laugh slips free after that and Clyde huffs, amused. Being together with

Tyler this time around when we visit is much easier going and everyone's full of smiles. I love it.

"Grab the Kool-Aid, sister," he orders on his way out. I swear my face may break with how my lips are pulled back so far, grinning like a loon at the nickname he's given me.

Sapphire Knight

I don't care if everyone doubts me,

as long as I believe in myself.

- @progressivesoccer

Tyler

"Will you please tell me already?" Kadence tries again. It's the fifth time since we've left the house. I'm getting the impression she's not a fan of exercise or surprises.

"I wanted us to have a chance to check out the ranch and then talk about it on the way back."

"How can we talk about *it* if you won't tell me what we need to discuss? Your brother doesn't have a building full of women or anything, right?"

"No more creepy movies with Clyde while I'm helping Nate with fence repair."

Her shoulders bounce in a small shrug, while her eyebrow props up like it's my fault she was subjected to watching some horror movie with my brother. She could've come along with Nate and me to replace the pickets.

"And we'll talk about *it* once we get to where we need to be. We're almost there anyhow."

I had to get Clyde's consent to even tell her about his side business. He thought it'd be better to show her and be able to thoroughly answer any questions she may have. If we hadn't been together for this long and him know how serious I am about her, he'd never had agreed to it.

The walk from the house isn't too far, and the breeze is refreshing as we trail under a cluster of trees toward a small shed heavily surrounded by brush and vines. If you didn't know what to look for, you wouldn't notice it. And that's exactly how it's supposed to be. My dad built the small building when Clyde was a baby and times got rough for him and my mom, trying to have enough money to keep up with the ranch.

My mom was a good woman. She never approved of my father's 'side hobby' as she liked to call it, but she knew he had his reasons to do it. No matter how important following the law was to her, it never came above her love for her family and seeing that they had all they needed.

My father taught my brother the ropes at age ten and carried on the tradition with Nate and me. We can all work everything and help out if needed and we have many times. I'm not as involved as I used to be now that I'm away most the time. I like to give Nate shit for sitting on the porch all the time, but he's really just keeping watch when Clyde's off doing stuff. Our father always had someone outside, just in case we had an unexpected or unwanted guest show up.

"Oh God, I was right, wasn't I?" Kadence mumbles as we head around the side to the only door.

Rolling my eyes, I grin at her dramatics. "No, Pretty. You trust me, right?"

"Of course, or I wouldn't have come this far."

"Good, because I'm trusting you too, with the well-being of myself and my family by letting you in here."

Swallowing, she glances at me warily and nods.

"It'll be fine, I promise." Using the old bent up key, I unlock the top lock and the bottom and then pull hard to get the door open. I don't know if someone smaller than myself would be able to wedge the heavy metal door open enough to even get inside.

There's room for us to each squeeze inside through it, barely. I hold my hand out, gesturing for her to lead the way.

"Wha-what is all this?"

The opening lets in plenty of light, the shine glinting off the copper. I flip on the battery-powered lantern so she can see everything better.

"Is Clyde a scientist or something? What is this contraption?" She waves at the pipes and huge copper barrel, glancing over all the glass Mason jars we use to store the liquor in.

Chuckling, I pull her into my side and kiss her forehead. "No. Kay, this helps us make moonshine."

"To drink?"

"Yes, it's liquor."

"You make it?" Her eyes grow wide, excited.

"Yep, all sorts of flavors too."

"Geez, this is amazing. I've heard of people making it before, but I've never actually seen how they do it."

"You haven't watched it in a movie or anything?"

"No, I read, remember? TV isn't my thing. I've read a bit about it, but it was mostly just about the actual liquor not about the process or the machines that are used."

"Well, this is it. And it's illegal, hence all the caution and not telling you about it the first time we visited the ranch."

"No, I get it. I'm not generally excited about breaking the law in anyway, but this is neat. I don't understand why it's illegal in the first place. People have beer and wine kits; this should be allowed, too, as long as people are cautious. It can be dangerous, right?"

"Yes, very. Our father always made sure we were extremely careful though, and it's made us responsible moonshiners."

"There are so many layers to you, Tyler Owens."

"Good layers, I hope?"

"Yes. I don't want to hurt your feelings, but when I first met you, I thought you were just some dumb jock with one thing on your mind, besides football. You've done nothing but prove me wrong each day. You have so much underneath that outer shell. I don't get it; how am I the lucky one you chose?"

"Pretty, you know I'm the one who's lucky. I love you, woman."

She grins, popping up on her toes to press a soft kiss to my mouth. "I love you, too, Ty. Thank you for trusting me."

I nod and gesture to my father's creation. "Do you have any questions about this?"

"Can we make some moonshine? I haven't tried it before, and you have me curious. Oh, and can we do a yummy flavor, like strawberry?"

"Not right now, it's a process. One day I'll definitely teach you, though."

"Ohhh, another ranch visit?" She mutters happily following me back outside.

Latching the two locks, I turn to her. "Yes. Is that okay, if we come here when we have time off?" I don't want her to get bored, but I need to be here when I have the chance to.

"Absolutely."

"I don't want you to think we can't ever go somewhere else or stay on campus if you want. I just know my brothers need as much help as possible, so I like to come home when I can and pitch in."

"You're such a good man, Tyler. I understand, and honestly, I love it out here. When I visit my dad, he stays in a big house they call 'the compound' that was built for him and the other bikers. Anyhow, it's like this." She gestures around us. "Lots of trees, land, and no one bothering them. I love it."

"I'm a little uneasy knowing you're around a bunch of bikers, especially if they're all as big as your dad," I mutter as we begin our trek back toward the house. I probably sound like an over possessive ass, but what if they hurt her? She's pint-sized compared to her dad.

"It's not like that when I'm there. I mean sure a few have flirted with me..." I shoot her a glare, and she laughs. "They would never go there; my dad would turn ballistic. But what I was getting at is it's not scary. It's like having five dads, all there ready to protect me if needed and they make sure no one is ever disrespectful. I usually load up my Kindle before I visit and just read and relax the entire time I visit."

"That doesn't sound so bad, besides the flirting bit." It comes out a bit gruff, but I can't help being a little peeved at other guys chatting it up with her.

"It's really not at all, and I didn't even realize they were flirting with me until my dad told them to stop during one of my visits."

That's what I mean. She has no clue just how beautiful she truly is, and not just that, she's so damn sweet inside too. It's way too soon to put a ring on her finger, but it's definitely in the overall plan. Hopefully, I get picked up by a good team this year, and she can move away with me. Flirting bikers can't compete with a man who loves her like I do and will be able to spoil her with anything she dreams up.

"You're um, happy, right?"

"What do you mean? Of course, I'm happy. I don't think I could be any happier right now. Well, maybe if you were naked and dancing, but that's beside the point."

"Don't rule it out; I can dance. The helicopter counts, right?"

It makes her laugh, and I adore that sound coming from her lips.

"I mean are you happy being with me, as my girlfriend? If the NFL called me up and asked me to go somewhere, are you content with us and do you love me enough to pack up your belongings and come with me, if I asked you to?"

"Geez, we're covering all sorts of stuff this trip, huh?"

I nod, waiting for her to think it over and respond.

She replies immediately, thank God. "Yes, to all of it. I'd pack my things and not look back because I can't stand being away from you for two days, let alone an entire football season."

"Good answer." Beaming a bright smile her way, I reach out and brush her hair back behind her ear as we get closer to home.

"Just good?"

"More like the absolutely perfect answer. I don't want to scare you off, but someday I hope that I get to ask you. I want you beside me wherever this road takes me."

"Good answer," she replies cheekily and winks.

"I think my brothers have been rubbing off on you." Grinning, I open the front door for her.

"It is possible," she acknowledges as Clyde comes around the corner.

"What's possible?"

"I was telling Kadence that y'all are rubbing off on her."

"Oh yeah, she likes us more, but she told me not to tell you." His mouth pulls up in a smirk, and she huffs.

"I did not!"

It's never ending around here; someone's always getting hassled.

KADENCE

"She knows, I take it?" Clyde asks, nodding my way.

Tyler letting me in on the family secret has nearly floored me. I tried not to come off as too surprised about it all, but really, I was. Never in a million years would I have guessed that they make moonshine. I want to learn how. The machine they use is impressive considering his father actually built it by hand. They're a family of many talents so it seems.

"Yep, I showed her everything."

"Do you have any questions?" He mumbles, gazing at me curiously.

Nate comes in, interrupting us, "Hey, sister." He greets me with the nickname he and Clyde have given me.

"Hey."

"She knows now," Tyler shares.

"You do?" Nate gazes at me, his eyebrow hiked up.

"Yep. It's official, I know."

"You're becoming a smartass." Nate grins, and Clyde rolls his eyes.

"She was sweet before, this is your fault," he mutters.

"Guys?"

"Yeah?" I get their attention.

"*She* is right here. I've always been a bit of a smart aleck but being around your constant horseplay and smack talking has indeed

Freight Train

brought mine to the surface with you. Now that we have that out of the way, when can I learn how to make moonshine?"

Clyde beams at me, a proud look in his gaze. Nate laughs, and Tyler pulls me into a hug, kissing my forehead.

"Soon, little sister, just don't run off telling anyone."

"She's not going to say anything." Tyler sticks up for me.

"I won't, I promise." The guys each nod at my declaration. I've learned that a promise to the Owens brothers from someone they trust, is pretty much gold. You don't make it unless you absolutely mean it. "Can I tell my dad though?"

"Hell no. Why would you want to involve him?" Clyde's hand rests against his hip, on guard.

He and Nate have no idea about who my dad is, only Ty. "Because he belongs to a motorcycle club that always has a bar fully stocked with liquor for their members. I think he'd like to take some back when he visits if you would let him. And if they like it, I'm sure his club would buy some whenever my dad comes through town."

"If Ty thinks it'd be a good fit then maybe next time your father's around, he can stop over for a meal, and we can have a chat."

"Sounds good. When he visits again, I'll ask Ty to text you."

He nods and just like that, I've helped their ranch out, only they have no idea yet. I know the President of my dad's club—Viking—and he'll buy cases and cases of liquor from them each visit for his own club, and if he likes it enough, he'll send it to other clubs. Clyde's about to become a whole lot busier, and hopefully, it'll help with the tax problem that I've heard Tyler speak to Nate about.

Sapphire Knight

**It has little to do with the number on my shirt
or the roar of the crowd. But everything to do with the
dream in my heart and the desire to give everything I have.**

- Quick Quotes

November passes us in a flurry, the leaves turning to beautiful colors around campus as Alabama gears up for December. Two weeks until classes are out for winter break and two games left for Tyler to play until the end of college football season. It's bitter sweet, knowing that another semester has nearly come to an end and another season for him is almost over.

My father visited again for Thanksgiving, and we spent it at the ranch. It was a little nerve-racking at first introducing him to Ty's brothers, but he ended up hitting it off well with Clyde. I think they're both just a touch rougher than Nate and Ty and it gave them some common ground. Plus his brothers sort of freaked out when they found out that my father is 'Chaos' the football player. I never thought men would go all 'fangirl' mode, but it's possible when it comes to sports figures.

In a house full of men that at one time were all athletes, it was a bit overwhelming watching the game after turkey dinner too. If we were in an apartment, the cops would've been called; they were so dang loud. I've never understood why people yell at the TV when games are on. Do they think the team can hear them? Well, with those four, I'd almost believe that the Patriots could've heard them cheering, even all the way from Alabama.

In the evening, I got to meet Ty's cousin, Dallas, for the first time. He was funny and fit right in with the three brothers. He brought over a deck of cards, saying it was a Thanksgiving tradition in their family to gamble away pennies and pretzels while playing poker every Thanksgiving evening.

I don't know how they were able to keep so active all day. With the turkey and pie that Clyde prepared, I might add, I felt like a giant couch potato. The food was amazing. He truly is a good cook, and at everything, it appears.

For the first time in years, I felt like I was family like my father and I belonged somewhere. My dad has his club, and I have Brianne, but this was different.

Tyler

Another team just called to inform me that they've been looking into me. Is this normal? It was with the colleges, the scouts tried to get me to attend schools all around the world, but the NFL now, too? I didn't expect to hear from anyone this far out from the draft, but I just hung up with the third NFL representative.

None from the team I want. Well, I want two different teams, so I'm hoping that if people are going to start calling, my team picks will end up being one of them.

"Was that Green Bay just now?" JJ pulls his sweatpants on as we all get changed after practice.

Nodding, I pull my hoodie over my head, still shaken from the unexpected call.

"You should've told them that their team sucks."

"Right now, no team sucks as far as I'm concerned. I want that contract and playing time."

"They aren't going to guarantee that you get time on the field, bro, no way."

"We'll see about that." Grumbling, I slide on my Nike slip-on sandals. "You know if Green Bay called you, that you'd sign."

"Nope, I'm holding out for Tennessee or Atlanta."

Rolling my eyes in disbelief, I zip my duffle bag closed as Chandler steps beside me.

"Campus police left me a message while we were on the field."

"Oh yeah? What did they want?" It's been radio silence from them over the past month.

"They found Briggs. The police in Florida have him detained."

"Florida? No shit? About time they figured it out. I was worried he'd disappeared for good at this rate."

He nods. "They asked me to get ahold of Lila to see if she'll press charges along with the college."

"Wow, I'd wondered where he scampered off to. Good thing it was a few states away. I can't believe he didn't get busted for doing it down there as well."

"Yeah, me either. What a piece of shit," JJ agrees.

"I'm just happy that he hasn't been around here. It drove me crazy inside having him near Kadence. Do you think Lila will press charges since she's had some time away from it all?"

Chandler runs his hand over his face. "I'm not sure. The cops said they weren't able to give me any other information about the case. Since the dean took care of it and we're not involved with it, we're not privy to any of the info they have. Fucking pisses me off. They should tell anyone who wants to know. Briggs is dangerous, especially to women and it's like they want it to be one big secret."

"That blows, but they're probably keeping it private until they have all their ducks in a row. If they want any chance of getting him in trouble, they need time to build a case against him."

"They've had plenty of time; he's been on the damn run. There's no telling if he hurt anyone else during his vacation in Florida and who's fault would that be then? We reported it and yet they didn't take it as seriously as they should have. It's ridiculous. We should've done something to him at the ranch when we had a chance to, months ago."

"Shhh, man, I know you're livid; hell, we all are, but don't let anyone hear you talk like that. The dean should've let us all go on record; then they would've had more against him. I get that he was trying to protect us, but it probably would've helped."

"He could've been fired if they found out he did that shit too. Completely against the college code of conduct for faculty. I know because I checked it out."

I'm not surprised at all that Chan's been doing his research on it all. I swear he was a damn lawyer or something in another life.

"Have you spoken to Lila about any of it? She could really cement the case against him. So could Haley, they both need to talk and press charges against him."

He shakes his head, clearly upset at thinking about them.

"You okay, man?"

"I'll be fine. I mean, Lila should be mad. I was the dumb one thinking that she and Haley wouldn't find out about each other. They have every right to hate me." He's lucky neither one went crazy and chopped his dick off or anything.

"Dude, you did it for a good reason, though. It's not like you just go out and date a bunch of women all the time, and you're one of the most decent guys I know when it comes to respecting women. People were getting hurt, and you were trying to help both of them, along with all the other women on campus. Who knows how many Briggs really threatened."

"I was so stupid to start falling for them both. I should've just broken it off when Briggs disappeared. Now they're both hurt, and they hate me. Lila won't even look at me, and Haley answers her phone just so she can hang up on me each time. I feel like such a damn loser, hurting them."

JJ smacks his back lightly "Give the chicks a little time and then talk to them both. Lay it all out on the table, and they'll get it."

"And if they don't?"

"Then they don't realize the type of dude they have right in front of them C, and you move on." He shrugs.

"I think he's right. Definitely call them and let them know about Briggs. It'll be a way to at least get them to speak to you, and maybe you can talk some commonsense into them. Then you just have to choose one."

"Hard to believe, but you're probably right. The fucked up part is that I don't know who to choose when it comes down to it."

Shaking my head, I lay my hand on his shoulder. Poor dude, he's never been so torn. "Hey, why's it hard to believe?"

"Because a few months ago, I was the one telling you to be a one-woman man if you wanted to be with Kadence, I never thought we'd be trading spots."

"Me either. But I wouldn't give her up for the world."

JJ butts in, trying to make the situation a bit lighter for Chandler, "And for the love of God, tell Owens that Green Bay sucks."

"Actually, they're not doing that bad this year," Chan replies and JJ groans in protest.

This has been an ongoing argument for the better part of our friendship. We all like different teams and we all play football, so in the end, we all think we're right, and the others are wrong. Get my brothers going about it, too, and the argument never ends.

"Whatever, let's get out of here."

Coach Stratton pops his head into the main locker room and shouts, "Owens! Office."

"Looks like I'm not leaving just yet." Muttering, I shoulder my duffle bag.

"No worries, bro, we'll catch a ride with Kash or Niner."

"All right cool, see ya," I reply and trek over to the coach's office. His door's open so I peek my head in through the doorway. "Coach? You wanted to see me?"

"Yes, come in."

Sitting in the same chair as the last time that I visited his office, I stare across the intimidating desk at him. "Yes, sir?"

"Do you have any plans for Christmas, Owens?"

My tight muscles relax. That's not at all what I was expecting him to call me into the office about. If anything, I'd figured the dean had called him to let him know Briggs had been found, but apparently not. As far as I know, Coach still has no idea that it was Chandler, JJ, and me who turned Briggs in to the dean and got the whole mess started. In a way, I'm glad he doesn't know because we'd have gotten into deep shit from Coach for not telling him first. With how the dean and campus security screwed it all up, though, maybe telling Coach first would've been the best idea.

Hell, even Chandler's right. We should've messed Briggs up some more at the ranch. I'm not a vindictive guy, but there's no telling who else he's hurt since he's been MIA. A broken knee or ankle would've taken him out of football and slowed him down enough for the cops to maybe have gotten to him easier.

"Just the usual. I'll be hanging out with Nate and Clyde and hopefully Kadence."

"I'm glad to hear things are working out with you two. She's a nice young woman with a good head on her shoulders. Speaking of Kadence, her daddy likes to call me weekly to check up on you."

"Really?" This was the first I'd heard of it. I'm shocked; I honestly thought her father approved of me and even possibly liked me. Thanksgiving was a blast with him visiting, and my brothers thought he was a decent guy.

"Yep, Chaos is convinced you're going to go pro and keeps asking me if I have a clue where you'll be headed. It seems he believes that daughter of his will be following you, wherever you end up going."

"No shit?" It slips out, and I backtrack, "I mean, sir." I'm excited he thinks that she'll come with me, but Chaos thinks I'll go pro? I'm damn near giddy inside that those words left his mouth, that's a huge compliment.

"Do you have any ideas on who you'd like to be picked up by?"

Yes, definitely, I always have since I was a kid. "Yes, Coach, the same teams as before—New England or New Orleans."

He nods as if he was expecting that answer. "I've been following them this year, and I think New England would be a better fit for you right now based on their roster and current records."

"I hope so; they're my top pick." Not to mention I've been a die-hard fan for most of my life.

Freight Train

"New Orleans doesn't have much in the bank right now, so I'd skip them. They won't be able to pay you enough—what you're worth."

"Sir, has anyone called you? Is that why you're talking to me about this?"

"No, and they damn sure better not call me. It's too early for them to start harassing me. I'm telling you this because I'm not blind." He points his finger at my chest, emphasizing his point. "You're a damn good player, and above all, you've managed to stay humble somehow. You've got just enough confidence to shake off anyone that tries to put a dent in you, but not too much to make you lazy. Not many men can pull that mix off. You're going to go places, twelve; that I'm sure of. You keep playing like you have been in these next two games and you'll have first round picks chomping at the bit for you."

Nearly choking in surprise, my voice comes out rough, "First round picks?"

Holy shit.

"Yep, like I said, you've got it. So go home and think long and hard about what you want in your future. You'll most likely be picked up before the draft even takes place, but if you wait, you may be offered a longer contract and more money. If that's not as important to you and it's more about the team, then you may want to choose before April rolls around, and you're sitting beside that phone waiting to hear who's just picked you up."

It's like I'm ten years old again and have won the state tackle football championship for the first time. My nose clogs up, tears flood my eyes, and the only thing that runs through my mind is how incredibly grateful I am. How is this my life? I've been through trials and tribulations, and in the end, so much good has come into my life.

Kadence and I have spoken about it, and in the next few months we'll find out just how serious she is about us. I want her with me, every step of the way.

"I need to go, Coach, I'm sorry."

"You all right?"

"Yes, I just have a lot to think about is all."

"Give Clyde a call. He'll be able to help bring you some peace inside about your decisions and then get a good night's sleep. These next two games are yours, kid."

I know what that means. I'll be playing most of the game, and I'll be running the ball. Coach obviously wants me to go out with a bang, and I'll be making him look good in the process. Teamwork's not just about you and the man with the ball or the guy who needs to be blocked, it's also about the relationship you have with the coach. He can make your career, just like the quarterback can.

"I appreciate it. I'll be here first thing for practice."

"I know you will."

"Bye, Coach." He nods, dismissing me and I hurry out to my truck.

He's right; I should call my brother. He'd know what I should do. What if he tells me to go, though? It'd mean leaving him and Nate to take care of the ranch by themselves. However, with enough money, I could hire a hand to give them the help they need in my absence.

Pulling up to the house, I head straight for my room. I'm starving, but I need to get this call out of the way before anything else.

"'Sup O," Niner greets as I pass through the kitchen. He's busy making a triple layer sandwich and plate full of cut up, raw broccoli.

"Hey, man," I nod, not stopping.

Once I'm finally able to lie back on my mattress, I dial Clyde.

"Did you hit someone?" He answers sounding mildly amused with a bit of irritated mixed in.

"What? No."

"You don't usually call during the week."

"Oh." Chuckling, I inhale a deep breath. "I didn't think of that. Coach just stopped me. Thinks I'll go pro."

"No shit." He doesn't sound too surprised.

"You knew?"

"Well, I had a suspicion. I mean, it's what you've been working for the better part of your life. You haven't failed at it yet, so I figured something good would come from it."

"That's not all. He said I have a chance of being a first-round pick."

He whistles a long low whistle, now surprised.

"Yeah. He said I might have a chance to be signed by others before, and possibly my top team."

"Damn, Ty, I'm really proud of you."

Jesus Christ, is he trying to get me choked up now as well?

"Thanks. I didn't tell Coach, but three teams have already called."

"Holy shit, and you haven't told me?"

"I wasn't taking them that serious. I just thought it meant they'd keep me in mind for the draft in a few months."

"You idiot."

Annnd there's my older brother.

"He made it sound like there's a chance that New England could call me since they rarely get first-round picks."

"You have to do it, Ty. Follow your dream."

"If I move all the way up north then I can't help you with the ranch."

"And if you don't move, I'll feed you to the cows."

"Be serious, Clyde. Think about what I'm saying."

"I am, and I've figured out how to keep things going thus far, haven't I? Do you have any clue how proud our parents would be of you if they heard this? Tyler, sign the contract if they offer it. I'm so damn proud of you. We'll always be here, and I'll do whatever I have to with the ranch. It'll always be there and always be *home* for you."

Stupid ass, he has me choked up with his words.

"Ty, you there?"

"Yep," I say gruffly. "Thanks and I'll be able to hire someone to help you and Nate out."

"Let's not worry about that right now. Just take it one step at a time, okay?"

Freight Train

"All right."

"Now save me a ticket, and I'll come watch you play this weekend."

"Thanks, Clyde."

"It's what I'm here for," he replies and hangs up.

That statement has never been truer. I may not have a mother or a father alive anymore, and so help me, do I miss them, but I have Clyde, and he's shown me one hell of a good example of what a father and a brother should be.

Sapphire Knight

Do your job.

- Bill Belichick

Talking with Clyde left me a little choked up, but it had to be done. He gave me that small boost of confidence to go in the right direction. I needed him to tell me that he's okay with whatever I decide on doing and hearing it come from him directly, made my anxiety over this huge decision dissipate.

I know what I want, but only if Kadence is on board. If not, then we need to figure out an option we'd both be happy with. It's only been a few months, but I feel like we're meant to be together for the rest of our lives. Christmas is nearly here, and everything inside me wants to propose to her, but something tells me that she'd say no. Not because she doesn't love me because I know she does. But because it's the next step, and there's nothing 'normal' about

Kadence. She marches to her own beat—not anyone else's—and that's one of the many things I respect about her.

What could I do that would mean forever but not freak her out too badly? I want her to know that I'm completely serious about her now and I always will be. Another thing about proposing is that if her father's here, he may break my arms and my face for moving her in that direction so quickly.

My thoughts are interrupted by a knock on my bedroom door.

"Yeah? It's open!"

Niner's head pops in. "Hey, you okay?"

"Yeah, I'm cool, why?"

"'Cause you stormed through the house so quick, I thought you were going to shit yourself or something. Thought I'd come see if you needed my Imodium or anything."

That gets me laughing. I probably looked like I was about to shit my pants with how I blew him off in the kitchen. "No, man; I'm good. Just had to talk to my brother about some stuff."

"Oh okay, everything all right with you guys then?" I'd told him before how Clyde likes to keep everything to himself instead of letting me and Nate help him however we can.

"We're fine, but can I talk to you about something?"

"Of course, man." He comes in and sits on my desk chair. "What's up?"

"I want to do something special for Kay for Christmas, but I'm not sure what to do."

"You mean she's not pregnant?"

"No, why would you think that."

"Oh thank Christ. You were so serious, and with you talking to your brother, I thought it was something big."

Chuckling, I shake my head. "You've been watching too many movies, bro."

"It's that stupid *Maury Povich* show; it's on at night when I can't sleep."

That has me cracking up. "So back to Kadence, I keep thinking I should propose to her, so she knows how serious I am. If I get signed or drafted, I want her to come with me, and I'm wondering if I need to put a ring on her finger to get her to come with me."

"I don't know; she's not superficial like that. I think if she knows you love her, then that would mean way more than some ring with a stone in it."

"I could tattoo her name on my body?"

He rolls his eyes. "Then she wouldn't speak to you for a week. You trying to cement her to you or freak her out?"

"Okay, then I'll save that for after we're married," I mumble, and he laughs at me.

"What about a teddy bear or something?"

"Dude, it's Christmas. 'Here's a teddy bear, now move across the country with me.' No!"

"You're really going that far?"

"Stay on track, Niner. What can I do for Christmas that will mean a lot to her? I'm asking her to basically pack her stuff up and give up her life so I can live my dream."

"How about a necklace? Like a locket or something? Chicks love that sort of stuff."

"That's a good idea, maybe one with a book charm or something so she knows I pay attention to her."

"That's good, man, but how about a promise ring? It means a lot, but it's not proposing marriage right then, It's saying you plan on it later down the road."

"Holy shit, Niner, you're a genius! Do they have diamonds in them?"

"No. I bought one for a girl in high school; it was a plain band with a heart on it."

"Wow, what happened to her?"

"We'll leave that one for another day." He shakes his head.

"All right. So what if I get her a ring with a birthstone?"

"That's a little kiddish, don't you think? That'd be something I'd get my little sister if I had one."

"Right...umm..."

"What about you go with the book idea and get something inscribed on the inside of the ring?"

"Damn, you're good at this."

He shrugs.

I pull up a random jewelry store on my phone and start scrolling through their section of promise rings.

"What about this?" I pass the phone to him.

"An anchor?"

"That's kind of what she is to me—my anchor."

"Not bad. What are you going to get inscribed?"

"My heart, my soul, my forever."

"Yup, you'll be getting laid with that one." He nods making me chuckle.

KADENCE

"No, you must have the wrong number." I hang up and turn to Tyler. "Did you give my number to any NFL people?"

"No, of course not. Why? Is that who called just now?"

Sitting with our group at lunch, I take a bite of the juicy, Golden Delicious apple and nod. "Yup." I finish chewing "They said they were with Pittsburgh and asked if I was your girlfriend."

"You're joking."

"No, I wouldn't joke about something like this."

"I can't believe they called you," he quietly replies. "People have been calling me all week.

"Teams?" I gasp incredulously.

"Shhh!"

"And you gave them my number too?"

"No, I swear I didn't, I don't want them calling you."

"Then why are they?" I shoot him an irritated glance. "I can't deal with headhunters for my boyfriend; they shouldn't know anything about me."

"Look, I didn't say anything, okay? But like it or not, Kay, you're a part of my life. You're going to be in the spotlight eventually."

"I don't want to be; it's hard enough fending off my father's fans." All the fake people are trying to be friends and offer you things, then when someone finds out your phone number, the constant calling, the crazy fans who start harassing you. I've been there, and it's not fun in the least bit.

"Let's talk about this somewhere else."

"Where?" I ask, standing up and gaining our friends' attention.

Ty flashes a fake grin at everyone and pulls me over toward the bathrooms where there isn't anyone in close listening range.

"You of all people should know what that lifestyle's like. I was hoping you'd be able to help me adjust to it."

"What's that supposed to mean? That type of lifestyle? My dad kept me hidden from it as much as possible."

"I don't understand why you're getting so upset; it was one phone call."

"Because it means that other people know who I am too. It's not going to be just one, it'll become a dozen, then a hundred, and so on until it's nonstop people calling and harassing me to speak about you."

"I'm so sorry to be putting you out," he replies sarcastically. He's never spoken to me like that before, so it flairs my temper even more.

"Maybe I'll just tell them all that I'm not your girlfriend then." Stubbornly, I cross my arms across my chest, getting defensive.

"Well maybe, that's a great fucking idea then," he growls and storms off, slamming through the cafeteria doors on his way out.

I swear every eye in the entire place is on me. Nosey bastards. They should mind their own business. Tyler and I shouldn't concern any of them.

Brianne tosses mine and Ty's food in the trash bin and makes her way to me. "You okay, woman?"

I shrug. What can I really say? Am I okay? Not really.

I'm sorta pissed and freaking out over this whole football thing. It was okay to think about it but with one phone call, the reality sets in. He's going to go pro, and if I want a life with him, it'll be in the pro spotlight. Women will constantly be throwing themselves at him and attempting to cause trouble. They're relentless and will do anything to try and drive us apart. Then there are the headhunters and organizations that'll harass me, thinking if they win me over then Ty will choose them or that we'll have loads of money to donate to whatever causes they represent. I'm starting to get why my dad just up and decided to become a biker. He was fed up with it all. He merely wanted to live his life, and that meant he had to basically disappear. I get it now.

"Do you want to go sit outside and talk about it?"

She's a good friend, and I'll need to talk about it with someone—possibly her—but not right now. I'm too upset that I may say something that I don't really mean. Tyler's already pissed at me over me freaking out, that he just tore out of here like his ass was on fire.

"Thanks, lady, but not right now. I think I just want to go back to the room, put in my headphones and lose myself in some good music."

"You should go find Ty."

"And say what?"

"I don't know, but I've never seen him upset like that when it comes to you. Don't let something good slip away because you're're too busy being stubborn."

"How do you know it was my fault?"

"You forget I've known you since second grade. I love you, but you can be hardheaded when you want to."

Absently, I nod, hearing her but not really listening to what she's saying. Should I go find him? He should be the one to apologize to me. I'm not changing his life completely; it's the other way around.

"Look, if not him, then maybe call your dad. He's a guy; maybe he knows how to deal with Ty?"

"Yeah, probably. Thanks, Brianne. I'll see you later." It comes out monotone, but I have too much going on in my head at the moment.

"Wait, you don't want me to come with you?" She asks, resting her hand on my arm, appearing a bit more worried about me.

"No, I'm okay, really. I want to be alone and just think."

She nods, "Okay, text me if you need anything."

"Thanks." I smile a small smile as she hugs me and then makes her way back over to Kash.

Leaving the cafeteria, Jada and her groupie trash all stare and giggle as I pass their table.

Like they have any clue what our conversation was about. Losers.

I walk well into the night until my feet feel like they may fall off, before deciding that it's a good time to head back to the dorms. The few hours I've gotten to myself didn't accomplish much, besides a dozen texts from various people asking what I was doing or where I was. It also made me realize that I may have overreacted just a bit at lunch with Tyler, but I couldn't help myself. It's a huge deal, and when they start calling other people on your behalf to try and sway you, well then that's seriously a big thing. As in it doesn't happen often, and they've obviously been watching Tyler a lot longer than we've thought. NFL teams don't just call up college players and multiple teams at that.

There's so much of me that's happy for him and proud of him, but also a nagging part that makes me not want to share him with everyone. I already have to share him with so many people during college; I can only imagine how much less time we'll have together when he's playing pro. Which makes me wonder if it's all worth it.

There's a possibility we're not meant to be together. As much as I want us to be, there's always that chance. Don't get me wrong. I love Tyler. I love that guy so much, but will it be enough to last over the years through the trials and tribulations life brings?

This is our first blowout over something that didn't have to do with my safety, and instead of talking through it, working it out like rational adults, we're apart. No doubt, we're both busily sulking over having our own angry feelings. I want to reach out to him so we can work through it, but I did that the last time, and damn it, I want him to get ahold of me. This is his deal; he should be reassuring me that everything's okay.

Another thing to worry about is, where on earth is he going to sign to? What if it's like Arizona or Seattle or someplace like that? I'll be miserable no matter how much I love Ty, and in the end, it'll break me. Is it entirely too selfish to ask him to pick within a few specific teams? If he wants me to move along with him, then it should be partially my decision, too, right?

I know he has certain needs, like making enough money to help his brothers, but what Tyler doesn't realize is his level of talent. He'll make a grip of money no matter what team picks him up. He's just that good. I'm too selfish to give him up, but it frightens me knowing there's a chance of me being miserable and dragging him through that as well.

Am I really that self-centered to ruin his life as well?

No. I would never allow myself to hurt him that way. I love him. Why can't that fact alone be enough to get through our issues? Instead, we have to argue and make up and work to stay together. Is this what a real relationship is? Work? Don't get me wrong; I'll do it. I just worry inside that my love won't be enough for him.

Jada and her butt-buddies are sitting outside the dorm when I make my way back. Giggles erupt from them as I pass, and I can't hold it in any longer. I've had a shitty day, and I'm not going to take any crap from them.

"What the hell is your problem?"

"Hmmm? Who, us?" Jada asks, acting as if I'm losing my mind. Her smirk makes me want to yank her ponytail out and poke her in her stuck up nose.

"You're the only pack of dogs around, so I'd say that's a yeah you."

I've had my fill of her and her friends thinking it's acceptable to be ugly to people they deem beneath them. I may be a book nerd and keep to myself a lot, but I don't tolerate any type of bullying toward myself or other undeserving people.

She sputters, climbing to her feet, balancing in what must be five-inch heels. They make her tall enough to tower over me. I'd say they put her at five-ten or so. "You little bitch! Calling us dogs? Who do you think got put out the back door today at lunchtime? Owens couldn't get away from your prudish ass fast enough. I wouldn't be surprised if he's texting me tonight to come over."

"Ew. No wonder he never liked you. You smell like garbage, act like garbage, and speak like garbage."

Her friends gasp, their gazes shooting towards her, waiting for a reaction. They're not used to people standing up for themselves against their little group.

"I'll make you eat those words you little tramp!" Jada hisses, storming at me in her obnoxious shoes. She makes it three steps in my direction when a wall of muscle appears in front of me. He just came out of the dark like Superman or something.

Tyler stands tall, his voice booming in the quiet night. "Jada, you touch one hair on my girl's head, and I'll make sure you're expelled. And you know how angry your parents would be if they thought you weren't being their darling angel and pissing off one of their favorite football players? It would bite you in the ass even more."

"She started it with me, Ty. I was just sitting here," She whines pathetically, and her cronies all climb to their feet, agreeing with her. They probably think that by backing up her story, it'll make me look bad.

"You're full of it. I was sitting right on the side of the building, making sure she made it back okay and I saw the entire exchange. You've turned bitter, and it's made you ugly on the outside as well," he replies angrily, turning to face me. "You okay?"

I nod.

"Are you mad at me?"

I shake my head.

"Want to go to my house?"

I nod again, and he grabs my hand. Jada glares something fierce the entire time we walk to his truck. She laughs as her friends make rude comments, but I couldn't care less. She's an idiot, and if this is how she treats people, then she won't be getting far in life. Chicks like her always end up meeting their matches, and it usually turns out pretty ugly.

The drive's silent and takes maybe two minutes. Part of me wishes it was a bit longer. I know the chat we need to have is serious, and I'm a bit chicken.

Freight Train

We unload and make our way to his room. He keeps hold of my hand the entire time. No more distance between us.

"Are you going to speak to me yet?"

"I'm not-not speaking to you. I was just keeping quiet while we were in front of those assholes."

He nods. "They're hateful. Her parents would be livid if they knew she acted like that."

"You know them?"

"Yes, they're a sponsor for the team, so I've met them. Big football fans and nothing like their spoiled daughter."

"Hmmm."

"She means nothing to me."

"I know, I'm not worried about that. But you see how they act when you aren't around? That's part of the reason why I was freaking out today."

"What do you mean? What do they have to do with our discussion from lunch? Did they say something to you earlier that I don't know about?"

"No, but they have a lot to do with my outburst actually. You just saw it firsthand how women can be when you're not around. How do you think they'll be when you go pro? It's irritating now, but they'll be like sharks then. I can't compete with that."

"People are assholes. I can't do anything about the way they act. I can, however, do my best to make sure you're protected and you have my word that I will. I promised you a long time ago that I wouldn't let anything happen to you, and I still won't. If anything, that promise is even stronger now. And you have no one to compete with, ever."

"Why *now?*"

"Because I fucking love you, that's why, *now.*"

Best answer ever, I think as I throw myself at him and basically attack him to kiss his cheeks everywhere.

"I love you too." Whispering, he walks us backward to his bed. He lies back, pulling me over top of him. We can't have a normal conversation it seems. He always has to touch me or something when we're alone, and I love that about us.

"Now tell me what else you were so upset about earlier," he grumbles, staring into my eyes as I prop myself up on his chest.

"Because," I respond, already getting choked up. I'm starting to feel selfish again and like I shouldn't have freaked out so badly. Now I have to admit to him why it all happened, and it doesn't seem like it should've been that big of a deal anymore. Glancing everywhere but at him, trying to hold the tears at bay and feeling a little embarrassed inside at how emotional thinking about everything makes me. "I'm going to lose you." It comes out as a mumble while tears spill from my eyes, running over my cheeks.

"Baby," he grumbles, pulling my glasses free, setting them beside us and then gently wipes his fingers under my eyes. The tears spill even more with him being so sweet. "You're not going to lose me. I promise that too. I'm not going anywhere that you can't come too. You're it for me, Kadence."

"You can't promise me; you don't know that. What if you're gone all the time, and then you get lonely? Women will start to look better to you and then next thing I know, you're divorcing me for some model or groupie."

He ignores my dramatics, being compassionate. "If I'm lonely, then I'll call you, or you can come with me, and we're married now?"

"You know what I mean," I grumble, and he wipes more of my tears away. The thought of not having him in my life is like this huge black cloud waiting to suffocate me, and he's the only one who can give me oxygen.

"Shhh, Pretty. Stop this. I love you, and you have nothing to worry about. I will do everything I can to make sure you're happy, and we're together—a lot, in fact. And I do promise you."

"You're not going to sign with anyone dumb, right?" As soon as the words leave my mouth, he starts laughing which makes me grin too. "Shut up; it's a legit question."

"I thought you knew which two teams I wanted to sign with?"

"Well yeah, I remember our talk about it. You wanted New England or New Orleans, but what if another offers you more money? You're so freaking good, and they all know it. They'd be dumb not to offer you some great options."

He shrugs. "If it comes to that, then I guess I make less money. As long as I have you, I'm able to take care of you and help out my brothers, then that's all I really need. I don't need a contract for twenty million dollars or anything crazy. I think we could live a very comfortable life with just a couple million, don't you?"

"Definitely. I could live a comfortable life on thousands right now," I reply, and he chuckles again.

"Okay good. I talked it over with Clyde, and if I get a chance to go with a team that I want, well then I'm going to do it, okay?"

"All right, but what if they don't offer you one? I think they will, but these are some of the bazillion questions running through my head right now. I need to cover some bases, so I'll stop freaking out so badly inside. This is huge and to be included, it has me all twisted up with excitement and nerves. I don't know how you can be so calm."

"If that ends up happening, then I'll let you know what's on the board as far as options go and we'll decide on something together. This is our future, not just mine. I want you happy with the decision too. And, I am excited inside. Trust me, I feel like I'm going to puke most days because it's becoming real, but I'm good at acting like it doesn't bother me. Part of my game face, I suppose."

"I'm so stupid sometimes; I shouldn't have doubted you. Thank you for thinking of me too in the overall plan." I overreacted. I know it, but he did too. That excitement he mentioned must've been bubbling up for him too. Those calls bring on so much more pressure than I ever would've imagined. The whole process will probably make my hair fall out at this rate.

At least it got us to really talk about things. I didn't realize I had so much worry filling me up inside, waiting for the chance to burst free. Just hearing him say that he's considering me and my needs through the whole process and that he wants me to be happy alongside him, helps ease my fears of this big change coming into our lives.

"Always, Kadence, always. You're nothing even remotely close to stupid, sweetheart. I think you're pretty damn amazing."

Ditto hot stuff…ditto." I wink and kiss him sweetly on the forehead like he does me all the time. "I love you so damn much, Ty."

"I love you too, Pretty, with everything that I am."

The conversation ends as our bodies take over wanting to be even closer than we already are. I can never have enough of this man, and if I'm lucky, he'll never be able to get enough of me either. His need for me is already insatiable; I hope it never wavers no matter what we end up facing together.

"You'll always be mine, sweetheart." The words whisper against my breasts as he nips at them through my shirt. "I'll love you with every breath in my body." His hands push the shirt up, exposing my thin bra.

Sitting up, I help rid myself of the material, and then he rolls us until I'm under him.

"I'm going to make love to you, Kadence."

"Yes, I want you so badly, Ty."

"Good, never stop wanting me, baby."

"I couldn't even if I tried. Each time I try to be mad at you, I think I fall a little deeper in love with you."

"I'll piss you off more then." His empty threat is said with him peeling away my jeans.

"You're so romantic," I chuckle and lift my butt so he can free me from my panties.

"And you're perfect. Every last inch of you is my favorite part."

"Even my toes?"

"Yeah, baby, even your toes." He ends his confession by pressing tiny, sweet kisses to the tops of my toes and feet. Eventually making his way up my calves and thighs, raining chaste kisses as he goes, he pauses to bite into my thighs right under my core. It's phenomenal, the way his teeth lightly press into me, just rough enough to cause goose bumps to overtake my flesh, everywhere.

My nipples grow hard, aching to have more attention bestowed onto them from his sinful mouth. Not one to be alone in my nakedness, I lift his shirt, freeing his magnificent body. He's delicious. I've never met another man that was so beautiful on the outside and just as gorgeous on the inside.

"I swear your body's heaven, babe." His voice is deep and a bit gruff, laced with his arousal and it does amazing things to my insides, hearing him sound like that.

"I could say the same about you." Biting my bottom lip, I push his jeans off his lean hips, exposing his glorious V. After being completely spoiled with him, I could never be satisfied by another man, this I know. He treats me like the most precious thing in the entire world while making love to me like he's the devil himself.

Tempting.

Erotic.

Lustful.

I can never get enough of him or be close enough. This is how I know that he's my forever. My heart already loves him with every last drop and my body has totally relented, letting him have his way with me completely.

His hardness bobs excitedly as his boxer briefs fall to his feet, and in seconds he's plunging into me. It's hard and fast and fucking amazing.

"I want on top of you, Tyler. I want to watch you with each move I make until you come inside me."

He nods, swallowing roughly at my admission and shifts, so I ride him. His large hands palm my breasts as my hips rock forward and back then left to right. He loves it when I go in all different directions, so I pick myself up a little and rotate my lower half to make circles on his cock.

He moans, over and over, quiet noises leave him full of pleasure. His eyes are watching me with each tilt and shift my body makes and has me working up a sweat quickly, panting as my own orgasm starts to show up.

He doesn't even have to move to make me hot all over. Just knowing that his full attention's trained on me is enough. My core aches, wanting to swallow him in farther. Strong hands make their way over my stomach, pausing to grip my hips tightly. He's getting closer; I can see it in the way his skin's flushed and the muscles in his neck growing more pronounced.

He's buff and sexy and feels so damn amazing with each drive, but most of all, I know he loves me, and that's what pushes me over. Witnessing the love shining in his beautiful sparkly gaze as I bring his body pleasure.

Sitting up, he pulls me into him more, wrapping his muscular arms around me, holding my body to him as he drives up into me powerfully.

"My God!" The moan leaves my lips as my orgasm barrels down full force, his hips grinding against my clit. The sensations are so blissful I feel like my mind goes to another place for a few seconds. He's right there with me as he races after his own satisfaction. One long moan as I ride my wave spurs him on the last little push he needed and his cock swells. His hardness pulses as cum escapes him and it has me crying out in ecstasy.

He's my everything.

You get to decide the legacy that you leave.

Tyler

Christmas time rolled around, and the phone calls stopped. To say I started to sweat was an understatement. I ordered Kadence the promise ring but decided to hold off on that too. I didn't want my promise to be her Christmas gift. My commitment should be separate. She deserves more because she is so much *more* to me.

So here I am, already at the end of January, trying to think of some way to give her this ring without coming off as a total sap or not doing enough, so it doesn't seem like that big of a deal when it is to me. What's in the middle and why have I let myself put it off so long? She deserved this back when we first got together. She's stuck beside me the entire time and has given me her full support. How I ended up with someone like her, I'll never know, but I'm so, so grateful.

Nate says to give her—and I quote—*a good dicking and then just slide it on her finger.* I can see why my brother's still single with that one.

Clyde, on the other hand, (yes, I broke down and asked him too) suggested that I should cook for her and maybe put it inside a cake or something.

Yeah, *NO.*

Clyde's answer to everything is food. If he ever ends up married, he's going to have to roll the chick around from stuffing her full of food all the damn time. Kadence thought I was bad about it. She has no idea what Clyde's woman will go through. *Poor lady.*

Kadence had such a great time when we'd swam at the pond, and she loves the ranch as much as I do, so I was thinking about doing it there. Maybe laying out a blanket, bringing some snacks—'cause let's face it, my brother has rubbed off on me a bit—and then just tell her how much she means to me. I should probably light a fire and bring marshmallows, she loved those too, and she gets cold easily. Oh, and chocolate sauce too. She can dip them in the sauce, and I can also use it to lick off her.

That sounds fantastic. I should've thought of this sooner.

A slap on my shoulder shakes me out of my wonderful thoughts of her covered in sugary chocolate sauce. "Yoo-hoo, bro, you were in la-la land. Care to share?" JJ grins and turns back to the video game that he and Niner are busily playing.

"I was just thinking about—"

"Kadence?" Niner interrupts, his eyebrow cocked.

Freight Train

JJ laughs. "Go figure; I'd be surprised if you have a cock between those legs anymore."

"Shut up, dickface. I'd whip it out, but I don't want to hurt your feelings," I retort and Niner snickers. "I was thinking, JJ, have you heard anything new about Briggs? Do you know what went down after he was finally caught?"

"Nope, I know nothing, bro. The last thing Chan said to me about it was that he'd called the police office again, but they still won't tell him jack. Lila and Haley want nothing to do with any of it, and he's a wreck trying to get them to press charges. He admitted to me that he'd called one of them twenty-two times one night."

"Shit, such a mess. I'm glad Briggs is off the field and away from campus at the very least."

Niner grumbles, staring me down. "I can't believe it happened to so many females and no one wants to come forward. Next time something like this goes down, you two better say something to me. I'd like the chance to punch him too. No fair you get to have all the fun."

"Promise man," I start to reply, but my phone goes off, signaling an incoming call. It's an out-of-state number, one that I've never seen before. Glancing back at the guys, I hold it up, "I gotta get this. I'll be back."

They nod as I stand and swipe my finger across the screen, answering as I head toward my bedroom.

"Hello?"

"Yeah, I'm looking for Tyler Owens."

"Speaking, can I help you?"

"Well, I'm hoping so."

"Okay." I drag out the word, not having a clue who it is, but apparently, they know who I am.

"I'd like to discuss a few things with you if you'd be open to it?"

"Excuse me, but who is this?"

"My name's Brandon...Brandon Diamond, I'm the head coach for New England." As soon as the words leave his mouth, I want to scream and puke all at the same time. This is the one phone call I've been waiting for my entire life it seems like.

"Sir, whatever you need, the answer's yes."

They can offer me a ride on the bench and to only make a hundred grand the first year; I couldn't care less. Because I plan to work my ass off for that team every single day until they give me the shot that I so desperately want. This franchise makes careers, and I want football to be my future.

Coach Diamond chuckles at my response. "How about you fly up here for a visit and check things out?"

"I'd be absolutely honored, sir."

"Great. I'll have Rachel get on the line, and she'll get your travel all booked up. New England can't wait to see what you've got."

"Thank you," I reply and damn near die on the spot. One thing's for certain; I gotta get that ring on my girl's finger.

KADENCE

Valentine's Day...

Ty leads me toward the pond.

"So, just what are you up to, man hunk of mine?"

"We have lots to talk about."

"Oh, you mean like that trip you just took to Massachusetts? You keep saying it went good, but I know you're holding back details, mister, and you need to tell me all about it."

"There may be a few things I failed to mention." He pops a kiss on my forehead and smirks. He's holding back, and it's driving me crazy inside.

"I knew it!" My smile's wide as excitement floods my stomach. He said his trip went well and then left it at that. I had tests all day yesterday, so I was too distracted to get him to crack and tell me what really happened while he was out of town. "So, what did you think of Foxboro?" I always loved that area, all the trees everywhere, made it sort of majestic. Minus the snow shoveling, I can pass on that part even if it was like something out of a picture there in the wintertime.

"It was beautiful and cold. I can only imagine it in the spring or summer."

I nod. He'll fall in love with it there too. "I can't believe you got to meet with the head coach already. What did you think of him?"

"I've never been so intimidated in my life. Stratton is good, don't get me wrong, but Diamond, he's a legend."

"You will be one day too, Tyler, I know it."

He's amazingly talented, and for the number one team in the league to see it is extraordinary. I've met Brandon Diamond many times. He's a good man and definitely knows what he's doing. Ty would do wonderful having someone like Brandon around to coach him. My father loved being on the team with him in charge.

We get to the pond where someone has set up a blanket and a small stack of firewood already. It couldn't have been Ty. We barely arrived from campus an hour ago, and he's been with me at the house the entire time.

I gesture to the setup. "Oops, are we interrupting one of your brothers?" There wasn't anyone at the house with them, but clearly, someone has something planned.

"Nope, it's for us." He grins, pulling my hand until I sit in the middle of the blanket. This man is always surprising me with sweet gestures.

"Us? Did you have Nate or Clyde set this up?"

"Yup, I sure did, so just relax."

He's so freaking amazing and thoughtful. I remembered to pick him up a small box of chocolates, but I didn't plan anything out. I knew we were coming out here so there wasn't much I could do. I never thought of asking his brothers to help me do something, but now I know for future reference.

He sets down a wire hanger and an unopened bag of pink, heart-shaped marshmallows beside me.

"Ohhh, you brought snacks too!"

Freight Train

"I'm an overachiever." He shrugs making me laugh and tosses a new bottle of chocolate syrup down beside me.

"Clearly. I could eat this entire bag." I freaking love them, and I can only imagine how great they'll taste coated in the gooey, sweet chocolate syrup too.

He places the small pieces of wood together, stacking them to resemble a triangle and gets the fire going. It's not too cold out here, even in the middle of February, but the breeze is a bit chilly. The fire gives off the perfect amount of heat to make it comfortable.

"You brought me out here to roast marshmallows? I have to say, Tyler; this is the most romantic Valentine's Day I've ever celebrated. Thank you."

No one's ever done anything special for me, besides my dad. He'd send balloons or a stuffed animal for Valentine's Day, and one year, my favorite year, he had Nan go shopping and buy every topping she could find, and we made ginormous banana splits to celebrate. We were covered in sticky toppings, but each bite was delicious, and we got to make them together. I loved every minute of it.

"You're special to me, so I wanted it to be special for you. I know some guys go over the top with a bunch of flowers and all that stuff, but I wanted to do something where we got to spend time together. You're the best Valentine gift I could ever have."

It's so sweet and thoughtful I could kiss his lips off and then screw him senseless for being so damn amazing to me.

"I freaking love you, Tyler Owens."

"I love you too, Pretty." He smiles widely, those pearly whites lighting up his face and making him even more handsome to stare at. I don't know how it's even possible, but he pulls it off.

We get situated with me roasting a marshmallow, my legs wrapped in the blanket and Tyler's legs wrapped around me, holding me from behind. I'm toasty and feel oh-so-loved by my man. I couldn't imagine spending the day any other way. We may need to make this a tradition.

"Tyler?"

"Yeah, babe?"

"Thank you for this. I hope I can spend every Valentine's Day wrapped in your arms."

"Well, speaking of that. I do have a gift for you."

"But I thought you are my gift?"

He chuckles, the sound deliciously deep as he rests his chin on my shoulder. "Well yes, but I have something else too."

"If you brought graham crackers for these marshmallows and chocolate, I swear I'm going to have to remove your pants. Because damn, you planned this out well and deserve a reward."

He laughs loudly at that, his chest rumbling, making me smile as well and then leans in, kissing my cheek. "Turn around for a second." He removes his arms, and I twist my body until my hands are resting on his thighs and I'm facing him. He digs through his pocket for a minute, bringing out a small white box.

Earrings? Necklace? Bracelet? Ring?

My excitement level's about to burst, knowing those little boxes always hold something good. He opens his hand, laying it flat,

Freight Train

so the box sits right in the middle of his large palm. Coming from Ty, I know it's going to be something special. He doesn't ever do anything without thinking about it first, and I know this time will be no exception.

"Open it."

He doesn't have to tell me twice. Smiling widely, I carefully grab the box and open the lid. I'm cautious not to jostle it in case whatever's inside, isn't secured. My mouth pops open as I finger the delicate piece of silver out of the slot cut in the cushioned piece of leather inside.

"It's perfect," I whisper, pulling the ring free. "An anchor?" It's a silver band that resembles a knot and in the center is a small anchor.

"You ground me and keep me real. You're my rock, sweetheart. You're the only one that's got control of my heart."

My fingers brush over the inside, feeling the difference in texture. Flipping it around so I can see inside, I notice the script.

My heart, my soul, my love, my life.

"Oh my God, Tyler." It comes out in a breath, my eyes welling up with happy tears.

I love this man so much. He's beyond thoughtful, knowing exactly what to do to make everything so much more meaningful. He never makes me doubt, not even for a second about how he truly feels. He's always been that way, too, since the very beginning when he had me in that laundry room alone and admitted that he wanted me.

"It's true you know." He gestures to the inscription. "These words right here. You mean everything to me."

"I believe you; you're everything to me too. I'd be lost without you. I never had a clue just how lonely I was until I had you."

His mouth meets mine, softly, gently, lovingly, each caress full of unspoken promises.

"I didn't want to freak you out with an engagement ring," he admits, and my eyes meet his. I want to marry him, truly, but it's like he gets me. "Make no mistake about it; I will marry you one day, Kadence Winters. This is my promise that it'll happen, but I'll wait until you're ready for it."

All I can do is nod as he peppers kisses over my nose and cheeks. He takes the dainty ring out of my hand, laying my palm flat as he carefully places my promise ring on my right ring finger.

"One day, I'll put one on your left hand, and if I'm being honest about it, I can't wait. I love you."

"I love you." My lips tremble at his words, how he means them with every ounce in his body and he doesn't just tell me but shows me as well. He never makes me feel unloved or neglected, not even for a second.

How I could find a love so true is beyond me, but I'm so damn grateful. Every day of my life I'll spend it showing this man just how much he truly means to me, how unbelievably happy he makes me and how my soul completely belongs to him. Ever since that first day that I ran into him full speed, there's been no one in my life but him, and being here today next to him, I know inside that I want him to be beside me in my future as well.

"I have something else to tell you."

Freight Train

"There's more? I'm already blubbering; I don't know how much I can take." It comes out with a small giggle, my heart happy, full, and in love.

"Things went really great in New England. I wanted to make a commitment to you before anything else, so we have some stuff to discuss now that you know my intentions with you and our future."

"Okay." I'm dying to know what all happened on his trip.

"So, they've offered me a contract."

"You're shitting me." It bursts out before I can stop myself and he chuckles. "I mean, I'm not surprised, you're fantastic, but holy shit! They offered you a contract?" My voice grows in excitement.

He nods. "They did. I've been thinking about it for a few days, and I just can't believe it, honestly. It's a good deal too. The coach was welcoming, the team's amazing, and it'll be enough money for my family's ranch." He swallows and looks down.

"Then what's the issue, Tyler? That all sounds wonderful."

He nods again, growing serious as he meets my gaze. "It means nothing, though, if you won't go with me. My heart chooses to stay with you, no matter where that is."

"You think I won't go?"

"I mean, I hope you will, and I hope you'll be happy. But this is it, Kay, my commitment's to you. IF you say no deal, then I say no deal to them. If I agree to go and play for them, will you come with me?"

I hold my hand up, my new ring on full display. "You think you're going anywhere without me after the promise you just made me, you're crazy." I grab his hands in mine, smiling widely at the most thoughtful, caring, and gorgeous man I've ever met in my entire life. "You bet your sweet ass I'll go with you, and I'll love *you* every minute we have together, too. I'm a New England fan for life, but I'm also yours for life, Ty."

"You promise me?"

"I promise you with everything that I am. I'm yours..."

EPILOGUE

It's not about who's in your path.
It's about who's in your huddle.

Two years later

KADENCE OWENS

"Go, baby, go baby, goooooo!" My scream's so loud a few of the other wives glance at me. I couldn't care less; watching Tyler run that football all the way down the field is a thing of beauty. If anything, it's become more exciting over the years. I swear he keeps getting better with each season. I don't know how it's possible when he's already so full of talent, but it's happening.

"Momma, sit your hiney down," comes gruffly from my left side.

"Did you see that?" I ask Clyde excitedly.

"Yes. But woman, you're gonna make my nephew pop out earlier than needed if you don't calm down." Right as the words leave his mouth, I get a sharp kick to my ribs. Maybe the jumping and yelling wasn't such a good idea after all because it's getting this baby overexcited as well.

"Ohhhh." My hand finds the spot, and I sit carefully back into the comfortable club chair. No hard stadium seats for me. My belly's getting too big and my butt needs the cushioning of the seats the owner's box provides.

"See. I told you. We were all three big babies; you need to take it easy. My brother's crazy to let you up here when you're so close to your due date."

"You jinxed me." I send a glare his way as my son moves around, making himself comfy in my basketball-sized stomach.

Clyde's overreacting, which seems to also be an Owens brother trait. I'm not that close to going into labor, but they all act as if this baby's going to fall out of my coochie walking down the damn street.

"Just be happy Nate's not visiting; he'd have you on bed rest."

I roll my eyes. Nate's the most overprotective of them all, like a giant momma bear or something. "Ha. I'd like to see him try."

Grumbling, my gaze lands back on number twelve, *my* number twelve.

"I didn't get to tell you last time when you called, but I want you to know that I'm proud of you, kid."

Shrugging, I wave him off. "It's cool, thank you, though."

"I mean it, Kadence. A lot of people get married and give up on their goals, others get pregnant, and then they go to the backs of their minds even more. You stuck it out; even through being sick every day for months, you kept up with your classes. It's a big deal, and you should be proud of that."

"It was online, so it wasn't so bad."

"Don't sell yourself short. You got that degree, didn't you?"

"Yes."

"Then you're already a success in my book."

The side of my mouth hikes up. Clyde rarely doles out compliments, but when he does, I swear they're the type you feel in your heart. Typical Owens trying to make me cry from being sweet.

And it almost works as my eyes begin to water. "Thank you."

"Your dad tell you he's been stopping by the ranch on the regular?"

"No." Shaking my head, I meet his gaze. "He's been in Alabama?"

"Yep, a few times."

"Weird, he hasn't said anything." I wonder what that's all about. I know the club enjoys the moonshine, but for him to purposefully go on several rides out there? Has to be more. I need to call and check up on him.

"It's good for the ranch. I've brought on Dallas to help out more."

"I'm glad. That's too much land for you and Nate to worry about alone."

I've heard Tyler worry about his brothers constantly, being this far away from them. For the longest time, Clyde kept sending the checks back that Ty would send him to help out. Eventually, my husband got smart and started direct depositing them into Nate's account and having him use it for things they needed around the ranch.

"Well, pop out a few nephews, and they can come help out."

Swatting at him with my left hand he fake cringes like I've wounded him. "Jesus, watch out with that thing, you damn near maimed me! How can you even lift your hand, that rock's so big?"

That makes me laugh. I gave in to Tyler a year ago and married him, four months later, and the brat knocks me up. Now I'm six months into this pregnancy and wondering if I'll ever have another. This kid has made me sick, feel like I'm starving to death, overly emotional, and run out of clothes. Ty's been absolutely thrilled to see me shovel down food all the time and live in his clothes; I think it's a secret fetish of his.

"If your brother has his way, then there'll be about five more on the way." I shake my head, smiling as I think of Ty whispering to my belly the night before about how he plans to be the best daddy ever. He already is, and he doesn't even know it. I'm so lucky to have him in my life every day.

"Sister, haven't you learned yet? Ty always gets his way. He's an Owens; it's what we do." He winks, and I'll be damned if I argue.

With a devious grin like that and a heart of gold, who can possibly say no?

The End

Stay up to date with Sapphire

Email

authorsapphireknight@yahoo.com

Website

www.authorsapphireknight.com

Facebook

www.facebook.com/AuthorSapphireKnight

THE REAL HEREOS DON'T HAVE THEIR NAME ON

THE BACK OF A JERSEY.

THEY HAVE THEIR COUNTRY'S FLAG

ON THE ARM OF THEIR UNIFORM.

-Earl Dibbles Jr

#SupportOurTroops

Printed in Great Britain
by Amazon